HUNTER OF THE FAE

HUNTER OF THE FAE

MODERN FAE BOOK 4

E. MENOZZI

For everyone who has ever wished they were a wizard.

1

MY ex-boyfriend is a wizard. We were together for almost two years, and I never suspected a thing. In the four years since we broke up, we've kept in touch and even hooked up a few times. Still, I never guessed he was part of some secret wizard community. I thought I knew him, but he'd been keeping this secret from me the whole time. It wasn't like I knew magic existed until a few months ago, but that didn't stop me from revisiting every memory of our time together, searching for something I'd missed.

"Listen, Angie." Evie leaned across my open suitcase and intercepted my hand as I reached for the next shirt. "Willow is going to be here any minute. Before she gets here, I just want to make sure you're okay with all this. It's been...a lot."

That was the understatement of the century. "I'm fine. It's fine." I patted her arm with my free hand, then twisted out of her grip so I could shake out my favorite sweater, roll it, and stuff it into a packing cube.

"You don't sound fine." Evie shifted position so that she

could lay on her stomach, crosswise on the bed. She rested her chin on her hands as she stared up at me. "You know, you don't have to do this if you don't want to. I'll talk to Fiona for you. I can explain—"

I cut her off. "It's okay. I can do this." The doorbell rang, distracting Evie from pursuing the topic further.

Evie started to get up, but stopped when her aunt Vivian's cheery voice called up from somewhere on the first floor of the manor. "I'll get it!"

Evie flopped back onto her belly. "It's late for visitors... Could be one of Aunt Viv's friends or that nosy neighbor, MaryAnn. You don't think Willow would use the front door, do you?"

I rolled my eyes. Evie's boyfriend's inability to use the front door and pretend he was a human had been what had gotten me into this mess in the first place. I snatched my wrinkled skinny jeans from the heap of clothing on the bed. My fingers dug into the fabric and squeezed extra tight as I rolled them up.

Liam messed up, and I ended up swearing an Oath to serve the Faerie Queen and keep all their secrets, just like Evie.

"You're thinking about him, aren't you?" Evie asked.

"Liam?" I knew that wasn't who she meant, but it was who I'd been thinking about. Easier to talk about Evie's boyfriend than confront my feelings about being sent to spy on my ex for the Fae.

"No. Not Liam. Max." Evie shook her head. "Are you sure you're okay?"

A yipping bark from downstairs distracted me from the question. "Did your aunt get a dog?"

Evie sat up and faced the open door to the guest room. "No... And I don't think MaryAnn has a dog..." She scooted to the edge of the bed and started to stand.

"You don't think that demon lady is trying to infiltrate Lydbury Manor with one of her hellhounds, do you?" I was kidding, but the look Evie gave me over her shoulder made it clear that joking about demon attacks was not okay.

Luckily, the definitely-not-a-hellhound in question chose that moment to bound into the room, followed by the petite and athletic form of Willow, the most recent addition to our Humans Who've Sworn to Serve the Fae Club. Current membership: three. No. Five, if you counted Evie's aunt and uncle.

"Phew." Willow exhaled, interlacing her fingers on top of her head as she caught her breath. "This house is enormous, and that dog may have short legs, but she's fast."

The little bundle of fur accompanying Willow had bounced up on the bed and was turning around in happy circles, tail wagging madly. She bounced over to Evie, but when Evie reached out to pet her, she twisted and pranced back toward me. Then she jumped and landed directly in the middle of my clean clothes, scattering them everywhere as she stared up at me, clueless and adoring.

"Oh, good," Willow said. "She likes you."

My grumpy mood melted in the face of what appeared to be the most adorable corgi I'd ever seen. "Hello there, little ball of fuzz."

"Her name's Salty," Willow explained. "And she's yours. Gift from the pixies, via Arabella."

I paused scratching Salty's head and looked across the room at Willow. "Um...I'm leaving. Remember? Your girlfriend knows that. What am I going to do with a dog?"

Salty butted my hand with her wet nose, demanding I continue with the scratches.

Willow shut the door, then sat down on the end of the bed,

opposite Evie. "So, about that... You're meant to take her with you. For protection."

I glanced down at the wagging tan-and-white dog shedding on my black leggings and my best cashmere sweater. "Protection? Is this a joke?"

Evie sat up straight, tucking her legs underneath her. "Oh. I've read about this. Corgis are thought to be companion dogs for the faeries. Is that true, then?"

Willow shrugged. "Something like that, I think. Ari didn't explain much. She just handed me the dog and said I needed to give her to Angie and tell her that she should keep the dog with her at all times."

"I suppose this is Ari's way of sending one of the Queen's Guard with you to protect you." Evie smiled at me like this was some sort of honor.

Something about her smile combined with the adoring fur ball insisting on my attention made me snap. I shoved my suitcase toward the center of the bed and sat down in its place. "I'm not fine." I sighed. "I don't think I can do this."

Salty plopped down right on top of my favorite blouse and rested her head on my lap. This was going to be one expensive dry-cleaning bill.

Evie scooted closer to me so she could rub her hand up and down my back. "Aw, sweetie. It's going to be okay. Do you want me to go with you? I could—"

"No." I shook my head. "I should be able to face my ex-boyfriend. It's just..." I swallowed the lump in my throat. "It's easier to forget that it's over when I don't have to see him."

"I'm sorry," Willow said. "I should never have suggested that we involve you. I didn't know."

"It's not your fault." Evie frowned. "I'm the one who knew. I should have said no. We can still find another way."

I shifted Salty off my lap and stood, pointing to the floor. "Off."

Salty looked up at me with sad eyes, then hopped down from the bed. "You both did the right thing. I swore my Oath, just like you two did. If this is what Fiona needs from me, I can do this. It's not like she's asking me to go toe to toe with a demon."

Evie shivered. "Don't even joke about that."

"Sorry." I pulled my suitcase toward me. "It's just Max. And I just need to get some information from him. I can do this." I started gathering up my clothes. "I'll go. I'll get him to tell me what he knows about those magic traps that the demons want to use against the Fae, and that will be it."

"I almost forgot." Willow reached into the pocket of her jeans and pulled out a coin about the size of a quarter. "Arabella also gave me a few of these to send with you."

I took the coin from her and studied it as she fished two more out of her pocket. "It's blank."

"Are these the blood coins?" Evie asked.

"Blood coins?" I winced at the awful name.

"Yeah." Willow held one up. "Nigel and Gwawr made a batch for Arabella to test. They're pretty sure they got all the kinks out."

"How do they work?" I asked.

"They're all coded to return to Ari, wherever she happens to be when they're sent," Willow explained, handing me two more coins.

"You probably also need to tell her how you send them." Evie grimaced.

I had a feeling I wasn't going to like this part. "And maybe why you decided to call them 'blood coins'?"

"Oh. Right." Willow slid a small knife out of a pocket on

the outside thigh of her brown canvas pants. She unfolded the blade. "Don't worry, I won't waste one of your coins just to demonstrate."

My face must have paled at the sight of her knifepoint, but she'd drawn the wrong conclusion from my reaction. She could have all the coins she gave me back if she was about to do what I thought she was about to do.

Willow dug another coin out of her pocket, then pricked her finger with the tip of her knife. A drop of blood dripped onto the face of the coin.

I pinched my eyes shut. "Nope."

"Come on, Angie. Open your eyes," Evie said.

I peeked through my eyelashes as Willow whispered to the coin. All I heard was the last bit: "Love you." Then the coin disappeared.

My eyes popped open. "Where did it go? How did you do that?"

Willow was human, like me and Evie, but a little bit of Fae blood from somewhere way back in her ancestry had trickled down through her family tree to both her parents, and ultimately to her. She had what the Fae called earth magic, which I'd come to learn was characteristic of the Elemental Fae. But as far as I knew, having earth magic didn't mean you could make things disappear.

"I told you. They're all coded to return to Ari once you've imprinted them with your message."

I cringed. "And imprinting them involves bleeding on them and whispering sweet nothings in their ear?"

Willow blushed. "The first part, yes. But, Ari means for you to whisper—or shout—a cry for help should you need backup."

"And why would I find myself in a situation where I would

need to A, voluntarily bleed myself, and B, call for backup?" I glanced down at the dog curled up on the carpet near the bedpost. She thumped her tail against the floor and opened her mouth to grin up at me.

Evie and Willow exchanged a look. I knew that look. I did not like that look.

"Nope." I shook my head. "Fighting demons was not part of the deal."

Evie scooted toward me. "It's just a precaution. No one expects anything bad to happen to you. That's why we're sending you. No one knows that you're Sworn. You'll be fine."

"Look." Willow pulled out her phone. "How about we start a group text. No blood involved."

Evie nodded. "Perfect. You can keep us updated, and we can cheer you on. I love it."

Willow passed her phone to Evie. "Go ahead and put your number in."

Evie's thumbs danced across the screen. Then she handed the device to me.

I shook my head as I added my contact info. "You promised me this wasn't going to be dangerous." Unlike my best friend and her soon-to-be cousin-in-law—or whatever the Fae called it when your mate's cousin chose a mate—no one was going to describe me as athletic. I liked to swim. You didn't get sweaty when you swam. But running, Evie's favorite sport, was torture, and I wasn't in a hurry to test that whole "I'll run if a demon is chasing me" theory.

I handed the phone back to Willow. She glanced at Evie, then bent her head to study the screen.

"You're going to be fine," Evie said. "Just keep Salty with you, and if you need help, don't hesitate to call."

On cue, my phone buzzed in my pocket. I pulled it out and

cleared the message alert. Right below the text from Willow was the last one I'd received from Max. His dark eyes stared up at me from his profile picture, and something inside my chest ached. The next week was going to be torture.

I tapped his face and typed a lighthearted message, letting him know I was coming to town "for work." Then I set the phone to do not disturb, switched off the screen, and shoved it back into my pocket. I refused to obsess about how long it took for him to respond. This trip was strictly business.

———

MY LIFE HAD BECOME a series of never-ending meetings. I shut the door to block the chatter from the employees seated in the open floor plan and took refuge in my office. If I had realized that agreeing to run Silicon Moon would require me to attend so many damn meetings, I might not have been so quick to accept the promotion. Everyone was so needy. The minute I left the privacy of the hundred-odd square feet of space that I was allowed to call "mine," they started in on me with requests and questions. I didn't dare open my e-mail unless I wanted to face more of the same.

Rolling my neck to release some tension, I crossed over to the floor-to-ceiling windows that lined the wall behind my desk and pressed my forehead against the glass so I could stare down at the damp concrete grid below. If anyone in the office caught me doing this, they'd probably worry that I wanted to jump, but that was the furthest thing from my mind. I used the change in perspective to reset my equilibrium and clear my head.

From this angle, pedestrians appeared like inkblots moving across a game board. They flowed in both directions, pausing at street corners as cars streamed past. One bright-pink umbrella with green dots wove through the flow of pedestrians on the sidewalk. I followed it until it disappeared around a corner. The splash of color reminded me of Angie and made the corners of my mouth twitch up into a grin.

As soon as I realized where my brain was going, I refocused my thoughts and peeled myself away from the window. Then I flopped into my ridiculously expensive office chair. I only had a half hour break. I could spend all of it daydreaming about my off-limits ex-girlfriend, or I could put the time to good use and research my current pet project.

Pit of despair temporarily avoided, I shoved a hand into my jacket pocket and extracted a small black clothbound notebook. Tugging on the string marking my place, I opened the book and laid it on my desk next to the keyboard. In the process, I jostled the mouse and woke my screen. I gritted my teeth as I typed in my password. Nothing says love like a lick on the nose.

We'd been broken up for four years, but I still couldn't bring myself to change my password to a series of numbers, letters, and symbols that wasn't based on one of our inside jokes. Every time I typed my password, I was reminded of the vacation we took to Italy the summer before our final year at college. Angie was about to finish undergrad. I was about to finish my MBA. I'd planned to propose until I'd been reminded that I had a company to run, a sister to protect, and secrets that I could never, ever share with the woman I loved.

The memories hurt, but they served as a useful reminder. My family, the Wizard Society, and the Society's governing Council were the three most important things in my life. There was no room for love, at least not with someone who didn't have even a drop of magic in their blood.

I opened the browser and entered the set of keywords I'd

scribbled into the margin of my notebook during the last soul-numbing meeting. A few clicks led me to a site featuring a picture of a shop. The interior was cloaked in shadow, but a man stood behind the counter, facing the shelves lining the walls. His long gray hair was pulled back in a low ponytail and secured with a clip.

I zoomed in on the picture, trying to get a closer look. It had to be the same wizard. The one who had told me he could help my sister. He'd pressed a mysterious key into my hand, then disappeared down a dark alley with no explanation. I was so absorbed in my research that I didn't even notice Jayden standing in the doorway until he spoke.

"Max? Earth to Max? Hello?" Jayden tapped on the doorjamb to get my attention.

I glanced up from the screen. "Oh. Hey. What's up?"

Jayden's eyebrows shot up. He looked pointedly at the clock. "What's up? Your two o'clock appointment is waiting. That's what's up."

"All right, man. No need to be sassy about it." I flicked the mouse to lock the computer screen, not bothering to close my browser window first. Jayden knew about the key and the wizard. I didn't need to hide my sleuthing from him. "I think I found something."

Jayden studied me with narrowed eyes. "Was it perhaps the papers I left on your desk?"

"Papers?" I glanced down at the scattered scraps of paper that littered the area around my keyboard.

Jayden shook his head and stalked toward me. He stopped at the other side of the desk and tapped a stack of papers positioned on the far corner. The pages had been marked with colorful sticky flags. "Papers."

"What are they for?" I stood, slipped my notebook back

into my pocket, and buttoned my jacket.

"Honestly. What do you even do in here all day?" Jayden spread his hands and stared up at the ceiling like some avenging angel was going to drop down and save him from my thickheadedness. He sounded like my father.

"For starters, I'm not in here all day. You control my schedule. You know I barely have time to piss, let alone lounge about doing nothing in my office." I stepped around the side of the desk and picked up the stack of papers. "I was trying to dig up information about the key, if you must know."

"My, aren't we grumpy today?"

I sighed after reading the first few lines. "Sorry. It's not your fault that this was the first time my ass touched that seat since seven this morning." My eyes narrowed as I looked up at him. "No. Wait. It is your fault."

"If you think this is bad, you should see the number of people I have to turn away." He set his hands on his hips. "Are you going to sign that, or what? Jeffries is waiting in Gates."

"This is a release for Cortez's personal effects."

"Yes."

"Has anyone looked through those boxes?"

"No. Jelly was going to do it, but she called in sick, and I just got a manicure, so I'm not doing it."

I set the stack of papers back onto the corner of my desk. "Fine. I'll do it."

Jayden sighed. "Or you could just sign the papers and be done with it. The guy was an engineer for our parent company. He disappeared more than twenty years ago, before Silicon Moon even existed. Whatever he kept in his desk is going to be obsolete at this point. Let the widow have what she wants."

I flipped through the pages at the top of the stack. "What

is her name, again?"

"Something flowerlike. I can't remember."

It was right there on the first page. Lilium Cortez. I frowned. Lilium. I'd heard that name somewhere before. It wasn't a very common name. If she was in the Society, Morgan would know. I pulled out my phone to text her and saw that I had a message. Angie's face smiled up at me, all big brown eyes and luscious pink lips. I swiped it away, ignoring the temptation to open the message, and sent a quick note to my sister instead.

Why do I know the name Lilium?

Then I slid my phone back into my pocket, much too aware of the warm hardware pressing against the thin fabric next to my skin. I'd read Angie's message later. At home. Not here, under the harsh fluorescent lighting and the all-too-knowing gaze of my executive assistant.

"Stall," I said. "Give me the weekend to look through the boxes. If something gets out that shouldn't, I'll never hear the end of it from Marcella."

Jayden shuddered at the sound of my mother's name. "I think you're being overly cautious, but I agree, best not to incur the wrath of she-who-shall-not-be-named."

"Your loyalty is heartwarming, truly." At least one person in this place was on my side. Maybe. "Gates, you said?"

"Gates." He pointed in the direction of our main conference room.

"Marketing?" I tried to remember who he said I was supposed to be meeting with.

Jayden sighed. "Public relations. The Italians are using our tech in their rocket launch next week. Remember?" He pointed through the office door to the countdown clock that hung on the far wall of the open-floor office. Four days, twelve hours, and forty-nine minutes. The seconds ticked down as I watched.

"To infinimoon..." I grinned, letting my voice trail off.

"And beyond." Jayden pointed to the ceiling.

I chuckled as I squared my shoulders and rolled my neck, preparing for another gauntlet of meetings. "You'll come rescue me at two thirty?"

Jayden shook his head. "Jeffries has you until two fifty, then you have ten minutes to 'piss,' as you put it, before the daily check-in with the engineering leads."

"I hate you." I grimaced and headed for the door.

"You would be nothing without me," Jayden scolded as he followed.

"Tell that to Marcella," I shot back over my shoulder.

"Tell her yourself, you big baby. I deserve a raise," he whispered. Jayden knew that was out of my control. He was my assistant, but we both reported to my mother, who ran the technology division of Hunter Works, my father's corporate empire.

"Go whine about it to Kyle. And while you're at it, remind everyone that we're meeting tomorrow. Eight o'clock, my place. Make sure someone brings food. I'll pay for it, but I'm going straight to the gym after work and won't have time to order anything or pick it up." I turned down the hall toward the conference room and increased my pace.

My fingers brushed against the phone in my pocket as I walked. Brown eyes and unread words lurked there. My heart pounded against the wall of secrets I'd built between us that were screaming to be let out. Since that was impossible, I attempted to center myself by concentrating on the magic pulsing through my veins. The effort it took to channel my power and direct it into my palms forced all other thoughts from my head and erased all lingering emotions.

Pausing outside the conference room door, I fixed a welcoming smile on my face. Then I entered the room and focused on the team sitting around the table. "Sorry I'm late."

2

MY legs were aching, and I was starting to sweat from the long climb up the hill to Max's house, but Salty was still going strong. She eagerly sniffed all the smells and grinned at the compliments from passersby. Everyone wanted to tell me what an adorable dog she was.

"You are eating this up, aren't you?" I unzipped my raincoat and flapped it open, hoping it would cool me off a bit.

Salty paused midsniff to look up at me. Her mouth dropped open and her tongue curled out.

I stuck my tongue out at her, even though she really was too cute to be mad at. "They should have named you Sassy."

Turning at the next corner, the sidewalk flattened out as it curved around the side of the hill. I led Salty past rows of large houses, some so big that they'd been converted into studio and one-bedroom condos. I'd stayed in one on my last visit so that I could avoid the long uphill walk to Max's house from the hotels closer to downtown.

This time, I opted for a hotel. It fit better with my cover

story of being in town for work, and I didn't need the added temptation and torture of being near, but not with, Max. I'd gone straight to the hotel after my flight landed and spent most of the rest of the day trying to get my body to adjust to the time difference.

When I reached the park cut into the side of the hill, I paused to admire the skyline. The sun had gone down, and the city lights twinkled along the waterfront, providing a picturesque backdrop for the Space Needle. I let Salty sniff around in the grass while I snapped a photo to send to our Humans Who've Sworn to Serve the Fae group chat.

I couldn't exactly make that the official group name on my phone, so I was trying to come up with something shorter, catchier, and less conspicuous. Maybe something with our initials. Angie. Willow. Evie. AWE. Short for "AWEsome." That would work. I attached the photo and added a short message.

At least the view is nice… Wish me luck!

I hit send and waited a minute to see if either of them would reply. Below the AWEsome chat, I checked the message I'd sent to Max before leaving England. Still no response. The long, slow walk uphill had given me plenty of time to consider all the possible reasons he might be ignoring me. I picked apart every moment of my last visit, only a few months ago.

I was still kicking myself for visiting in the first place. I'd been the one to end things four years ago, just before graduation. I'd hinted about a future together too many times for him not to have noticed. Then he'd agreed to take a position in one of his father's tech companies on the East Coast and made his plans for life after graduation without consulting me. Maybe he'd just assumed I would go with him, but I'd had plans of my own. We'd fought. I left. He didn't stop me.

We hooked up before he moved to the East Coast, then

sent messages back and forth as we lay in our beds on opposite sides of the country, but never officially got back together. When he said he was moving back, I'd thought maybe that would be it. But it turned out he meant back to the West Coast, not back to San Francisco—and the two cities were over eight hundred miles apart. Still, I'd found an excuse to go up to Seattle to visit while Evie was in England. If she'd been home, she would have talked some sense into me.

I'd actually thought something had changed that weekend. I thought we were finally going to figure out a way to make it work. We hiked and danced and laughed and ate ice cream on the pier in the rain. We snuggled on the couch while we watched our favorite movie. I barely spent a minute in that condo I'd rented. But, I didn't hear from him after he dropped me off at the airport. Nothing for weeks. And he had ignored my latest text message.

I straightened my shoulders and rezipped the front of my raincoat. If I wasn't here to help my friends and honor my Oath to the Faerie Queen, I'd take a hint and go home. But I wasn't here for me. I had to swallow my pride and at least try to make contact with him before I gave up and left.

My phone buzzed. Hope gripped me for a moment, but I shook loose from its hold before I checked my messages. Good thing I did. It was Evie, not Max. Still, her message made me smile.

You can do it!

Willow responded with an image of a cartoon character waving a giant foam finger on one hand and a flag in the other.

I slid my phone into my pocket and tugged on Salty's leash. "Let's get this over with, shall we?"

The faerie dog yipped at me in response, then led the way

down the sidewalk to Max's house, like she already knew where we were going. I shook my head and followed. We'd only walked a few steps when my phone buzzed again. I decided to ignore it. I didn't need any more words of encouragement via text. But the vibrating didn't stop, and I recognized the muffled chime of my ringtone.

Steering Salty over to the edge of the sidewalk, I reached into my pocket to see who might be calling, only to find Evie's smiling avatar staring at me. I accepted the call.

"Isn't it after midnight over there? What are you doing awake at this hour?" I asked.

"Calling to check on you."

"I'm not even at his house yet." I glanced down the street, but I couldn't see his front porch from this angle.

"Good."

"Good?"

"Yes. Good. What's your plan?"

"My plan?" I realized that I hadn't thought much about tactics. I'd been too overwhelmed with my feelings.

"Are you just going to repeat everything I say?"

I groaned. "I don't have a plan."

"I didn't think so."

"Well, are you calling to gloat or to help me?" I tucked the hand holding Salty's leash into my armpit to keep it warm and used it to prop up the arm holding my phone to my ear.

"Help, I hope."

"Good. Then get with the helping. The clouds are spitting on me, and if I spend too much longer out here, my hair is going to be a frizzy mess. Besides, if one more person stops to pet this oddly intelligent dog, I'm going to tell them she bites." Salty tilted her head up at me and wagged her tail.

Evie sucked in a breath. "She'd never."

"She could." I raised an eyebrow at the faerie dog who had decided I was no longer of interest and had buried her nose in a tuft of grass. "You were only with her for a few hours. What do you know?"

"Well, I would be completely unsurprised to find out Arabella gave you a dog that can understand human speech, but I am pretty sure that Salty is not some sort of faerie in disguise. I've been studying up on Liam's kin. Only the High Fae can take an animal form, and they don't choose the form. Plus, it's almost always a predator of some sort. So, not a corgi."

"Dogs are totally predators."

Evie sighed. "Fine. I said I'm pretty sure. I didn't say it was impossible."

I dropped my voice to a whisper. "For the record, I'd really like to know if I'm walking around with a faerie on a leash." There was just so much wrong with that. Given how smart she was, I was already questioning having Salty on a leash even before Evie mentioned the slim possibility that she was a faerie in disguise.

"All right. I'll ask Ari in a few hours when she gets here to train with me."

I smirked. "The High Fae have animal forms, huh? When were you going to tell me what sort of animal it is that you're sleeping with?"

"I'm not."

"Not going to tell me? Or not partaking in that particular relationship perk?"

"Will you be serious?"

I laughed. "He's totally there, isn't he? Just tell me. Does he have wings or a tail? I mean, I'd understand the hesitation if he has a beak, but not if he's got one of those sandpaper tongues..." I let my voice trail off, knowing I'd already said enough to make her blush.

"Enough. We are not talking about this right now."

"Tell me the truth, that's why you're still awake at this hour, isn't it?" I couldn't help teasing her just a little bit more.

My question was met with silence, interrupted only by muffled sounds of walking and a door closing. Then Evie responded. "You win. I am now out of my warm bed and pacing the hallway because Fae happen to have excellent hearing, and I am fairly certain that Liam is no longer even pretending to be asleep."

I giggled. "Worried I'm going to give him some ideas?"

"While I appreciate your filthy mind, I would like to get some sleep tonight."

I snorted. "That's what she said."

"Honestly. You're worse than my brothers. If I admit that the answer to your question is tail not beak, can we talk about your plan?"

"Oooh. Yes. But, I demand more details, later." I switched the phone to my other hand and pushed the loop at the end of the leash down around my wrist so I could warm the hand that had been exposed to the weather. "Let's hear it. What's your idea?"

"Willow and I called her mom on the ride back from the airport. Bethany says—"

I interrupted her. "You said you wanted to sleep, and I'm freezing out here and getting drenched, remember? Give me the short version."

Evie inhaled before diving into her summary. "Right. Short version is, Max may or may not know about the boxes, so don't be the first to bring it up. Try to catch him doing magic, or get him into a situation where he has to admit to being a wizard. Then you can be relieved that he also knows about magic and try to get him to open up about his powers and his family."

"Get him to use magic?" I whispered the words into the phone as I glanced around to make sure no one was close enough to overhear me. "That's your plan?"

"It's a solid plan."

I kept my voice low. There was another couple at the far end of the park, but other than that, we were alone. "If he's been able to hide his powers from me for this long—"

Evie cut me off. "You didn't know about magic before. Would you have even noticed if he had?"

I liked to think that I would have been observant enough to catch something like that, but the truth was, you didn't expect to see magic when you didn't know it existed. Then once you did know, you saw it everywhere, and you were shocked that you'd never noticed before. "You're right."

"Okay, then. Step one, get Max to expose his secret to you."

I snorted. "Now who's the dirty one?"

"You are the worst. I love you, and I'm going to bed now."

"To bed. Not to sleep. Gotcha. Tail, huh?"

"I'm hanging up now."

"Love you, too." I glanced down to find Salty looking up at me as I hung up the phone and returned it to my pocket. "Ready?"

Salty turned in a circle, tail wagging like mad, then took off toward Max's house.

"That's it. You are officially creeping me out, dog."

———

I MADE IT HOME from the gym with about fifteen minutes to spare before everyone was scheduled to arrive for our usual Friday-night meeting. That was assuming that any of them arrived on time. I didn't really care how late they were as long as someone remembered to bring food. My stomach was already growling.

I unlocked my door, dropped my keys on the table in the foyer, and kicked the door shut behind me. Then I kept moving. The clock was ticking, and even though I'd showered after my workout, I needed to tidy up my house a bit. On my way past the door to my room, I tossed my gym bag inside and made a mental note to throw my sweat-soaked clothes in the hamper later.

Next stop was the kitchen. I raided my pantry for anything that looked like a snack that I might be able to serve or consume. All that was left was a half box of nearly stale crackers and a bag of tortilla chips. I checked the fridge. No salsa. Then I remembered that Morgan was on vacation.

My sister spoiled me. She usually popped in once a week to check on me and bring me some staple grocery items. While we caught up on what was going on with me at Silicon Moon and what was new with her now-retired famous child-actor husband and her secret charity projects, she stealthily checked my cupboards and fridge to see what I was running low on.

It was only slightly insulting that she didn't think I could take care of myself, but clearly, I couldn't, at least not while also running a chapter of the Wizard Society and a division of the company that was something of a front for the entire wizard organization. In my defense, this was supposed to have been Morgan's job, not mine. That dream ended when she sprouted horns on her fifteenth birthday, and we both found out what my mother already suspected.

Morgan was technically only my half sister. The most powerful wizard and head of the Society, otherwise known as my father, didn't know that my mother had been seduced by an incubus. That was a secret kept by exactly four people: my mother, me, my sister, and my sister's husband.

If anyone else found out, especially my father, then my family would lose its place on the Wizard Council. So Morgan and I swapped destinies. She hid her horns under a glamour and retreated from the spotlight, pretending her power was weak and not worthy of leadership, while I drew all eyes to me.

But Morgan hadn't popped in to drop off groceries, and I was stuck with whatever I could scrounge from the back of the fridge. Since she was on vacation, she probably wasn't checking her messages, either. I extracted a baggie that had wedged itself behind one of the shelves and was rewarded with a small but possibly salvageable hunk of mystery cheese. I tossed it onto the counter and checked to make sure I hadn't missed anything else edible.

The doorbell rang. I extracted my head from the refrigerator and checked the clock. I still had ten minutes.

"Coming!" I retraced my steps back to the door and shouted down the hall, "It's open. You can just let yourself in."

The words were barely out of my mouth before I reached the door. I opened it expecting to see Jayden and Kyle, and found Angie standing on my doorstep. She let the hood of her bright-red raincoat fall back to reveal her round face framed by her dark-brown hair cropped to chin length and striped with purple. The cut and color were both new since her visit a few months earlier.

"Angie?" I gripped the doorknob tight to keep myself from pulling her into a hug and kissing her glossy pink lips. "What are you doing here?"

"I texted. You didn't respond." She smiled as she shrugged

one shoulder. "I was in the neighborhood, so I thought I'd stop by and see if you were home. Bad time?"

"No." I shook my head to clear it. "I mean, yes, but come in." I stepped aside to let her walk past and only then noticed the small dog sitting at her feet. "You got a dog?"

She hesitated on the doorstep. "Yeah. Are you sure? I can come back another time. I probably should have called first."

"No. No, really." I set a hand on her shoulder and guided her inside. "It's great to see you. I'm sorry about your text. I meant to respond. It's been a crazy week. But that doesn't matter. I'm glad you're here. Did you walk? It's freezing out there. Hard to believe it's the end of May."

Somewhere in the middle of my babbling, I shut the door, helped her out of her jacket, and hung it up to dry on one of the pegs behind the door.

"That's pretty wet." She pointed at her jacket. "Are you sure you want it dripping on your wood floor?"

"Oh. Right." I lifted the jacket off the hook. "Maybe I should hang it in the bathroom instead."

"I can do it." She reached to take it out of my hand, and her fingers brushed against mine.

We froze like that for a heartbeat. Our eyes locked, and I started to lean toward her, unable to resist the pull of her. Then her dog yipped and broke the spell.

I blinked down at the furry reminder that Angie was off-limits. "I've got the jacket. Tell me about the dog."

"Oh. Is it okay to let her off her leash?"

"Sure. Do you want a towel or something to dry off her paws?"

"Yeah. That would be great." Angie bent down to unclip the leash.

I hurried to the bathroom to drop off her coat and grabbed

one of the cleaning rags I kept in the cabinet under the sink. When I stood up, I glared at myself in the bathroom mirror. Keep it together, Hunter.

I flicked off the lights and poked my head out of the bathroom. Angie was still crouched down in front of her dog. Her mouth was moving, but I couldn't hear what she was saying. I grinned.

"Here you go." I handed her the towel.

"Thanks." She dabbed at the dog's paws like this was the first time she'd ever attempted such a thing. "I know you're more of a cat person. I promise that Salty will be on her best behavior."

"Salty?" I didn't mind dogs, I'd just never had a chance to spend much time with any. Our family had been stereotypical cat-loving wizards. At least until my sister grew horns. My mom had to let Morgan move into the guest house, claiming she was allergic. Even with the glamour, Morgan had started freaking out our cats.

"She already had a name when I got her."

"What made you decide to get a dog? You always said you were too busy with work to take care of one." I'd always suspected that she didn't want a dog because she thought I didn't like dogs. If she finally gave in and adopted one, then I guessed it meant she was serious about it being over between us. I hated that she was moving on.

She shrugged. "I got a new job recently. It's a little more flexible. They encouraged me to get a dog, actually."

"Huh. That's cool. Is that why you're here?" If she was moving to town permanently, I was going to have a really hard time staying away from her.

"The boss and most of the company is in England. I'm just here on an assignment."

"International IP firm?"

"Something like that." She handed me the dirty towel. "Were you expecting someone else?"

"Huh? Oh. Yeah. I have some friends coming over for our weekly RPG." I fell back on my old cover story that I'd used in college when Angie and I lived together and our wizard chapter had a meeting at our place. "You're welcome to stick around."

She made a sour face. "It's not really my thing."

"Yeah, I remember." I grinned. "But Hannah and Grace and Varun will be here. You remember them, right?"

"Sure. Wow. I haven't seen them since... Well, yeah. It's been a while." The way her cheeks colored, I was pretty sure I knew what she was thinking.

The last time she'd seen my friends had been at Morgan's wedding. Angie and I had been apart for a year at that point. When I saw Angie walk into the ceremony and take her seat on the bride's side of the aisle, I'd panicked. I stood with the other groomsmen, trying to avoid looking at her. At the reception, I cornered my sister and called her a traitor for inviting my ex. Morgan had just rolled her eyes at me and walked away.

Officially, Hannah had been my date to the wedding. She was Morgan's best friend and maid of honor. We decided to go together because we were both still nursing our respective relationship wounds and knew the paparazzi at the wedding would devour any hint that either of us was moving on with anyone new. We made our entrance at the party, her the up-and-coming fashion designer, and me the heir to the Hunter family fortunes. Then, inside and free of the press, we went our separate ways. Angie and I circled each other for most of the reception before ending up half naked in a supply closet.

I tried to ignore the wave of desire brought on by that memory. "Stay. I'm sure they'd love to see you and catch up."

"I don't want to crash your party."

"Look. I know you're hiding a book in that bag of yours. No one will care if you curl up and read while we campaign. I want to hear more about this new job of yours."

"I can't stay late." She looked down at her dog, then glanced up at me out of the corner of her eye.

I guessed at what she wasn't saying. She wasn't here to hook up. "They'll be gone by ten, and I'll drive you back to your hotel. You'll be in bed by midnight." I won't try to take your clothes off, as much as I want to.

"I can get a cab. You don't need to do that."

"It's no trouble, really."

The doorbell rang, cutting off her chance to object and giving me only a few seconds to prepare to face the knowing looks of all my friends who would assume Angie's presence meant we were getting back together. Only Jayden knew about the promise I'd made my mother. If this got back to her, I'd have a lot of explaining to do.

Sure enough, the first to arrive were Kyle and Jayden. Kyle grinned as Salty rushed out to run figure eights around their ankles. Jayden took one look at Angie and narrowed his eyes to glare at me.

"Salty, come." Angie bent down to lure her dog back into the house.

While she was distracted, I shot Jayden my best "we'll talk about this later" look.

He responded with an arched brow, and I knew it was going to be a long night. When he spoke, it was all sugary gush. "Angie. What a surprise. Max didn't tell us you were in town."

Angie was still crouched down, keeping hold of Salty's

collar. "It was sort of a last-minute thing for work."

Kyle bent down to scratch the dog between the ears. "Is he yours? What's his name?"

Angie let go of Salty's collar so the dog could nuzzle Kyle. "Her name is Salty."

"Aww. What a cutie."

Jayden continued to glare at me over their heads. I needed to get him away from Angie so I could explain. "Why don't you come help me with the snacks in the kitchen?"

"Sure."

I pushed him ahead of me down the hall. Behind us, Kyle said, "She seems like a great guard dog."

"What makes you say that?" Angie's voice hid a hint of defensiveness, which seemed odd, but I was too busy worrying about what I was going to say to Jayden to give it much thought.

"Good instincts, that's all. We used to have..." Kyle's voice disappeared as I shut the kitchen door.

Jayden didn't hesitate before turning on me. "What is she doing here? We're supposed to be having a meeting, and you know your mother forbid you from seeing her."

"Shh. Keep your voice down. I know. She texted me yesterday, and I forgot. Then, when I remembered, I didn't have a chance to respond because someone had me in meetings all day today. I didn't expect her to show up on my doorstep. It's not like her. Something must be up, but I haven't had a chance to find out what."

"Whatever it is, it's not your problem." He frowned and shook his head.

"She's still my friend." Or at least I wanted her to be. I couldn't stop thinking about her, and I definitely hadn't stopped caring about her.

"Don't give me that. I've heard the stories. Reliable sources have informed me that any time you two end up in the same room, it's only a matter of time before your hands are all over each other." He wasn't wrong.

I sighed. "Just, don't tell Marcella. Please?" I hated that I had to beg my assistant not to tell my mother on me. "I'll drop Angie off at her hotel after you all leave. We'll talk. That will be it. I promise."

"What about our meeting? I thought you found something?"

"I did. We're still going to meet. It will just be undercover, like the old days."

"Like the old days?" Jayden's eyebrows lifted.

I remembered that he hadn't gone to graduate school with the rest of us. "Back at Stanford, we used to put everything into the context of a role-playing game so no one caught on. Angie sat through hundreds of our meetings and never had a clue."

"An RPG?" Jayden lifted a hand to his chest. "You expect me to pretend that I'm pretending to be a wizard? I did not sign up for this."

"It's fun. You're going to love it. Now help me with these snacks, and let's get back out there before Kyle says something he shouldn't."

"Kyle knows a reg from a wizard. He's not the problem. Your ex is the problem." Jayden grabbed the two bowls and stared at the meager contents. He glanced between the handful of stale chips in one and the woody carrot sticks in the other. "You weren't kidding. This is sad."

"I warned you." I picked up the remaining platter of mystery cheese and cracker scraps and followed him back into the living room.

3

THIS was not what I'd signed up for. Seeing Max again and knowing that he was totally over me was one thing, but having to face all his, formerly our, friends? Nope. I perched on the edge of Max's couch as Kyle, who I had thankfully never met before, asked me polite questions about Salty. I did my best to answer as vaguely as possible, but my mind was in the kitchen with Max and his assistant.

Jayden and I met the last time I'd visited Max, and I knew he didn't like me. He may have pretended to be sweet, but I could tell he had not been happy to see me here. And when that doorbell rang again, it would be announcing more people who probably didn't want me here. They were protective of Max. According to them, I broke his heart. I have no idea what he told them, but the heartbreaking had been mutual that night.

I needed to get out of there. Stopping by unannounced was a very bad idea. I'd call him tomorrow and try again.

Kyle distracted me with another question. "So, you don't

live in Seattle?"

"No. I stayed in California after I graduated. I had a job in the Bay Area."

"I take it you went to college with Max, then?"

"We met when I was in undergrad at Berkeley. He was in grad school at Stanford."

Kyle squinted at me. "Are you two...together?"

"We were."

The doorbell rang just as Max and Jayden emerged from the kitchen.

I sprang up from the couch. "Hey, um, Max? I think I'm just going to..."

Max set the plate he was carrying down on the table. "Let me get the door. I'll be right back."

He hurried away and left me standing there, facing Jayden.

"I think I'm going to go," I said.

Jayden attempted to look sad. "Oh. That's too bad."

Kyle stood up and crossed his arms. "If she's leaving, I'm leaving, too."

The false pity on Jayden's face turned to genuine concern in an instant. "What? Why? No." He rushed over to Kyle and caressed his arms, trying to coax him to stay.

Kyle jutted out his chin and glared at Jayden. I was glad I wasn't the only one who could see through Jayden's act.

Max walked back into the room. "What's going on?"

Grace Shin, clad in her signature black hoodie and jeans, stood behind Max. Next to her was a tall woman with red hair and freckles. She looked familiar, but I couldn't remember her name. They were both focused on Kyle and Jayden. So, I wasn't sure they'd spotted me yet. I considered using Jayden and Kyle's disagreement as a distraction that might allow me to slip out unnoticed, but Salty took off toward the newcomers, wagging her majestic tail and trotting in circles around their feet.

"Look at you!" Grace cooed at Salty and bent down. "Max, you didn't say you got a dog."

"She's actually Angie's dog." Max glanced past Jayden and Kyle, who were still hissing at each other in low voices. His eyes met mine and sent a jolt to my core.

"Angie?" Grace looked up.

I stepped around the coffee table and waved. "Hey."

Grace looked to Max, then back to me, uncertain what to make of my presence.

I decided to save her from having to ask. "I'm in town for work and happened to be in the area, so I stopped in to say hi. But, I'm going to go because you all have plans, and I had a long flight. I should really get some sleep."

It wasn't until I finished speaking that I realized I was going to have to squeeze past them to get to the door, and Max had put my coat in the bathroom. Meanwhile, my traitorous faerie guard dog was licking Grace's hand and begging for more rubs. Extracting myself was not going to be easy.

Rather than giving in to Salty's demands, Grace stood and wiped her hand on her jeans. "Don't go. Please? I haven't seen you in forever. Plus, Hannah is going to be pissed if she finds out she missed you."

Seeing Grace was one thing. I really wasn't ready to face Hannah.

"I can drive Angie back to her hotel if she wants to go," Kyle said.

I turned toward him to find he still had his arms crossed. Jayden was pouting. Even though I suspected that Kyle thought he was sticking up for me, I knew he was only making Jayden hate me more.

Someone knocked on the front door, then called out as they opened it, "Hello?"

"Hannah, get in here!" Grace called out. "Angie's here!"

"Angie's here?" Hannah's flawless tan face peeked in from the hall. "Ahh!" She waved her hands in the air. "Let me get these boots off, and then I want a hug."

The woman that Grace arrived with winced at Hannah's excitement. She kissed Grace on the cheek as she squeezed past her and plopped down on the couch.

Max caught my eye and raised an eyebrow.

I nodded. "All right. I'll stay. But I really don't want to interrupt your game."

Hannah rushed in and hurried over to me. She was six feet tall with movie-star good looks and a model-thin figure. She was also Morgan's best friend and had known Max since he was in elementary school. Hannah had fans and millions of followers, but she still was one of the most generous people I knew. You had to be pretty nice to cover for your date when he wanted to sneak off and hook up with his ex in a closet at his sister's wedding.

She threw her arms around me and squeezed as she whispered in my ear, "Please tell me he grew a spine and you two are getting back together."

I smiled. "Nope."

She groaned. Then she held me at arm's length so she could get a better look at my outfit. "Not bad, little angel. Loving that blouse. That cut is so hot right now, and you have the perfect shape to pull it off."

I beamed at her praise. "Well, I learned it from watching you."

"Oooh! Did you catch my livestream today?" Her fingers squeezed my arms.

Max and Grace were talking in low voices just beyond Hannah's shoulder. I wanted to know what they were saying. "I missed it. I was on a plane. But I've got it marked to watch later. Good stuff?"

"Great stuff. In fact...I think I have some samples in my bag. I'll hook you up."

"So is Angie playing with us, or do we only need characters for Jayden and Kyle?" The woman with the freckles on the couch had a box open on the coffee table. Papers and dice threatened to crowd the snack bowls off the far edge.

"Chill, Callie. Varun's not even here, yet, and we still need to eat," Hannah scolded the woman who I now recognized as Callie Barrington. She'd been in Max's cohort at Stanford, but they had never been close, so I didn't know her very well.

"I'm not playing. I think I'll just hang out for a bit and then catch a cab back to my hotel." I glanced around, searching for Salty, and found her curled up at Max's feet.

"Then don't make a character for me," Kyle said. "I'll drop Angie off and circle back to pick up Jayden." He'd finally uncrossed his arms and had one slung across Jayden's shoulder.

Jayden had one arm around Kyle's waist. The other held his phone up to his ear. He finished his call and hung up. "Varun's on his way and says he has plenty of food for everyone. He says to tell Angie 'hi' and that she better not leave before he gets here."

"Good. It's settled, then." Grace clapped her hands together. "You're staying."

"And I'll bribe you with this if you'll stay and let Max drive you home after the game." Jayden pulled a hardcover out of his messenger bag and held it out to me.

"How did you get this?" I took the book from him, cradling it in my palms so I could study the cover art.

"I have my ways." He waved a hand as if it were nothing. "Do we have a deal?"

Hannah peeked over my shoulder. "Is that what I think it is?"

"It's not supposed to be out for weeks." I tore my eyes away from the foil-embossed cover long enough to glance at Jayden. "Are you sure?"

He shrugged. "Just give it back when you're done."

I hugged the book to my chest. "I'll be extra careful with it."

Salty barked once, drawing everyone's attention. Then the doorbell rang.

Hannah tugged on my arm. "That will be Varun. Put that down and come help me get some plates."

I set Jayden's bribe down on Max's bookshelf and followed Hannah into the kitchen. She found the cabinet with the plates on the first try, like she was familiar with the layout. I smothered the little spark of jealousy before it burned me.

"How have you been?" she asked. "Really?"

I shrugged. "Fine."

"Fine?" She shot me a look that made it clear she did not believe me. Then she handed me a stack of plates. "He told me that you came up to visit a few months ago."

"He did?"

She'd moved on to the silverware drawer and was scooping up forks and knives by the handful. "He wasn't going to, but I stopped by with Morgan before she left for vacation, and he was a mopey mess. She threatened to cancel her trip unless he told her why."

"Oh."

"Yeah. Oh." She shut the drawer with her hip and dumped the cutlery on top of the stack of plates, then moved on to the fridge. "So, are you going to tell me what's up with you two?"

"Nothing."

"Nothing?"

"Nothing."

She searched the fridge and sighed. "Seriously? I can't believe he doesn't have any ketchup." She shut the door and turned to me. "For the record, Grace and I are rooting for you guys to work it out, whatever's going on. You two are the power couple of the century, and you deserve to be together."

I scowled. "That's really nice, and I appreciate your enthusiasm, but I think it's really over this time."

She arched an expertly shaped eyebrow at me. "You don't want to be with him?"

"He doesn't want to be with me."

She laughed. "Uh. No. I do not believe that for one minute."

I shifted the plates in my arms. They were starting to get heavy, and I was frustrated enough that I kind of wanted to throw them. "Tonight is the first time we've talked since I left. He didn't call me. He didn't text me. Then, when I texted him to let him know I was in town, he read it and never responded."

"Huh." Hannah took the stack of plates from me. "That makes no sense."

Varun walked in carrying two large paper bags. "Angie! It really is you!"

Hannah set the plates down on the center island. "Are we setting everything out in here, then?"

"Yes." He put the bags down and returned his attention to me. "Max said you were here for work. Did you finally decide to join the rest of us and move up here?"

"It's just an assignment. Not permanent."

He scowled. "Who do I have to talk with to make it permanent?"

That was not the reaction I'd been expecting. I'd thought that they all hated me for breaking up with Max. They'd all avoided me at Morgan's wedding, and now they were treating me like a long-lost bestie.

Max walked in with Grace and saved me from answering. "I put Callie in charge of getting Jayden and Kyle up to speed. Burgers first and then campaigning? Or campaign while we eat?"

"I can't stay long." Hannah glanced at the shiny black bangle on her wrist. When she twisted her wrist up, a digital display flashed on, and I realized that it was some sort of new, fancy watch and not a bracelet. "I have to make an appearance at a club for a thing."

"Campaign while we eat, then." Max glanced at me. "Is that okay with you?"

I waved a hand. "Yeah. No problem. I have a book to read."

"Just like old times, man." Varun sighed as he dug around in the bags. He emerged with two paper-wrapped packages, both marked with a "V." He set one on his plate and handed the other to Hannah. Then he grinned at me. "Welcome back, Angie."

ONCE EVERYONE WAS SETTLED around the table with food, I pulled the key out of the back pocket of my notebook and set it in the center of the table. Then I flipped to the page I had marked. Under the table, Angie's dog set her head on my foot.

I glanced over at Angie, who had curled into the armchair next to the gas fireplace with Jayden's peace offering. She'd tucked her feet up underneath her as she munched on fries with one hand and turned pages with the other. If I had the power to freeze time, I probably would have stopped it right there so I could have had a few more minutes to savor the feeling of having everything just right.

When I agreed to take over as heir in place of my sister, I had promised my mother that I'd end things with Angie and marry for magic. Even if we found a cure for Morgan, my mother was not going to let me out of that promise.

"All right. Let's pick up where we left off last time, shall we?" I got a thrill from the extra challenge of hiding our meetings in plain sight. I gestured to the center of the table. "We've been put in charge of uncovering the source of a plot to destroy all wizards. We have this key, but we don't know where to find the object it unlocks, or what secrets it hides. And we just discovered that the wizard who gave us the key works at an undercover magic shop in the heart of the city."

"Oh, really?" Jayden leaned forward in his chair. "Is this what you found out?"

I glared at him, then cut my eyes toward Angie.

"Where is this shop?" Callie asked. "Can we go there?"

"The shop is hidden. Does anyone have any spells they'd like to try?"

Callie glanced over her shoulder at Angie before answering. "I think we should try a revealing spell."

Hannah sighed. "Too easy. We should find someone who can lead us there."

"And how do you propose we do that?" Varun asked.

"I've been doing some research." Grace interrupted, then paused, waiting until she had everyone's attention before continuing. "In the, uh...in the library of ancient folklore. I think we should try a divination spell on the key, but my, uh...character doesn't have the right sort of magic to do that.

So, I was thinking that maybe Kyle might be willing to give it a try?"

"Why Kyle?" I asked, curious about whatever Grace found in the Society's lineage records that might have made her think that Kyle might be able to do more than just control the element of air.

"Well, in the library, I found this note about a certain type of wizard that has the ability to see into the future as well as see hidden aspects of an object."

"My character can do that?" Kyle asked. He was doing an excellent job playing along, much better than Jayden.

Grace nodded. "I think it's worth a try."

I rolled the dice a few times and made some notes in my notebook to make it look like I was working within some sort of game mechanics in case Angie was paying attention. I snuck a glance at her to confirm that she was still absorbed in her book.

"All right. Kyle takes the key and attempts his spell." I pushed the key toward Kyle.

"Now what?" Varun asked, leaning forward.

I jumped in with a plausible story. "Kyle closes his eyes and concentrates on the key, trying to unlock its secrets."

Kyle held the key between his fingers and stared at me.

I stared back until he took the hint and closed his eyes.

His lips pressed together as he focused. The room fell silent as we watched and waited. When his eyes popped open, he started to speak.

I shook my head to silence him and handed him the dice. "Would you like to roll to see how that turns out?"

Kyle rolled a six. His eyes met mine, and he tilted his head. "What does that mean?"

I tapped my finger against my lips. It didn't really matter

what the number was. I wanted to know what he'd seen, but I had to be the one driving the game. I stated my question, making it sound like I was informing them, rather than asking. "The spell worked."

Kyle nodded and opened his mouth to confirm, but I shook my head.

Hannah checked her watch, then pushed her chair back from the table. "I hate to do this, but I have to go."

"Already?" Varun sighed. "We were just getting started."

"I know. I'm sorry." Hannah made an apologetic face.

"Let's take a quick break. I want to talk with Hannah before she leaves." Grace stood and started collecting the empty plates from the table.

Callie tugged on the sleeve of Grace's hoodie. "We should probably get going, too. I have an early shift tomorrow morning."

Grace frowned, but nodded, then followed Hannah into the kitchen.

"Maybe we should all go and pick this up tomorrow when Max doesn't have company." Varun kept his voice low and jutted his chin in Angie's direction.

"You guys don't want to know what Kyle saw?" I asked.

"I can just tell you."

"That's not how this works." Callie's eye's darted between Kyle and the spot where Angie was still curled up on the other side of the room.

Hannah and Grace returned from the kitchen, heads bent toward each other and whispering. Callie stood and intercepted them.

Varun pressed his palms against the table and leaned back. "Come on, you two. Let's go."

Kyle handed me back the key. "I'll text you."

"Sounds good. We'll reconvene tomorrow." I slid the key into the pocket at the back of my notebook and secured the strap.

Varun walked over to where Hannah and Grace were saying goodbye to Angie, and Callie moved toward the door, leaving Kyle and Jayden alone with me.

Jayden cringed. "We may have an issue with meeting tomorrow."

"What's that?" I asked.

"The widow's lawyer called again. They want to know what's taking so long."

"I thought you were going to give me the weekend to go through the boxes?" I waved to Callie, Grace, Hannah, and Varun, who were standing at the door, ready to leave.

Jayden nodded. "I did. I told them I'd ship everything on Monday. That means you've got some work to do tomorrow. See you at the office at nine?"

I groaned and rolled my eyes as I realized what he was doing. He was making sure I didn't spend any more time than absolutely necessary with Angie. "Yeah. Nine tomorrow."

"I'll get the coffee." He slipped his hand into Kyle's and started walking toward the door.

"See you then." The others were already heading to their cars when I opened the door to let Kyle and Jayden out. That had not gone as well as I'd hoped, but Kyle's reaction to the key made me think that we were still making progress.

Angie was standing in the hall with her tote when I shut the door. "What was that all about?"

"Remember I mentioned that this week has been crazy? Well, one of the Hunter Works engineers went missing like twenty years ago. He was part of the department that got spun off into Silicon Moon. Somehow we ended up with all his stuff, even though he was long gone before Silicon Moon was even a thing. Anyway, a few weeks ago, he turned up dead. Now his widow wants his stuff, but I'm nervous about sending her a bunch of boxes when I have no idea what's in them."

"Sounds like a lot of work."

I shrugged. "It needs to get done, and apparently it needs to be done fast. I'm not about to ask someone else to come in on the weekend when I can just do it myself."

She squinted at me. "But you're the CEO."

"Yeah, and you're an ambitious corporate attorney. You know you'd do the same thing."

She shrugged. "I guess, but that's not really the same as being the CEO."

"No, but..." I had an idea—one that might salvage my weekend and give me a valid reason for hanging out with her more. "Since you're the IP expert, do you want to help? It could be a contract job. Does your new firm let you do those?"

Angie frowned. "Yeah."

I wasn't sure how to read her reaction. "I can pay you."

"It's not exactly how I'd planned to spend my weekend, but..."

"Please?" I gave her my best impression of Salty's puppy dog eyes. "It'll be way more fun if we do it together." I clamped my jaw shut once I realized what I'd said and hoped she wasn't thinking about what else we could be doing together, because I definitely was, and Jayden had already warned me. I could not go there.

"You are not going to convince me that searching through dusty old boxes of papers together is going to be fun." She had either missed or chosen to ignore my accidental innuendo. "But, you're right. If you think there may be design docs in there, you should have someone from your legal team looking at that stuff. Not you. No offense."

"None taken. You're absolutely right. So you'll help?"

"I'll help. Text me the address, and I'll meet you there in the morning." She glanced at her watch. "But if you want me there at nine, you better drive me back to my hotel. It's late."

I hurried to grab her jacket and my keys before she could change her mind and call a cab. As we walked out to where I'd parked my Jeep in the driveway, I fought the urge to put my arm around her and tuck her against my side. I did manage to beat her to the passenger door. I opened it and waited as she lifted Salty up and slid into the seat.

Once she was settled, I walked around to the other side and climbed in. "So tell me about this new job of yours."

"There isn't much to tell. Evie got a job working for a sort of wealthy and powerful family. They have a lot of secrets." She paused, and I felt her eyes on me. "Evie convinced them they needed a lawyer."

"They're British?"

"They're sort of international, I guess you could say." Her jacket crinkled when she shrugged. "I'm dealing with their business in the US."

"So is this a temporary thing? Or a permanent thing?" I stopped at a stoplight and glanced over at her profile.

Her front teeth pulled at her bottom lip. "A little bit of both, I guess."

"I suppose once you're in, you're in." I knew a thing or two about powerful families with secrets.

"Something like that."

"Well, I'm glad you're here, and I really appreciate you taking the time to help me tomorrow."

"Hey, Max?" She turned her head toward me, but the light

turned green, and I had to focus on the road.

"Yeah?"

She stayed silent for several blocks. "You know you can trust me, right?"

I pulled my Jeep into the loading zone in front of her hotel and shifted into park. "Yeah. I know."

"Okay." She unbuckled her seat belt.

I shifted in my seat until I was mostly facing her. My fingers ached to reach out and touch her cheek and smooth away the frown that had settled at the corners of her mouth. "I'm sorry I didn't call after your last visit. I thought about it a lot. I just could never decide what to say."

Angie's frown deepened. "When you figure it out, let me know. I'll see you in the morning. Don't forget to text me the address." She opened the door, slid out of the car, and disappeared into the hotel before I could respond.

4

WHEN I opened my eyes, the first thing I saw was a pink tongue. Hot dog breath washed over my face. I groaned and rolled over to check the alarm clock. Then I did the plus-seven math to decide if I should bother trying to call Evie to catch her up on things.

My phone buzzed on the desk where I'd left it plugged in to charge. When I sat up, Salty stood and started running around in circles on the top of the bed.

"Chill, dog." I swung my legs out from under the covers and stood to stretch. "Human needs first, then I'll deal with you."

I scrolled through the increasingly desperate texts from Evie and Willow on our group chat. I sent a quick response to let them know I was alive and would call in a half hour, then I headed for the shower. While I waited for the water in the shower to heat up, I frowned at myself in the mirror.

I should have been happy that I'd managed to survive an evening with Max's friends and extract myself without succumbing to the temptation to stay. Not that he'd offered. He hadn't even made a move that could have been interpreted as anything more than friendly, and his weak attempt at an apology for not calling didn't help. I fussed with my hair and pouted my lips. The whole thing was pointless.

Even though I wanted to linger in the comforting embrace of the hotel's endless supply of hot water, I needed to walk Salty and call my friends to give them an update. I counted to three and turned off the tap, then hurried through my usual routine, trying not to obsess about my outfit, hair, and makeup. I was going to work, and I planned to keep it strictly professional. Of course, it wouldn't hurt to make sure Max knew what he was missing out on.

I checked the address of Max's office, scouted a route that would allow me to swing by one of my favorite purveyors of caffeine and pastry, stuffed my essentials into my tote, and bent down to consult with my guard dog.

"Ready?"

Salty yipped in response. I had no idea what that meant, so I took it for a yes and reached for her leash.

"Sorry about this, bud." I clipped the end to her collar and stood.

She shook herself thoroughly from head to fluffy fox-like tail.

"My feelings exactly." I sighed. "Let's do this, huh?"

Once we were outside the hotel, I called Evie. She picked up after the first ring.

"Angie?"

"Wow. That was quick." I stuffed my second earbud into my ear and flipped to the navigation app on my phone so I wouldn't miss the cross street that led to my favorite local cafe. I knew enough about the city to know where I wanted to go, but not enough to get there without a map.

"How did it go last night? Tell me everything."

"It went about as well as you might expect from a sponta-neous reunion of all the friends your ex won in the breakup. You know, like if you suddenly found yourself at the same resort with everyone from Connor's annual ski trip? About that good."

Evie groaned. "Ugh. I'm sorry. We should never have asked you to do this."

"I don't know. Maybe it wasn't that bad? It's hard to say. Grace and Hannah seemed genuinely happy to see me. I think Varun was ready to hire me. It was really only Max's assistant, Jayden, who was openly not a fan. He did give me a copy of the new novel in the Emma Fierce series, though."

"What? Wow! That's not out until next month."

"I know. He decided to bribe me with his early copy after his boyfriend offered to leave early and drive me back to my hotel. That may have influenced his generosity a bit."

"His boyfriend took your side?"

"His boyfriend could tell that Jayden was being a massive jerk to me, and he didn't want anything to do with making me uncomfortable."

"Nice."

"Yeah. I feel like I need to pull poor Kyle aside and have a talk with him about his choice in men. Then again, who am I to be giving advice on that?"

"Max may be clueless, but he's a good guy."

"He is," I grumbled. "This sucks so hard."

"I know. Have I apologized, yet?"

"Only about a million times."

"Were you able to get any information out of him?"

"Nope. But I'm on my way to meet up with him now."

"Breakfast?"

"No. Work. He asked if I'd consult on some IP thing. I agreed, but only because it's a decent excuse to spend more time with him. I think his assistant is going to be there, though."

"It may be a good thing to have someone as a buffer to keep things from getting too awkward."

"You mean to keep me from throwing myself at him?" I grinned.

"We both know you are way too stubborn for that."

"You're right." I sighed, wishing it weren't true. "He was such a damn gentleman last night when he dropped me off. He didn't even hint that I could just stay at his place."

"You broke up with him. What do you expect?"

"I expect him to realize the error of his ways and get down on one knee and beg for forgiveness, damn it." That comment caused a few heads to swivel my way as they passed me walking down the sidewalk.

"It could still happen," Evie said.

"Do not go there."

"Sorry."

"You're starting to sound English with all this apologizing. Stop it."

"Sor— Uh. Okay."

"Better." I stopped outside the coffee shop and peeked through the glass on the front of the building. The line wasn't terrible. "I've gotta go. I'll text you later with an update."

"Okay. Just keep Salty with you and keep your eyes open for any signs of magic use."

I paused in the process of looping Salty's leash around a bike rack. "What if I need coffee? Is it okay to leave her tied up outside?"

Salty lay down and set her head on her front paws, then stared up at me with her big brown eyes.

"She's a guard dog. She'll be fine. I don't think the demons are going to try to attack you in a cafe while you're surrounded by other humans, especially since they have no reason to be targeting you."

"Yet." I finished securing the leash and rubbed Salty's head.

"You'll be back here safe and sound before they ever know what you're up to."

"Let's hope so. Nigel's mother sounds like a peach."

"If peaches were deadly and poisonous."

"Exactly." I'd heard about Evie's encounter with her and had no interest in meeting the succubus leading the demon clans in their attempt to eliminate the Fae.

"Just be safe, okay? I worry about you."

I caught a glimpse of my reflection in the glass door as I pulled it open. "You should be worried about Max. He's the one who's not going to be safe once he takes one look at me in this outfit."

Evie laughed. "That's right."

"Love you."

"Love you, too."

I hung up and stepped behind the last person in line, then directed my attention to my phone screen. After scrolling through my playlists to find the perfect amp-up mix, I glanced outside to make sure Salty was okay. A couple with a toddler had stopped to admire her, so I figured she was fine and focused my attention on deciding between the dozen or so types of pastry in the display case. The whole place smelled like dark roast espresso and butter. Heaven.

My stomach growled. It must have been loud because the person in front of me turned their head. When our eyes met, my jaw dropped open. I fumbled with the controls on my phone, trying to pause my music.

"Hello, Jayden."

"Angie." He glanced around like he expected to see Max with me and looked visibly relieved when he realized it was just me. "How are you this morning?"

I didn't get a chance to answer before he had to place his order, so I waited for him to finish. He handed over two travel mugs and asked for one large coffee and one cappuccino. I guessed the cappuccino was for Max. That was his drink. But I had to admit I was surprised at Jayden's no-frills order. For some reason, I'd pegged him as one of those complicated alternative-milk and no-sugar-sweetener types.

He moved away to allow me to order my mocha along with two chocolate croissants, which was really the bare minimum amount of chocolate required for what I was facing this morning. Though I did plan to give one of the croissants to Max. It would be entirely too cruel to enjoy our mutual favorite pastry without sharing, and I wasn't about to give him half of mine. When I caught Jayden looking at me, I realized he probably thought both were for me because he probably didn't know that we'd crossed paths on the way to the same destination.

"Planning to do any sightseeing today?" Jayden asked when I joined him at the pickup end of the counter, his question confirming that Max hadn't filled him in about my addition to their weekend project.

"Oh, I don't know. Maybe later." I shrugged and wondered how long I could keep him in the dark. "Thanks for the book, by the way. I'll be sure to get that back to you before I leave town."

He waved a hand. "No hurry. It's just going to sit on my

shelf with the others."

"You weren't going to read it?" My eyes widened in shock.

He grimaced. "I never read my sister's books."

"Leia Reyes is your sister?" I must have shrieked a bit because he cast a nervous glance at the other customers nearby. Luckily, it was just a woman bent over her baby in a stroller and a guy decked out in spandex with a bike helmet and earbuds in his ears. They didn't seem to notice my excitement.

Jayden's jaw clenched. "Yes."

"But, she's amazing. Her books are..." My hands flailed as I tried to find words to describe the detailed world-building, lush descriptions, and swoon-worthy heroes that Evie and I had initially bonded over when we stumbled into each other freshman year in the library.

"Entirely too fantastical for me." He stepped forward to retrieve his large coffee from the barista.

I stared at the back of his head, newly convinced that he was, indeed, a monster. I was so lost in my loathing that I almost didn't hear my name.

A woman with pink-streaked hair piled on top of her head handed me a bag stamped with the cafe logo. She grinned at me. "Love your hair."

"Thanks." I smiled back. "Same."

"You had a coffee order, too, right?" She leaned back to check the order receipts pinned to the back side of the counter.

I nodded. "Mocha."

"Right." Her grin widened. "Let me grab that for you."

Jayden frowned. He was still waiting on Max's cappuccino.

My new pink-haired friend returned with my drink just as the barista slid the second half of Jayden's order onto the counter.

She handed me my mocha, then checked the receipts again to confirm who the other drink belonged to. "Cappuccino to go for Jay?"

"Thanks." Jayden stepped forward and plucked the cappuccino up. Then he paused and turned to me. "Nice catching up with you."

Before I could respond, he was threading his way through the crowded cafe. I thanked the pink-haired woman, dropped another dollar in the tip jar, and hurried after Jayden. I was going to have to break the news to him before he caught me following him and thought I was a stalker or something.

I lost sight of him as I made my way to the door, but caught up with him as soon as I walked outside. Or, more accurately, Salty had caught him in her leash, and he was trying to extract himself without spilling either of the drinks in his hands, or getting too close to Salty's panting tongue.

"Need some help?" I asked.

He glared at me. "Yes, please."

I bent down to unfasten the knot attaching the leash to the bike rack. "We might as well walk together. I think we're heading in the same direction." I stood, leash in one hand, mocha and pastry bag in the other.

"Is your office near Silicon Moon?"

"For today, my office is Silicon Moon. Max asked me to help you guys go through the boxes. It's kind of my area of expertise."

Jayden's face paled. "He didn't."

"He did." I took a long sip of my mocha. I was definitely going to need more chocolate for this. "Shall we?"

———

THE ELEVATOR DOOR OPENED, revealing two grumpy humans,

both bearing coffee, and one ecstatic dog. Angie and Jayden stepped forward at the same time, realized they weren't going to be able to walk through the door together, and had a momentary stare down until Salty rushed forward, breaking the impasse.

I hid my amusement by squatting down to pet Angie's dog as she ran to greet me, tail wagging. When Salty stopped in front of me, panting and wiggling from nose to tail, Angie's boots stopped alongside. She bent to unclip Salty's leash, and I glanced at her. Our eyes met.

Our faces close enough that I had to concentrate on pinning my heels to the ground to resist the urge to lean forward and kiss her. She smelled amazing, like vanilla and sugar. The plunging neck of her blouse moved just enough to give me a glimpse of the top of her breast. My mind filled in the missing details, and my body reacted, making it so I was going to have to adjust myself if I didn't stop picturing her naked.

"Do you mind if I let her run around?" Angie asked. She gave no hint that she recognized my lusting or my distress.

I shifted things loose as I stood and hoped she hadn't noticed. "No. Not at all."

"Thanks." She held up a brown wax paper bag stamped with a smiling and dancing coffee cup. "I got two. Want one?"

My mouth watered at my guess as to what was inside the bag. "Hell yeah. Thanks."

Jayden was staring at me. When he spoke, his voice was mocking. "Thanks for the coffee, Jay. Sorry I forgot to tell you I hired my ex as a consultant."

"Thanks." I took the insulated mug he offered me. "And sorry?"

Jayden grunted. "I'll go get the forms she needs to sign." He pivoted and stalked away.

"I don't think he likes me," Angie whispered.

"Don't worry. He's like this with everyone." I waved her toward my office. "Come on. Let's eat while those are still warm."

As she moved past me, I reached out a hand to touch the small of her back, where her bright-red blouse billowed as the smooth fabric glided across the seat of her dark-wash denim. Then I caught myself and pulled back. I let my palm hover in her wake just long enough to be sure that she hadn't noticed what I'd been about to do. My hand flexed against my will, so I shoved it into the pocket of my jeans to keep it from rebelling further.

I blinked my eyes closed and shook my head to clear it. Torturing myself with Angie's presence was probably a very bad idea. Jayden would be sure to inform me exactly how bad of an idea this was as soon as he got me alone.

When I opened my eyes, Angie was standing next to the wall of windows behind my desk, staring down at the street below. "Wow. Nice view."

"Yeah. Best part of the job." I motioned to my desk chair. "Have a seat."

She eyed the chair, then me. "Are you sure?"

I shrugged. "It's just a chair. Besides, I like the view from here."

I bit back a cringe. I sounded like a lovesick teenager. I needed to get it together. If Jayden heard me dropping lame lines like that, he'd never let me hear the end of it. At least Angie hadn't picked up on my awkwardness.

She plopped down in my chair and set her coffee alongside the bag of pastries on my desk. "Are you going to freak out if we get crumbs on your desk?"

"Nah." I tried to play it cool, but she knew me too well.

"Did they give you napkins, at least?"

She laughed. "Yes. I grabbed some napkins."

We divided up the napkins and the pastries. I'd finally got my teeth around my first bite of the most perfect chocolate croissant in the city when Jayden returned. He slapped a few pages on the desk near Angie's elbow. They still smelled of hot toner from the printer.

"Nondisclosure and standard contractor agreement. Do you need a pen?" He stared past Angie at her dog, who was lying in a beam of light filtering through the windows. His eyes narrowed.

"I've got one." Angie set down her croissant and wiped off her hands.

Salty lifted her head from her paws and looked at Jayden.

"You can wait until after you're done eating." I patted the side of my leg and dangled a bit of croissant crust above the floor to get the dog's attention. She sat up but didn't come over to investigate.

Angie took a sip of her coffee, then leaned over to dip her hand into the tote bag she'd set on the ground near her feet. "No. It's all right. Better to get this out of the way. Jayden's right. This sort of thing is important." When she sat up, the glint of light on metal caught my eye. She popped the jeweled cap off an emerald-green pen, revealing a fountain tip.

I glanced at Jayden and grinned as his jaw went a bit slack and his eyes widened. He gaped for a moment, visibly torn between his admiration of Angie's taste in writing instruments and the fact that, as my loyal assistant, he'd sworn to hate her, and possibly also her innocent and adorable dog, forever.

Angie caught him looking. "Would you mind also getting me a copy of your employee agreement? Ideally, the one that this particular employee signed so that I know what we're dealing with here?"

Jayden closed his mouth and nodded. "Of course."

He hurried out of my office without another look at me, and Angie bent over the nondisclosure form. I watched her face as she started to read. Then I took another bite of my croissant and pulled my phone out of my pocket to text Jayden.

Why were you staring at Angie's dog?

It didn't take long for him to respond. Kyle thinks there's something up with that dog, and I agree.

Something like what? I responded. Then added: Familiars don't just attach themselves to humans without magic.

You think I don't know that? Watch. That. Dog. I'll be back in fifteen, and if I catch you smooching, I'm telling your mother on you.

I grimaced at my phone.

"Something wrong?" Angie slid the cap onto the pen and set it on top of the signed papers.

"No. Just...family stuff." I hated lying. I decided that was going to be the last one. No more lying to her unless it was to keep my family's secrets. It was bad enough that I couldn't tell her the real reason we couldn't be together. I could at least be truthful about everything else.

"Morgan?" she asked.

"No. Morgan's great. She's on vacation." I slid my phone into my pocket. "Ready to get to work?"

Angie gestured to her unfinished croissant. "Couple more minutes?"

"Oh. Yeah. Sure. Sorry." I sat back and ran a hand through my hair. My eyes strayed to Salty, who was still sitting up. "You don't usually see a lot of purebred corgis in shelters.

Must have been pretty lucky to find her, huh?"

Angie shrugged as she finished chewing and swallowed. "Oh, I didn't adopt her. She was a gift from a...friend of a friend, I guess."

"I thought you said you adopted her."

"Nope."

"Huh. Interesting." Now I was squinting at the dog, but not from suspicion. The feeling making my leg twitch was decidedly more like jealousy. I wanted to ask about this "friend of a friend," but I wasn't sure how to formulate the question without sounding like a possessive jerk.

She took another bite and sipped her coffee. "You remember Evelyn, right?"

"Your roommate from college? Sure. Of course."

Angie took another sip of coffee. "She's living in England now, with her aunt and uncle. She got a new job and has a boyfriend who lives there."

"Oh. Wow. Really? That's cool." I tried to sound enthusiastic, but her comments seemed more like they were leading to a change in subject than to a story about how she got her dog.

"Yeah. I went to visit her after I...uh...left here."

"Oh." We were beginning to stray into dangerous territory. The weekend she was referring to had only been a few months ago. It was amazing, and perfect, and it could absolutely not happen again, no matter how much I wanted it.

"Anyway. Evie's doing well. Salty was a gift from one of her new friends, this woman named Willow who used to live in Alaska, but now she works with Evie."

I knew Angie had dated both women and men, but for some reason, I hadn't expected her to have replaced me with a girlfriend. Things between the two of them must have been moving fast if they were already at the "giving pets as gifts" stage of the relationship. She hadn't said she was dating anyone, but then again, we hadn't talked since her last visit. "Is that how you two met?"

Angie nodded as she finished the last bite of her pastry. "We sort of all work together now, I guess." She paused for a sip of coffee. "It was actually Willow's girlfriend's idea to give me Salty. Her girlfriend is Liam's cousin. Liam is Evie's new boyfriend..." She waved a hand. "Never mind. This is probably way more than you wanted to know."

Relief that I had no business feeling swept over me. "Sounds like you're getting to work with friends, at least."

"Yeah. That part is great." She wiped her hands off. "Okay. I'm ready. Which way to the boxes?"

I stood and collected the garbage, stuffing the used napkins into her empty coffee cup. "I hauled everything to the conference room while I was waiting for you and Jayden to arrive this morning. I thought it would be more comfortable to go through everything in there."

"Sounds great." She picked up her tote and slung it over her shoulder. "Lead the way, boss."

I groaned. "Okay. I don't care what Jayden made you sign, but you really don't need to call me that."

Angie laughed. "I was kidding. Technically speaking, I am my own boss in this arrangement."

I sighed with relief. "Good. That makes me feel better. I am very not comfortable with the idea of you working for me. Let's just get this done so we can go back to being..."

She stepped closer and tilted her chin up so she could look me in the eyes. "Friends?"

My eyes snagged on her lips, hating that word and knowing that if I gave in and kissed her and Jayden walked in, he would go straight to my mother. "Yeah. I suppose. Friends."

5

HE still liked me. I could tell. What I couldn't figure out was why, if he was working so hard to keep his hands off me and worried about who I was dating, he completely froze up as soon as I mentioned my last visit. Something was going on with him. Maybe it had to do with this whole wizard secret of his, or maybe it was something else. Something more. Something that had him spooked.

I pulled dusty objects out of boxes and sorted them into stacks on the conference table as I tried to figure Max out. I didn't need much brainpower to separate the desk trinkets and dried-out old pens from the battered notebooks and file folders stuffed with papers. Max was doing the same thing at the other end of the table.

Jayden had propped open the door to the conference room, probably so he could monitor us, then retreated to his desk, most likely so he could throw darts at a copy of my photo pinned to his cube wall. Max may think that his assistant was like this with everyone, but his icy attitude seemed particularly intense when it came to me.

Max emptied out the box he'd been working on and set it in the stack by the door. "Another one done. Only..." He scanned the room. "One? Really? Is this the last box?"

I extracted a file folder stuffed with loose papers and set it with the others we'd found. "I think so. I just finished this one. Do you want me to take the last one?"

Max had already lifted it up onto the table in front of him. "No. I'll do it. Why don't you take a break."

I grinned at him. "You are entirely too nice. I'm on the clock. You're paying me by the hour, and I'm not giving you a friends and family discount."

"Well, in that case." He stepped away from the table and gestured to the last box. "It's all yours."

I tapped my chin with my finger, pretending to think, and watched his eyes darken as they focused on my mouth. "On the other hand, you are paying me an awful lot to sort through this junk. Perhaps it would be a better use of my very expensive time for me to get started on that mountain of paperwork."

We'd pushed anything requiring closer examination to the center of the table. In the process, we'd created a mound of old notebooks, rolls of paper that could be product design documents or inspirational posters, and file folders that threatened to spill their contents out onto the floor. Most of it would probably end up shredded in a dumpster, but I was secretly hoping I might discover at least a couple of treasures so that Max could justify the expense of hiring me.

"Excellent point." Max tossed the lid of the last box into the corner by the door. He shook his head as he stared down at the contents. "This guy was such a pack rat."

"Why do you even still have all this?"

"I have no idea." Max sighed. He lifted a metal cube out of the cardboard box and held it up to examine it. "Looks like one of those puzzle things."

I glanced up from the file folder I'd pulled toward me. Salty got up from where she'd been dozing and wandered over to Max. He set the metal cube on the edge of the table and bent to scratch her head.

"You probably want to go for a walk, huh?" he asked my faerie dog.

Salty accepted the rubs but kept her eyes on the cube like she was trying to tell me something. It didn't look magical or dangerous to me. Then again, it could be one of those magic boxes I was supposed to be finding for the Fae. But that would be way too much of a coincidence. There was no way it was going to be that easy.

I flipped open the file folder and scanned the page on top. "What did you say this guy's name was?"

"Cortez. Emilio Cortez." Max straightened and stretched, causing the fabric of his dark T-shirt to pull tight across his muscled chest. "What do you say we get some fresh air and maybe some lunch once I'm done sorting this last box?"

I almost didn't hear his question because my eyes were busy feasting on his body, and my mind had stuck on that name. I reached into my tote for my phone. "Yeah. Sure. That sounds great. Hey, I totally forgot, but I need to make a quick phone call. Do you mind if I use your office?"

"No. Go ahead. I'll keep an eye on Salty, if you want."

"Yeah. Thanks." I stood. "This shouldn't take long."

"Cool. If you see Jayden out there, let him know that we're going to break for lunch soon."

I nodded, already swiping and tapping my phone screen to open the AWEsome group chat.

Urgent update. Call me now.

My phone was ringing by the time I stepped inside Max's office. Willow's profile photo appeared on my screen. I shut the door and headed toward the windows.

"Hello?"

"Hey." Willow was breathing hard like she'd been jogging. "What happened?"

My phone beeped at me. "Hang on. Evie's calling. Let me add her in."

"Ang? Are you okay?" Evie asked before I could say a word.

"Yes. I'm fine, but I need some info. Willow, you still there?"

"Yep."

"Great. Arabella and Nigel's father, his name was Emilio, right?" I scanned the top of Max's desk while I talked. The papers I'd signed were still where I'd left them, and so was the letter I'd seen.

"Yeah, why?"

"Did his death get reported?" I asked.

"Yeah. We thought it would be a good idea to let any family know, so Eve's aunt put the word into the right ears and got it in the news and everything. Why?"

I skimmed the letter while Willow confirmed what I'd already guessed. "Well, would you believe that he used to work as an engineer for a company owned by Max's father?"

"You're kidding."

Evie gasped. "Woah. No way."

"Yep. His widow, someone named Lilium Cortez, is asking for his stuff. So I've been going through boxes with Max all morning, and you'll never guess—"

"Wait." Evie cut me off. "Did you just say Lilium?"

"That's right. I'm looking at the letter from her lawyer right now. Max had it on his desk."

"Where's Max?" Willow asked.

"In the conference room."

"Are you alone?" Evie asked.

"Yes. I'm in his office. Why?" I ran a hand over the back of his leather desk chair.

"Could his office be bugged?" Evie asked.

"It definitely could be," Willow said. "Angie, be careful what you say, okay? Don't mention the M-word or the F-word, or—"

Evie interrupted. "Just let us do the talking, okay?"

"Sure. Fine. Talk." I rolled my eyes.

Evie cleared her throat. "Lilium is Nigel's mother's name."

I gasped. "No way."

"Yep. If she wants Emilio's stuff..."

Willow finished her sentence for her. "She must think there's something in there of value."

"Shit." I pivoted to face the conference room as I realized it was possible that Max really might have been fondling one of those magic boxes earlier.

Evie sighed. "Yeah. I am so sorry. You really are right in the middle of it. We should not have sent you."

"No. Not that. 'Shit' because I think there is something in there." I walked over to the window next to Max's office door to see if I could see the conference room from here.

"What?"

I waved one hand in the air, trying to find words to explain what I'd seen without saying anything that might give away what I knew about magic and the Fae. "One of those things, you know?"

"One of the boxes?" Willow asked.

"Yeah. Maybe. I don't know." My front teeth worried my lower lip as I considered if it would be possible to sneak that cube thing out of here—and if I did, what I would do with it.

"Shit." It was Eve's turn to swear.

"Exactly." I grumbled the word.

"Does Max know?" Eve asked.

"I don't think so." I replayed Max's reaction in my head.

"Well, find out. Then see if you can get your hands on it, or at least make sure that Lilium does not get her hands on it."

"Okay." I glanced at the door. "I should go."

"Good luck." Evie used her most cheery and upbeat tone.

"Be careful." Willow's sign-off was more command than warning.

"I will." I hung up and slid my phone into my back pocket. Then I started to pace.

Someone knocked on the door. When I turned, I found Max had opened it a crack and poked his head inside. "Everything okay?"

"Uh, yeah. I just needed to check on a work thing with Evie. All good."

"Great. I checked with Jayden. We were thinking we'd order some fish-and-chips from the chowder place down the street. Then we can take Salty for a walk and go pick them up. Does that work for you?"

"Yeah. Sounds great." I looked down at Max's feet but saw no sign of my guard dog. Willow had warned me to keep her with me at all times. "Where is Salty, anyway?"

"Oh. I left her with Jayden."

My chest clenched, and I tried not to panic. I opened the door wider so that I could slip out, past Max, only to be faced with a sea of light-gray cubicle walls. "Which way?"

Before he could answer, Salty bolted out of a cube about halfway down the row directly in front of me. She ran toward the sound of my voice.

Jayden popped up and hurried after her. "Come back here, you."

Salty slammed her little body against my shins, and I bent down to stroke her fur.

"It's cool. I got her." I looked up to find Jayden standing a few feet away, scowling at Salty. "I'll just go grab her leash. I left it in my tote bag in the conference room."

"I can get your bag for you. Then you can look at the menu and decide what you want." Max's offer was kind but would require leaving me alone with Jayden.

"You said fish-and-chips?" I scooped Salty up and cradled her in my arms. She was shaking.

"Yep."

"That sounds perfect. Be right back." I hurried toward the conference room before he could ask any more questions. Deep-fried cod actually did sound good, and it was probably what I would have picked out even if I hadn't been eager to get Salty away from Jayden and snag a few minutes alone with Mr. Cortez's stuff.

The metal cube was still on the table. Max had moved it into the pile of old coffee mugs and awards. I plucked it out and held it up to the light. Salty squirmed in my arms, so I set her down. The metal had a dull silver sheen like it had never been polished, or like it had tarnished with age. The sides weren't solid but made up of a labyrinth of winding segments, bent and worked to create the shape of a cube. When I twisted the cube, the flesh of my fingers was visible through the gaps. I could see why Max had thought it was a puzzle.

I set the cube down on top of the file folder I'd been looking at and reached into my tote to get Salty's leash. I was tempted to slip the object into my bag to hide it, but it was too unique. Max would definitely notice it was missing when he began to box up the personal items.

While I was occupied, Salty circled the table, sniffing. I held out the leash and called her to me, but she sat down instead, nose pointing up at the table. It was the same thing she'd done when Max had found the cube.

"Weird little dog. What did you find now?" I walked over to where she sat, just under the mounds of old office supplies that Max had made from the contents of the boxes he'd gone through.

It looked identical to the one I'd made. A few staplers, twenty-odd old pens, the stub of an eraser, and binder clips of all sizes, and that was just the bit that was visible. I sifted my hand through the pile, spreading it out. One of the staplers fell onto its side, revealing what looked like a playing card stuck to the bottom.

"Are you ready?" Max asked from the doorway.

I glanced up. "Yes. I just got distracted."

"It's a lot of junk, mostly. Don't worry. We'll get through it faster on a full stomach."

"You're right." I plucked at the card with the edge of my fingernail until it popped out and fell onto the table.

"Did you find something?" he asked, moving closer.

The face of a horned demon stared up at me as a naked man and woman in chains gazed longingly at each other. I'd seen something like this before, in a movie or a book.

"A tarot card?" Max asked. "That's odd. How'd you find that?"

"I was looking for a paper clip." I said the first thing that came to mind, even though it was a total lie. "Let's eat. You're right. We can deal with this later."

Max picked up the card and studied it while I clipped on Salty's leash. He took the small notebook that he always car-

ried with him out of his pocket and removed the elastic holding it shut. Then he slid the card inside, closed the notebook,
and returned it to his pocket.

"Not going to send that one back to the grieving widow?"
I asked.

He shook his head. "Who knows how long it's been stuck
to the bottom of that stapler. Probably wasn't even Emilio's.
I mean, how many engineers do you know who dabble in
tarot?"

I squinted at him. Emilio had been more than an engineer.
He'd been a powerful wizard. Max must know that. His question was meant to make the idea seem ridiculous, but it had
me wondering exactly how many of Max's engineering staff
were also wizards.

WE STEPPED OUTSIDE into the spring sunshine, waiting for a
break in the weekend foot traffic before merging in and starting toward the chowder place. I tried to think of something
casual to talk about, but my mind was still fixed on trying to
figure out how Angie had found that random tarot card.

I knew Angie didn't have any magic. I had made it a point
to check when we got back from that vacation in Italy. I'd
cross-referenced her ancestry with the lineage books in the
Society's archives, desperate to find anything that might give
me a reason to challenge my mother's demand.

Her parents didn't have magic. Her grandparents didn't
have magic. There wasn't so much as a dabbler in homeo-
pathic brews in her entire family tree. Yet, somehow, she'd
shown up with what Jayden swore was a familiar, and she'd
pulled a tarot card streaked with old magic out of a mound of
rusting office supplies.

As my old gymnastics coach used to say, once is luck, twice is coincidence, three times you got it. Or, in this case, if she showed one more magic-related affinity, something was definitely up. I'd have to keep my eye on her until I could be sure it was all just coincidence and nothing more. It wasn't like I could just bring it up and ask: So, magic...discuss.

"What do you know about tarot?" Angie's question startled me out of my thoughts.

I supposed that was one way to start the discussion. The only problem was, I'd promised myself not to lie to her unless I was doing it to protect my family. I grimaced. "My sister was into it for a while. I learned a few things from her. Why?"

Angie swerved to avoid some folks walking toward us on the sidewalk. In the process, her shoulder brushed against mine. "Just thinking about that card and how it got there. That image was pretty creepy."

I curled my fingers into a fist to squelch the urge to grab her hand and keep her close. "Well, I can ask my sister about it, if you want. Not sure it matters much, though."

"Is that why you kept it? To ask her about it?" Angie glanced at me out of the corner of her eyes.

I'd kept it because I wanted to show it to Jayden and see if he could get a read on any of the magic. Something about it felt like that key. It was a long shot to think that the two might be connected. Emilio had been a wizard, no different than a lot of the Silicon Moon employees and the folks who worked in the other companies my parents owned. That stapler could have belonged to any of them, and that card could have been stuck there long before that stapler landed on Emilio's desk. Still, if the owner of that key was a former or current employee, it would make finding out what it unlocked that much easier.

"No. I just thought it looked interesting, and I'm not about to send that stapler back to the supply closet with a creepy surprise attached."

"Probably a good call." Angie tucked a purple lock of hair behind her ear, giving me a better view of her profile.

"We should cross up here at the corner. The chowder place is one block that way." I snuck a longer look at her when she turned her head to see where I was pointing.

The sun was out, and we'd left our jackets at the office. Her blouse pressed against her torso when the wind blew, and the fabric was doing nothing to hide the curve of her breasts and the dip of her waist. I considered how close we were to her hotel and was tempted to ditch the food and Jayden and all my various responsibilities, including the promise I'd made to my mother.

My phone vibrated in my pocket, but I ignored it. "Are you planning to stay in the Bay Area now that you have this new job? Sounds like you're going to be traveling a lot."

"I haven't decided yet." Angie paused to let Salty sniff at a street tree.

"This is the place." I gestured to the sign on the next store-front. "I'll go grab our food if you want to wait here."

Angie nodded, so I jogged ahead and ducked inside to pick up the food. Jayden had already paid, which meant I only had to wait for the guy behind the counter to finish taking a phone order. He handed me two paper sacks. I thanked him and slipped a few dollars into the tip jar.

Angie and Salty were standing outside when I emerged into the sunlight. "It smells so good in there."

"Best fish-and-chips in the city." I held up the bags. "This place is my favorite."

"You seem to be really settling in here." She sounded a little sad.

I shrugged. "I don't know about that. I spend most of my time at the office and the gym. I'm usually only at my apartment long enough to sleep, eat, and shower."

"How are you liking running a company?"

"About as much as I expected." I paused as a memory surfaced. "Following in my parents' footsteps and eventually taking over responsibility for Hunter Works was always the plan. I'm not even sure I bothered considering what else I might have done instead."

"Kayak guide?" Angie grinned.

"Mountain climber." I managed to keep a straight face until she shoved my shoulder.

"Liar. You were terrified the entire time we hiked that mountain range in Italy. You couldn't wait to get back to the hotel."

"I admit that I may have been trying a bit too hard to impress you, but I seem to remember that I wasn't the only one who benefitted from my eagerness to get off that mountain." I scanned my badge on the card reader and held the glass door open so Angie could enter.

She blushed and tried to hide it by letting her hair fall across her cheeks, but I'd seen the color there. Her fingers drifted up to her neckline, and I wondered if she was also remembering the locket I'd given her for our anniversary. It hadn't been the ring she'd been expecting, but she'd worn it every day until we finally broke up, almost a year later.

The elevator ride was tense, and I began to worry that I'd made a mistake bringing up those memories. My phone vibrated again, breaking the silence, and reminding me that I'd ignored the last message.

As we stepped out of the elevator, I slid my phone from my

pocket to check the screen, just in case it was a message from Morgan or my mother. Instead, it was an update from Kyle, sharing what he'd seen when he'd used his power on the key. I opened the message and realized he'd sent it to both me and Jayden.

"Problem?" Angie asked, pausing to look back over her shoulder.

I hadn't realized I'd stopped walking. "Uh. No? I don't think so." I slid my phone into my pocket but kept my hand around it. "I'll just go grab Jayden and tell him we're back. Meet you in the conference room?"

"Sounds good. Do you guys have any plates? This could get kind of messy." She held up the already-grease-splotched bag.

"Yeah. I'll grab some from the mini kitchen." I pivoted toward Jayden's desk and pulled my phone out to study the image Kyle had sent.

"Where is she?" Jayden stood when I got to his cube. He searched behind me and checked my office before catching a glimpse of Angie as she entered the conference room. "Did you see Kyle's text?"

"Yeah. I just saw it. But what does it mean?" I stared at my phone screen, trying to make sense of the photo of a drawing Kyle had made on a scrap of blank paper. It looked like a symbol of some sort, or an icon.

"It's what he saw. He's been trying to draw it since last night. We think it's some sort of a seal or a crest."

"Did he remember anything else?"

"I was on the phone with him trying to find out when you walked over. I hung up because I thought she might be with you." He waved his phone in my face. "This is progress. You need to wrap that up and get her out of here so we can get to work on this new clue."

"Since when are you so amped to help me out with this project?" This had been my pet project for almost a year. The wizard who'd given it to me said that this key would lead me to a cure for Morgan. I'd begged my friends to help me, and they'd agreed even though I wouldn't tell them why it was so important. Grace and Hannah had been on board from the start, treating it like a game or an adventure, like a real-life RPG campaign. The others had been less enthusiastic and barely contributed to our group chat.

"Since my boyfriend's superpowers got you the clue you needed to move forward. Now we can finally talk about something else besides that crusty old key."

"Fine. You're right. Let's go eat some lunch, and I'll see what I can do to wrap this up. We can probably just shred all those papers and claim they contained proprietary information or something."

"I'll be right there. Let me just call Kyle back and make sure he's not mad at me for hanging up on him."

I grinned. "Kiss and make up. Your chowder is getting cold."

My emotions warred within me during the short walk back to the conference room. On the one hand, I was enjoying having an excuse to spend time with Angie and would be happy to stare at her and keep her company while she examined every paper in that room. On the other hand, Jayden was right. This was our first breakthrough in months. I was already itching to get started on image searches to see where it would lead.

I found Angie bent over a stack of papers while she fidgeted with that metal puzzle cube I'd found in one of the boxes. I almost didn't want to disturb her, but she hadn't even started eating her lunch. I could tell she was waiting for me.

"Hey, sorry that took so long."

She looked up from the papers to meet my eyes. "Oh. No problem. You gave me enough time to find something potentially interesting. This looks like some sort of schematic or design for something. Does it look familiar to you?"

She slid her chair aside so I could stand next to her. A small symbol caught my eye at the bottom of an engineering design for an early prototype of our inertial measurement unit. Among wizards, it was the equivalent of a signature, and everyone had their own. The folks in the engineering department used them to sign off on completed work that included any sort of magical component. This one matched the drawing Kyle had made.

6

FEELING like I'd justified my hourly rate, I pushed the stack of papers away and dug into my sandwich. Whatever this was, it must have been important to the company, because Max had been a little dumbstruck when I showed him the plans I'd found. And that was just the first file folder. My mouth watered, and not just from the delicious fried fish assaulting my taste buds.

I lived for projects like this one, where I got to come in and help save someone from making terrible mistakes that might cost them millions in lawyer fees down the road. Investigative work was like a treasure hunt, and it almost never came with any drama. I wasn't the one who would have to deal with the angry widow. Especially in this case, I really hoped I would never have to confront her.

My good vibes deflated a bit when Jayden joined us in the conference room. He took a seat on the far side of the table, keeping well away from me and Salty, who lay curled at my feet. I let Max fill Jayden in on what I'd found.

He'd passed the engineering documents over to Jayden as soon as he'd walked in. They'd exchanged a look I couldn't interpret. Then Jayden had proceeded to turn his attention to his phone. It didn't seem like he cared.

Max started to lay out a plan of attack for finishing up the project while we ate, and Jayden alternated between scowling and typing out messages with his thumbs. I wasn't even sure he was paying attention to the conversation. He'd barely taken a bite of his chowder.

Max turned to Jayden to summarize what we'd just agreed on. "Jayden, you take the plans we already found, scan them, and send them off to the team. Meanwhile, Angie and I will box up the rest of this mess—office supplies in one bin and desk trinkets in another. Then you can take the office supplies back to the supply closet and label the boxes to ship to the widow while we go through the rest of the notebooks and folders. Okay?"

Jayden nodded. He slid his phone into his pocket, gathered up the engineering plans along with his untouched lunch, and stood. "Got it."

I savored my last bite of fish and watched Jayden through the conference room windows until he turned into the maze of cube walls and only his head was visible. "Seriously, what is up with him?"

"What do you mean?" Max crumpled up his sandwich wrapper and stuffed it into the empty bag.

"If I had an assistant like that, I'd fire him and find someone with a better attitude."

Max laughed. "He's really not that bad. I mean, he is giving up his Saturday to play chap—" Max cut himself off. He stared at me with wide eyes for a split second before correcting himself. "To help."

"He thinks we need chaperoning?" I asked. My heart fluttered against my ribs. Evie kept reminding me that I'd been the one to break up with Max. Maybe Jayden was just being overly protective of his boss. They were friends, after all.

"Don't let him know I told you that." Max walked around the table until he was standing next to me. He jutted his chin at my empty wrapper and pile of greasy napkins. "You done with that?"

I blinked up at him. If I moved an inch, we'd be touching. I forced myself to look away and busied my hands with tidying up my trash. "Yeah."

His hand reached down to take the garbage from me, and our fingers touched. My grip on the crumpled wrapper tightened.

"I can take that from you." His voice was a low rumble just above my head. His fingers were still splayed on top of mine.

I wet my lips and swallowed, then forced my fingers to let go. "Right."

Jayden was right. We definitely needed a chaperone. I focused on the pile of file folders in front of me and didn't dare look up.

Max dangled a small square package in my field of view. "Want one of these?"

On closer inspection, the square turned out to be a pouch that contained a single hand wipe. I held my hand flat underneath, and Max dropped it into my palm.

"Thanks." I glanced up to find him grinning at me.

"No problem." He crumpled the trash into a tighter ball and tossed it across the table, toward the garbage can near the conference room door. We both groaned when he missed. "Want to start with the office supplies? I'll grab a box."

"Sure." I stood and walked over to meet him next to the pile of blank notepads and writing instruments that I'd made earlier. "We should probably just throw out most of these pens."

He set an empty box on the table next to me, then returned for the trash can. We stood side by side, scooping things that could be reused into the empty box and dropping old pens and bent paper clips into the trash can.

I was about to toss one oddly twisted paper clip into the trash when Salty butted her head against my leg. I bent to scratch her behind the ear, and she sniffed at the bent metal. It didn't look like anything to me, but I knew better than to ignore her sense of smell after she'd located that tarot card.

"Do you think she needs to go out?" Max asked.

I looked up and found him staring down at us. I palmed the twisted paper clip and shook my head. "No. She's probably fine. I'll just get her a treat for being such a good, patient doggo."

I stood and walked over to my tote, expecting Salty to follow me, but she seemed distracted by something Max was holding in his hand. I dropped the weird bit of twisted metal into my tote, now unsure if it had meant anything at all, or if she'd really been interested in whatever Max was still examining.

"What is that?" I asked as I dug around for the package of dog treats Willow had given me.

"Hmm?" He turned his head toward me, blinking like he'd forgotten I was there for a moment. "Oh, it's just an inertial measurement unit. This one might be broken or something. I'm going to set it aside for now and have Jayden see if it's worth saving."

I couldn't tell if I'd just caught him using magic, or not. It was frustrating being the only one in the room with no sense for magic. I was anxious to get back to the paperwork. That was where my special powers could actually be of use.

"Looks like we got everything over here," he said. "Let's add the stuff from that other pile."

He carried the box and the garbage to the other end of the table while I fed Salty a treat. Then I joined him. The stapler still lay where I'd left it, so I picked that up first and dropped it into the box. When we were done with the office supplies, Max put the full box outside the conference room and grabbed an empty one.

"Do we need to be careful about how we pack this stuff?" I held up one of the gem-shaped glass awards.

"Probably. But for now, let's just clear this all off the table and into a few of the empty boxes. Jayden can decide if he wants to repackage everything, or if he wants to give that job to one of the interns."

Max and I moved to opposite sides of the table, each working on filling a box with Emilio's personal stuff. As I worked, I thought about how weird it was that I was fondling all of these things that had belonged to the man who had been Nigel and Arabella's father. Two people who terrified me. One because he was half demon and his mother was bent on destroying the Fae, and the other because she was easily the fiercest warrior I had ever seen in real life. It didn't help that she lacked Willow's sunny and warm disposition. There was just no way to know where you stood with her until she was pointing a sword at your rib cage. I still hadn't quite figured out why my best friend liked her—especially since she'd nearly killed Evie when they first met.

I wished I could tell Max how strange this was. Hey, did you know that this Emilio guy sired a half demon and a Fae warrior princess? Oh, and I've met both of them. Yeah, I know. Crazy, right?

I hated that Nigel's evil mother was going to get all of Emilio's stuff, even if most of it was junk. I felt like I should be snapping a few photos or sneaking off with a few odd bits to take back to his two offspring. Instead, I kept glancing over at the metal cube Max had found. That was the one thing I needed to make sure didn't make it into one of the boxes that would be shipped to Lilium.

Jayden returned but stopped in the doorway. His eyes were on Max, waiting for him to pause and look up. I wasn't sure Max had even noticed that Jayden was standing there.

"These boxes are done, if you want to take them." I pointed to the stacks we'd made next to the conference room door.

Jayden flashed me a cold but polite smile. "Thanks. I'll just check with my boss, first."

"Okay." I bit my lip to keep my mouth shut and prevent an unwarranted apology from slipping out.

Max earned about twenty bonus points for his reply. "What Angie said sounds good to me. Those two are ready to go back to the supply closet. These will need to be repackaged and shipped to Emilio's widow. We should have them done by the time you get back."

I grinned, then hid my reaction when his eyes darted to the table near me. I followed his gaze to the whatever-he-called-it that he'd been so absorbed with earlier.

"Oh, and can you have a look at that IMU, as well? It seems like we may be able to salvage it."

Jayden looked where Max was pointing, and his eyes narrowed. He picked up the object and stared at it, just as transfixed as Max had been. I wished Willow had sent me with some sort of magic decoder glasses. I'd have to text her and ask her if anything like that existed. If it didn't, some-one should definitely invent it. Then again, maybe the Silicon

Moon engineers already had, and they were keeping them all for themselves. Maybe the plans for the decoder glasses were somewhere in Emilio's notebooks.

I capped my box and set it on the stack with the others destined to be shipped to Lilium. "Max, I think I'm going to get started going through the files, if you don't mind."

"Yeah. I'll just finish up with the last of this stuff and then I can help."

Jayden left with the IMU thing, plus the boxes for the supply closet, as I grabbed a stack of files and sat down next to the papers I'd already reviewed. I'd left the metal cube on top of the stack, and I wanted to keep it within reach while I skimmed through the files and sorted everything into two stacks. Things that looked promising I set aside to review with Max. Copies of old employee benefit pamphlets or other preprinted and clearly expired materials went directly into the shred pile.

Even though we weren't talking and seemed to be absorbed in our respective tasks, I couldn't help being painfully aware of Max's body moving around near me. It didn't matter if he was on the other side of the room, or right next to me—even with my eyes closed, I knew where he was. My skin seemed to pull toward him like a compass needle pointing North.

The tension grew until Max's phone started vibrating and broke the spell. He paused to check it, typed something, then returned to putting the last of the desk trinkets into a box. The silence built for about a minute, then his phone buzzed again, and he repeated the process. My nerves were already on high alert, and after it happened for the third time, I started cringing. I waited until the fifth time before I commented.

"Sounds like something urgent. Do you need to go deal with that?" I asked.

"Sorry." He finished typing and slid the phone back into his pocket. "Do you want to get dinner tonight?"

I blinked at him. That was not the response I'd been expecting. "Uh. Sure?"

"Cool. Grace and Hannah and most of the group from last night are thinking about getting together for dinner. I said it would have to be later because we're working on finishing this up." He gestured to the mound of paper occupying the center of the table. "When they found out I was with you, they suggested that you join us."

"Oh." It was a pity invite. I considered saying no, but if I did, then he would know that I had only said yes because I'd thought he was asking me on a date, or at least asking to spend more time with him. Alone. Away from his grumpy assistant who had decided we needed a chaperone. "You don't have to invite me to tag along with you and your friends. I'll be just fine on my own."

"You're just going to go back to the hotel, order room service, and watch a movie, aren't you?" He grinned.

I tried to act like that wasn't my plan, even though it totally was, and we both knew it. "I saw a restaurant I thought I might try."

"Uh-huh. Which one?"

"I can't remember the name. I'd have to look it up." I tried to remember any of the signs I'd passed on my way to the cafe.

"Just come with us." Max tilted his head to one side, eyes wide and pleading.

I looked away from his face, knowing I was going to give in if I let him stare at me like that for a moment longer. Sitting up in my chair, I tried to see out through the glass separating the conference room from the cubical area. When I responded, I kept my voice low. "Is Jayden going to be there?"

Max chuckled. "Probably."

I made a face.

"Come on. You two can geek out on fountain pens or something. He'll be your best friend in no time." Max pressed his palms on the table and leaned toward me. I tried not to stare at the point where his short sleeves exposed the skin that stretched across his flexed biceps.

I swallowed my desire to let the tip of my tongue trace the lines of that muscle. "I don't need a new best friend."

"Just come with us. Please?"

I could never resist his "please."

"Fine. My bubble bath will have to wait until tomorrow."

He shivered. "Hotel tubs are disgusting."

"If you think that, then you're just not going to the right hotels."

His phone vibrated again. "How much longer do you think we'll need?"

I looked at how much I'd completed versus how much there was left to do. "All night."

"Yeah. Let's give it another couple hours and then come back tomorrow and finish up."

"If you can put that phone away and help me out, we may be able to get through this faster."

"Just let me—" He stopped talking and stared down at his phone screen. "Uh. I need to find Jayden. I'll be right back. Will you be okay for a bit without my help?"

He was already halfway out the door before I could respond.

———

"JAYDEN." I HISSED HIS NAME as I approached his cube. Then I cast a contained ball of firelight and sent it zooming ahead of me, keeping it well below the cube walls. Once it reached his cube, I exploded it, creating a flash that I hoped would attract his attention but not Angie's. It was a risk, but a sudden flash was something I could explain away, if necessary.

Jayden's head popped up above the cube wall. He searched until he spotted me, then he gestured to the flash, pointed to the conference room, and shook his head. As if I didn't know the rules about doing magic in front of regs.

"Are you checking your messages?" I waved my phone in the air as I closed the distance between us.

"I've been working on that other project you gave me." He had the old IMU on his desk along with the kit of herbs and potions he kept hidden in the back of his file drawer. He'd taken the usual Society training for wizards with earth magic, but he'd also been taught by underground wizards, ones who'd either been kicked out of or never bothered joining the Society.

I gestured to the mess he'd made. "And you're worried about me being conspicuous? What if Angie walked over here? Not to mention, isn't most of this stuff banned by the Society, anyway?"

He plopped down into his chair and leaned back. "If Angie leaves that conference room, I'll know about it. Now, what's all this about my messages?"

I didn't want to ask what sort of magic he was using to monitor us. I should have assumed he had something rigged up. "After you shared Kyle's drawing with the rest of the group and told them about the seal I found on Emilio's engineering drawings, Varun got online and logged into the Hunter Works engineering department archives. He searched for any news articles or photos of Emilio and posted copies of what he found. Look."

I held out my phone so Jayden could see the image on the screen. Most of the articles that mentioned Emilio had been written by the PR team and focused on highlighting a bit of our regular tech development. Those didn't contain anything helpful, except one that included a picture of the engineering team. At the time, it was only five people—four men and one woman. One of the men was Emilio. He was positioned at one end of the group. The man standing closest to him had long hair pulled back in a low ponytail and a slightly crooked nose. He looked like a younger version of the wizard who'd given me the key.

"You wanted a picture of Emilio? Is that what you're so excited about?" Jayden scowled. "I could have got that for you."

"No." I pointed at the man with the ponytail. "This guy is who I'm excited about. I am pretty sure this is the wizard who gave me the key. He knew Emilio."

Jayden snatched my phone from my hand and flicked his fingers across the screen to zoom in on the wizard with the ponytail. "Does it say what his name is?"

"Marcus Shaw."

Jayden handed me back my phone. "Never heard of him. Did Varun find anything about him?"

"He's looking now." I slid my phone back into my pocket. "We're getting closer. I can feel it."

"You think these two had some conspiracy going to overthrow the Society?" He tilted his head to one side and stared at some point in the distance. "Maybe this whole group was in on it together."

I'd forgotten about my cover story for the key. I'd told my friends that the Council was concerned there might be a group of wizards working against the Society, and they were trying to figure out who might be included and what they might be plotting. That was true, but it didn't have anything to do with the key I'd been given. I'd only claimed it did because I couldn't tell my friends that what I was really after was a cure for Morgan. Something to stabilize her very strong and very difficult-to-control powers. Something that might allow her to pass as a regular wizard without having to go to the demons for help.

"Maybe." I shrugged.

"Are you going to tell your parents what we found?"

My parents were two of the twelve wizards who sat on the Council. The Council positions were hereditary, for the most part. Every once in a while, a new family was added, but someone from the Hunter family had been the head of the Council for the past five generations. My father was the current head wizard, and I was supposed to take over from him when he retired. That was the reason I'd given my friends to explain why I'd been chosen to help with this investigation.

"I think I'll wait until we have a little more information." I glanced toward the conference room. "I should probably get back in there. Once Angie's done going through all the files, we should be done with this and ready to go to dinner."

"Angie is coming with us to dinner?"

I held up both hands and pretended to be innocent. "Don't blame me. Grace and Hannah asked me to invite her. You'd know that if you checked your messages."

Not that I would ever tell Jayden, but I was thrilled that Angie had agreed to go. Even though I knew there was no future for us, I missed spending time with her. I wasn't ready to let her go completely. As impossible as it seemed, maybe there was a chance for us to be friends.

Jayden scowled at me. "This is a bad idea, and you know it."

"We can be friends." I almost managed to make it not sound like a question.

He shook his head. "Neither of you wants to just be friends. You're not fooling anyone, and you're only going to hurt her when you pull away again. Consider that if you truly care about her like you say you do."

I crossed my arms. "You're wrong. She's the one who broke up with me. She's over me."

Jayden sighed. "Sure she is."

My heart betrayed me by speeding up at the thought that Angie might still love me. I ignored it because I didn't want to admit that Jayden was right about me wanting Angie back, and not just as a friend. "It's just a bunch of friends having dinner together. It will be fine."

"Famous last words."

I shook my head as I walked back to the conference room. By the time I returned, Angie had sorted almost all the file folders into two stacks. There were still some notebooks and loose papers scattered around the center of the table, but she appeared to have gotten distracted by the contents of the notebook she held in her hands. She was so absorbed in scanning the pages that she didn't even look up when I walked into the room.

"He sure was a fan of composition notebooks." The one she held was the same black-and-white-speckled variety as almost all of the others.

She set the book down on the table, pressing the spine open to reveal the pages she'd been looking at. Her lips were set in the same firm line that had preceded most of our infrequent arguments. It was the look I'd come to associate with the last few months before she finally got fed up and broke up with me. The best course of action was to figure out what

I'd done and apologize.

Even though I wasn't entirely sure what that was, I jumped straight to apologizing. "Sorry I had to leave you to deal with all this on your own."

She shrugged one shoulder, but her mouth remained tense. "This is what you hired me to do. You have a company to run. Totally understandable."

Okay. Not that, then. "How's it going?"

"Pretty good. I think we can dump all of this." She gestured to a small mound of printed papers, brochures, flyers, and miscellaneous empty file folders on her right. Then she motioned to the larger stack on her left. "This is all stuff I need to go through with you. But there are a few obvious things that jumped out at me. Like this." Her finger jabbed at the open notebook.

I walked around the table so I could take a seat next to her. "What's that?" I asked.

"I was hoping you could tell me."

The page was covered in cubes, like a child who was just learning about perspective in art class had decided to practice drawing three-dimensional boxes. Some had swirling designs on one side. All around and in between them were notes scribbled in pencil, written in a nearly illegible script. I couldn't understand what about boxes drawn by a dead former employee could possibly have made her mad.

"They look like boxes."

She sat back in her chair and folded her arms across her chest. "What I'm trying to figure out is if these sketches and notes are related to some Silicon Moon engineering project. Honestly, that's the question for nearly all of this stuff, but I just happened to be trying to figure this out when you walked in."

I dragged the notebook closer so I could attempt to make out some of the writing. The first thing I recognized were the symbols scattered among the words. He was writing about magic. My heart sped up, and my hands started to sweat. What was this guy thinking leaving this sort of thing lying around for anyone to find?

Then it dawned on me. Angie had been reading this. She'd been reading it because this guy's widow wanted all of these notebooks. We didn't know if he'd married a regular human. We couldn't send all this out into the world. I panicked.

But if I wanted to keep it, I would have to claim it all as proprietary information belonging to the company. If I did that, Angie might begin to realize that we did more than just make guidance systems for rockets. And she'd already read some of this stuff. Just because she didn't have any magic didn't mean she couldn't recognize someone talking about spells. Not when it was all written out like this.

I flipped forward a few pages and then back a few pages. It was all more of the same. I cringed as I crafted a response in my head. "It doesn't look like a Silicon Moon project, but it could have been something he was working on for Hunter Works. I'll need to check."

Her mouth softened a fraction. "You've never seen anything like this before?"

"Have you?"

She shook her head. "But I don't run an engineering company that is trying to build an elevator to the moon."

I squinted at the drawings. Maybe she thought they were cargo containers for the elevator project. Maybe she didn't recognize the symbols as Elemental runes. She was the most logical person I knew. The last person I would expect to end up with videos from underground wizards in their recommended viewing queue.

"While I cannot officially confirm that is actually one of our projects, I can say that nothing I see here would be helpful on that particular project."

She leaned forward until her shoulder brushed against mine and twisted the notebook so that we could look at it together. "First off, you could confirm it, if you wanted to. I'm signed a nondisclosure. Remember?" She kept her voice low. "Second, if you're saying you know that none of this would be helpful on that project, then do you know what this is?"

"I honestly have no idea."

"Honestly?"

"Honestly."

She sighed as she collapsed back into her chair. Her hands gripped the armrests, and her lips twisted into a scowl before relaxing into a closed-lipped smile. "I think I'm hungry. Maybe we should wrap this up for today."

"Do you want me to help you sort through this last bit, first?"

She shrugged. "I'll sort through the rest if you can find a container to shove all that into. I'd recommend shredding it."

"Sounds good." I found an empty recycling bin and started shoveling papers into it.

7

WHEN Grace paused to take a bite of her taco, I glanced around the table. Max was deep in conversation with Jayden and Kyle. The music was too loud to hear what they were saying, but I caught a bit of what Varun said when he leaned over to join their discussion.

"You don't need earth magic for that, you need fire magic. Wait. Maybe he was a fire wizard." Varun slapped the table.

"You think everyone is a fire wizard because that's what you are." Jayden took a sip from his cocktail and rolled his eyes.

"Well, not everyone can be as fancy as our fearless leader and claim more than one element." Varun shoved Jayden's shoulder. Then Max said something I couldn't hear, and their voices lowered to a level that blended with the steady thrum of the folky guitarist strumming away in the corner of the restaurant's patio dining area.

I swallowed the last of my chips and took a long sip from my water, still not quite believing what I'd just overheard. It wasn't just Max. They were all wizards. Maybe even Grace and Hannah. This whole time I'd been surrounded by magic and had no idea.

Grace leaned toward me. "That salsa is kind of spicy. I probably should have warned you."

"Huh?" I set my glass down and turned to her.

She pointed to the chili flakes stuck to the sides of the small serving bowl. "It's spicy, right?"

"Yeah. I love it." I reached over and stole one of Max's chips and scraped the last of the salsa from the bottom of the bowl.

Grace wiped her mouth with her napkin. "You seem distracted. Is something wrong?"

"Oh, no. I just..." If they were going to be casual with their magic talk, I decided I might as well confirm what I'd heard and see what sort of reaction I got. "I thought I heard them talking about wizards or something."

Grace's eyes went wide for a second before she covered it with a laugh. "Wizards. Right. They're probably just rehashing that game from last night."

I couldn't tell if she was surprised because they were talking about it here, or if she was surprised because she really did think they were just talking about their role-playing game. "Oh. Right. Listen, I'm going to the bathroom. If the server comes by and asks, I'm still working on finishing this." I gestured to what was left of the mound of rice and beans that came with my tacos.

"Sure. No problem. Do you want me to keep an eye on Salty while you're gone?"

"No, that's okay. I'm going to take her outside while I'm up." I slid my chair under the table, and Max turned to look up at me. "I'll be right back."

He nodded and returned to his conversation. My phone

was out and up to my ear before my feet touched the side-walk. I paced down the street until I was no longer in view of our table as I waited for Eve to pick up her phone. It was still well before dawn in England, but I didn't care. I needed advice, and I needed it now.

"Angie?" Eve's voice was low and heavy with sleep.

"Hey. Sorry to wake you up, but I need your advice."

"Okay. Hang on." The rustle of bedding was followed by some mumbled conversation, then a door closing. "Liam's awake, but I got out of bed anyway. What's going on?"

"I'm with Max and his friends, and they're talking about the thing again. They actually said the word. At a restaurant."

"Magic?"

"No, the other word."

"Sweetie, I was sound asleep a few minutes ago. You're going to have to help me out here."

I glanced around, then whispered into the phone. "Wizard."

"Oh. That word. Got it. That's great. What's the problem?"

"I think they're all...that. Grace and Hannah and Varun and his jerk-face assistant, Jayden. All of them."

"Oh!"

"Yeah."

"Can you text their last names to Willow? I'll have her check with her parents to see what they know about those families."

"Fine, but in the meantime, what do I say to Max?"

"Well...what if you confront him about it?"

"Just say that I heard what he was saying?"

"Say you know about magic."

"He's going to deny it, or ask me how I know." I'd reached the end of the block, so I turned around and paced back toward the restaurant.

"Let's see... You could tell him you have a friend with earth magic."

"Willow?"

"Sure. It's true."

"I already told him that she gave me Salty. Do you think it will be bad if he connects those two things together?"

"Well, you don't have to say who your friend is. But, you can be honest without mentioning the real reason you're there. If he knows he doesn't have to hide from you, maybe he'll finally tell you the truth."

"So, I tell him what I heard and ask him if it's true what Varun said about him being able to use more than one element—"

Eve cut me off. "Varun said what?"

I stopped walking at the point where I knew I would be visible to Max and his friends. "Do you want me to repeat that? Because if you do, I'm going to need to turn around and start walking again."

"Did you just say Max can control more than one element?"

"That's what I overheard Varun saying. Yeah."

"That's impossible."

"Are you sure?"

"Well...no. I'd have to ask Willow to be sure. I'm not an expert on this magic stuff. Not that she is, either, but her parents are, and—"

I interrupted. "Can you check with her about it, then? I need to go before they send someone to the bathroom to check on me."

"Sure. Text Willow the names. I'll call her as soon as it's light outside. Or...I'll tell her to join my sparring session with Arabella, and we can talk then. You'll be asleep anyway."

"Text me when you have info. If I'm awake, I'll call you."
I had a feeling that if I confronted Max tonight, we might be
up late talking. My pulse sped up, and I forced it to chill. Just
talking. "Thanks, Evie."

"No problem. Hang in there."

"I'm doing my best."

"Love you."

"You, too." I hung up with her and typed a series of names
into our group chat. Then I shook off my pep talk and headed
back to the table.

"Oh, good, you're back." Hannah looked up from her phone
as I approached.

"A couple of us are getting dessert, did you want anything?" Grace asked.

"No, thanks, I'm good."

Max leaned over when I sat down. "You can have some of
mine if you want."

I turned toward him to respond and found Jayden glaring
at me. Even though I'd already said no, that look made me
want to change my mind. I smiled. "Thanks. We'll see how I
feel after I finish my dinner."

Max reached over and scooped a bite of rice and beans off
my plate. He shoved it in his mouth, then made a face. "These
are cold."

I tried a bite. He was right, but the decreased temperature
didn't make them any less delicious. "More for me, then."

He scowled. "You sure you don't want me to order more?"

"Are you joking?" I paused long enough to realize that he
was not. "It's fine. Really."

Hannah called my name, and I turned away from Max to
see what she wanted. Out of the corner of my eye, I caught
him reaching his hand toward my plate, so I reached out to

catch his wrist. I missed, and the tips of my fingers slid under his palm just long enough to feel the heat radiating off his hand. I pulled my hand away, but he caught it, and held it up to examine my fingertips.

"Are you okay?"

I stared at him. The ends of my fingers pulsed like I'd been holding them over a candle flame. "I'm fine, but if you keep trying to steal my food, you're not going to be."

He ran the pad of his thumb over the top of my index and middle finger. The scrape of his skin against mine made me shiver. While I was distracted, he grabbed his fork with his other hand and snatched another bite. "You mean like this?"

Did he not realize that all his friends were staring at us? Jayden had set down his margarita, fingers curled into a fist around the stem, and leaned forward in his chair. I sensed Hannah and Grace staring at the back of my head, probably both wearing similar expressions to Varun's amused smirk.

I pushed my plate away from Max and grabbed the fork out of his hand before he could take a bite. "Nice try, Hunter."

I turned my back on him and positioned my body between him and my food, then went back to talking with Hannah as though nothing had happened. Keep it cool. Keep it friendly.

Hannah saved me by asking about which of the half dozen summer fashion "looks" I was most into and which I wanted most to die a fiery death.

"I'm so sick of boho." She sighed. "All those tiny flower prints and peasant shirts. Ugh."

I preferred solid colors over prints, but I had to admit I had at least one belted tunic dress in my wardrobe. "They can definitely keep you cool in the summer heat, though."

Grace waved a thin, long-boned hand. "We live in Seattle. You pack an extra layer regardless of the season. I've decided

I'm bringing glam back."

"Oooh!" Hannah leaned in. "Yes. I can totally see that for you."

Grace nodded. "I've been shopping at vintage stores, trying to build my collection. So if you see anything, grab it for me, okay?"

"Definitely. What about you, Angie? Planning on sticking with your 'ladies of rock and roll' look? If you move up here, you can probably make that denim work for you nearly year-round."

"Ha ha." I couldn't tell if she was making fun of me or complimenting me.

"Seriously. I wouldn't change a thing. Except maybe..." She unzipped her purse and dug around until she extracted two tubes of what appeared to be lip gloss. "I found my samples. They're from that new line I was telling you about. These are all wrong for me, but they would be perfect for you. Check it out."

I took the tubes from her and read the color labels "Ruby Spice" and "Blackberry Supernova." They sounded promising, so I swiped the wand of the first one against the back of my hand. "Oh, yeah. This is great."

"Told you."

I striped the second color next to the first. It was a little darker with just a hint of sparkle. "Not sure about the glimmer, but I love this shade."

Grace leaned closer to have a look. "Go with the glow."

"Try it." Hannah bounced in her seat.

"Let me finish eating first." I slid both tubes into my tote bag and took another bite. Behind Hannah, the server was making his way over to our table with a tray of paper bags and little ceramic pots. I knew what that meant. Churros.

Jayden better brace himself, I was definitely going to be sharing Max's dessert.

———

OUR PROGRESS ON FIGURING OUT what the key unlocked was making me a little bold and reckless. I didn't care what Jayden thought when I turned away from our conversation to check on Angie. She'd been gone a while, and I'd been distracted, worried that she was just going to leave without saying goodbye. I hadn't been paying any attention to her, even though we'd been sitting next to each other. I'd left her to talk with Grace and Hannah because that's what they'd wanted.

I'd been careless using my magic in an attempt to heat up Angie's food. It would have worked if she hadn't noticed my hand creeping toward her plate. I was sure that I'd burned her fingertips, but she didn't seem to notice. Jayden had, though. He started scowling when dessert arrived, and actually grumbled when Angie leaned over to lift a sugary fried pastry off my plate.

I was painfully aware of her shoulder brushing up against mine whenever she reached over to dip the end of her churro into the chocolate sauce. Her knee shifted and tapped against mine under the table every time she moved, but I didn't move away.

I was flirting with danger, but that's all it was. Harmless flirting. Angie and I had a history. Even if her fingers were sticky with sugar and chocolate, and I wanted to lick them clean, we were adults. We could contain the simmer of heat between us.

She didn't know about magic, and magic was my world. There was no place for her in my life except as a friend, and I was going to have to figure out how to deal with that. Even though Jayden was convinced it was impossible, I'd been paying attention. The way Angie was acting, I found it hard to believe that she still had feelings for me.

"Last one." Angie's fingers hovered over the plate.

"Go ahead." I grinned, planning to grab it before she could.

"Are you sure?" She flexed her hand, ready to pull it away if I said no.

My tongue darted out to wet my bottom lip. "I'm sure."

She lowered her hand, but I reached in at the same time. Our fingers tangled, and we pulled them apart, taking bits of pastry with us. We each ended up with roughly half. Her bite was a little larger than mine, but I didn't mind.

"Nice try, Hunter. I knew you were going to do that." She bumped my shoulder with hers as she reached for the chocolate.

"You did not." I dipped my half in the sauce before she could take it away, scraping as much as possible off the sides of the ceramic.

Varun laughed. "You're not surprising anyone. You do that every time."

"Do I?" I managed the question around a mouthful of churro.

"You really do." Grace rolled her eyes at me as she spooned the last of her ice cream into her mouth.

"You are so predictable." Hannah pulled out a compact mirror to check her makeup. She snapped it shut once she was satisfied that she was still ready for a close-up. "Sorry to bail, but I have to go. Club opening appearance."

"The busy in-demand life of a social media icon."

"Don't you know it." She struck a pose and a few heads turned our way.

Varun groaned. "Get out of here before you cause a scene."

"I'm going, but first…" She handed Angie her phone. "Digits, please. I'm not letting you disappear for ten years again."

Angie took Hannah's phone and bent her head over the screen. "I think it's only been three since Morgan's wedding."

"Whatever. It's too long, and you better not leave town without saying goodbye. Promise?"

"All right." Angie hit save on the contact entry and handed the phone back to Hannah. "Promise."

"Good." Hannah pointed at each of us in turn. "You all heard her. You are my witnesses."

"I want your info, too." Grace dug her phone out and handed it to Angie.

"Later, loves!" Hannah waved and tossed her hair over one shoulder as she made her way to the exit.

"I should be going as well." Varun stood and opened his wallet. He was counting out bills when the server arrived at the table to start clearing away plates.

"The bill's already been paid." The server lifted Hannah's plate onto his tray.

"What? Who paid?" I glanced around at my friends' faces.

"The woman who just left paid the bill for the whole table." The server pointed toward the exit.

"Tip, too?" Grace asked.

"Just the bill." He cleared a few more empty plates and glasses onto his tray until it was full, then walked away.

"She's good." Angie sat back and sighed.

"Extremely good." I shook my head. This was the third time in a row that Hannah had figured out a way to pay before any of us realized what was happening. It was becoming a trend.

"Let me get the tip, at least." Varun slapped some cash down on the table. "I'll do what I can to beat her to it next time."

"I'm the one who organized this, I should have been the one to pay. At least let me help with the tip." Grace dug her wallet out of her bag.

"Too late. Money's on the table, and I'm out." Varun grinned and waved. He did his best impression of Hannah's hair toss, even though he kept his own thick hair short and gelled into a wave that barely moved in the wind.

"I'm getting it next time," Grace called after him. She wedged her wallet back into her tiny purse and stood. "I have to go pick up Callie."

When Angie stood to give Grace a hug, Jayden pushed my shoulder. Once he had my attention, he bugged out his eyes and raised his eyebrows, like I was supposed to know what he meant. I shrugged. "What?"

He wiped the look off his face when Grace released Angie and turned to us to say goodbye. "Jayden, I can give you a ride, if you want. Your place is nearly on my way."

Jayden pushed his chair back from the table. "What about you Max, how are you getting home?"

"I left my car at the office. I'll just walk Angie back to her hotel and then drive home."

"Oh, that's right." He snapped his fingers. "I left my laptop at the office. I should probably swing by and grab it. Maybe I should walk with you two and get a ride home from Max."

He was a terrible actor, and I was done with his chaperoning. "Don't be ridiculous. You're meeting me back there in the morning. Leave it until then."

"If you're coming with, then let's go." Grace took a few steps away from the table and motioned for Jayden to follow.

Jayden scowled. "I'll call you later about that project."

"Or we can talk about it in the morning." I crossed my arms. Jayden's eyes narrowed.

"If you're planning on getting coffee again tomorrow, I'll meet you there, and we can walk in together." Angie smiled at Jayden. "I'll probably be able to finish that book you lent me tonight. So I can give it back to you in the morning."

That seemed to appease him. "Okay. Sure."

"Jayden, let's go." Grace was already halfway to the exit.

With one last look between the two of us, Jayden hurried after Grace.

"He takes his chaperone duties very seriously." Angie shook her head.

"Like I'm going to just strip you naked and take you on this table if he isn't here to keep me in line." The words were out of my mouth before I realized I was speaking aloud.

Angie snorted. "That's one approach."

"I wouldn't..." Except I wanted to. But not in front of an audience. Maybe it was a good thing we weren't alone.

"I know." She unfastened Salty's leash from the arm of her chair. "Come on. Let's go before Jayden comes up with some excuse and changes his mind about walking with us."

We walked in silence for a few blocks, and I started to worry that she was mad at me for suggesting we might hook up. I kept formulating apologies in my head, unsure about what exactly I was apologizing for, but certain that one was required.

Part of me wished I'd never agreed to switch places with Morgan. Even if the key did lead me to a cure for her, it would only stabilize her magic. My mother would never agree that it was safe enough to let my sister take over as the Hunter heir. And she'd made it clear that, since any children Morgan had with Brady would still be one-quarter demon, I was on the hook to produce the next generation of Hunters.

It didn't matter how I felt about Angie. She could never

know about my world, which meant it had to be over between us. I needed to accept that and stop flirting with her.

"Hey, so, I have a weird question for you." Angie's statement interrupted my thoughts.

"What's that?"

"I overheard a little bit of your conversation with Varun and Jayden at dinner."

"Yeah?" I knew they had been talking too loud. I thought through the conversation, trying to anticipate what sort of response would be best.

"Yeah. This is really weird, but...it sounded like you guys were talking about Elemental magic, and I have this friend... Well, I was curious what you knew about that stuff."

"About what stuff?" My heart slammed a warning against my rib cage.

"Magic. Wizards. The real kind. Not the kind in your games." She glanced at me out of the corner of her eye.

"You know." It was more of a statement than a question.

She nodded. "Just, you know, recently. I have a friend with earth magic. She explained a few things to me when I asked her about it. I didn't believe her at first, but...I don't know, it seems legit. And then you did that thing to my food."

"I thought you didn't notice."

"You burned my fingers." She wiggled them in the air between us.

"You didn't say anything." I wrapped my hand around hers and pulled her to a stop so I could examine them under the streetlight.

Angie shrugged. "I didn't say anything because I didn't know who knew. I told you that you could trust me."

She'd kept my secret, even though I'd never told her.

I glanced around. "We can't talk about this here."

She looked over her shoulder, and I realized we were standing outside the entrance to her hotel. "Do you want to come up?"

I was in so much trouble.

8

MAX hadn't said a word since opening the door to the hotel and following me inside. We stood shoulder to shoulder in the otherwise empty elevator, watching the floors tick up until the doors slid open to reveal the bland gray carpet and cream walls that welcomed us to my floor.

Salty ran out, and I followed. She led the way down the hall, and Max trailed, just behind my shoulder. I couldn't tell if he was mad, or just surprised. I hadn't planned on inviting him up, but I wanted answers. We were both adults. I wasn't going to jump him just because there was a bed in the room. I'd made the first move when I came to visit him months ago. I was not about to throw myself at him again, and risk being rejected.

I tapped my key card against the door pad, and the lock clicked open. I turned the handle and pushed my weight against the heavy door, only to have Max plant a palm on the face of the door and take all the weight off my shoulder.

"Thanks." I hit the light switch, then went around turning

on every bulb in the room just to make sure it was blinding-ly bright. I was going for interrogation lighting rather than mood lighting.

Max crossed to the window, took a brief look outside, then pulled the curtains shut. "Nice room."

"It's not bad." I unclipped the leash from Salty's collar and filled up her water dish in the bathroom sink. When I emerged, Max was pacing on the far side of the bed. "You can sit down if you want."

He studied the options and picked the desk chair. That meant I could either sit on the end of the bed, or I could squeeze past him to sit in the armchair in the far corner of the room, next to the window. Sitting on the bed would send the wrong signal. I needed to avoid the bed at all costs.

When I walked toward him, preparing to slide between his knees and the edge of the bed, he tensed. Every hope I had abandoned me in that moment. It was over between us. That flirting at dinner hadn't meant anything. He was so nervous about being alone in the same room with me that he probably would be on the phone to his assistant right now, asking for a chaperone, if I wasn't asking him about magic. That word focused me.

"So, what's the deal, Max? Are you a wizard?" I knew the answer. I wanted to hear it from him. I sat down in the arm-chair and folded my hands in my lap.

"What do you know about wizards? How do you know about wizards?"

"I met some people. Some stuff happened." I shrugged and waved a hand in the air. "But that's not my story to tell. Turns out that magic is real. But I get the impression that you al-ready knew that."

At least he had the decency to wince. "I'm sorry. It's not

something you just run around telling people. Especially people who don't have magic."

"People like me."

He nodded.

"So you are a wizard."

He nodded again.

"And Varun said you can control two elements. From what I understand, that's somewhat unusual."

"It's very unusual. But my family... My family has been the head of an ancient society of wizards for about as long as that society has been in existence."

"Your family is in charge of all the wizards?" I knew that as well, but I had to make it seem like I didn't.

"Not exactly. My father is the head of the Council that rules the Society. But there are some wizards who choose not to join the Society, and some who decide they don't like it and leave."

Willow's parents had left. They hadn't even told Willow she had magic because they were scared that this Society that Max's parents led would find out. It was hard to believe that Max would support a group that would make some wizards feel unsafe.

I leaned forward so I could rest my elbows on my knees. "Were you ever planning to tell me about any of this?"

He pressed his lips closed as he inhaled and exhaled. "No."

"Is this why you broke up with me?"

"You broke up with me." He stood and ran a hand through his hair as he paced in his corner.

I wasn't about to let him have the high ground, so I stood up as well and planted my hands on my hips. "Because you were keeping secrets from me. Every time I mentioned something about the future, about our future, you clammed up."

He muttered something that sounded a lot like, "Because we can't have a future."

"What did you say?"

He dropped his hand to his side and turned to face me. "We can't have a future."

"Why?"

He scowled. "My family has a reputation to protect."

I could tell it pained him to say it, but it didn't make the truth any easier. "You broke up with me to save some sort of wizard reputation?"

He lunged toward me, closing the distance between us in one step. "You broke up with me."

I jutted my chin up and squared my shoulders. "Because you already knew we didn't have a future and were too chicken to do it first."

"I didn't want to hurt you."

My hands flew off my hips as I raised them in an exasperated shrug. "What did you think was going to happen? You knew. The whole time, you knew." Tears stung the corners of my eyes, but I swallowed them, refusing to cry.

He caught my hands in his and wove his fingers between mine. "I'm sorry."

My chin trembled. I clenched my teeth to keep from caving in.

"I thought that maybe my parents might make an exception. This wasn't what I wanted."

"What did you want, then?"

He released one of my hands and brushed his knuckles along my cheekbone. "You."

My insides quivered. One more touch and all my resolve would crumble. I stepped back, putting some distance between us, taking my skin out of his reach. "You should go."

"Angie..."

I held up one hand. "You don't need to worry. I'm not going to tell anyone your precious secrets. I promise."

"Thank you. I really am sorry." He paused a moment longer, then turned to walk toward the door.

I wanted to let him go, but that wouldn't help me get what I came for. There were so many more questions I needed to ask him. The most important were for Fiona and the Fae, but the one that slipped out was for me. "Why?"

Max paused. "Why what?"

"Is there some sort of wizard rule that says we can't be together?"

Max pivoted to face me across the large expanse of white bedspread. "It's not a Society rule. It's just my family's rule." He paused. "I need to marry someone with magic."

I opened my mouth to respond, but he didn't give me a chance.

"Not just magic, but someone who can trace their magic all the way back to the source in an unbroken line. You said it yourself. Our family is one of the last who can control more than one element. The only way for that to continue is if we keep our bloodlines pure."

My disgust must have shown on my face.

"I know. It's terrible, and I hate it." His voice lowered to a hoarse whisper. "This isn't what I wanted."

"It isn't what I wanted, either." Not wanting it didn't change anything or make it better.

The corners of his mouth turned down, and he nodded once. "I'll understand if you don't want to come tomorrow. I can finish going through Emilio's papers without you."

"No." The word came out automatically and possibly sounded a bit too aggressive, judging from how his eyes widened. I adopted a softer tone. "I'm a professional. I won't let this affect my work."

If he cut me off from Emilio's papers, I wouldn't be able to copy the plans that I found. He hadn't seemed to recognize what I was sure were the initial designs for those magic traps, but he could have been hiding his knowledge.

"Well, I'll see you tomorrow morning, then." He turned to go, and Salty jumped up from where she'd been lying.

She chased after Max. When he stopped, she pranced around his feet, wagging her tail. He bent down to scratch her between her ears, and she leaned against his leg.

I walked around the bed to collect her so Max could leave. When I bent down, he looked up. My knee bumped up against his leg, and his torso twisted, causing his shoulder to knock into my arm, throwing us both off-balance. Then his fingers wrapped around my forearm to steady us.

Our eyes met, and his grip tightened. My heart sped as I realized how close my face was to his. I wobbled, and he set his other hand on my elbow to steady me. Then he guided us both to our feet, but didn't move away.

"Angie." He touched his fingertips to my jaw. They hovered there, barely skimming the surface of my skin but pulling at my center like a magnet.

I wanted to lean in. I wanted to run away. I really wanted him to kiss me.

"I wanted to tell you." He whispered the words.

If it had only been about magic, I probably would have caved. I'd wanted that to be the only thing keeping us apart. I'd thought that once he knew he didn't have to hide from me, everything would be all right. But, that hadn't been all he'd been hiding. "Now I know."

"Can we still be friends?"

"You don't get it, do you?" I pulled away from his touch and wrapped my arms around myself. "I thought we were going to..." I couldn't bring myself say the words "get married" out loud, but I wasn't the only one who had thought that. Everyone had. Another realization hit me. "Your friends all know, don't they? Grace and Hannah and Varun? Jayden. This is why he hates me, isn't it?"

This explained why Grace and Hannah had been so nice to me. They pitied me.

Max shook his head. "Only Jayden knows. The others probably suspect, but Jayden... Sometimes I think he works for my parents more than he works for me." He released a pained laugh. "You said that thing about firing him for his attitude. I'm not sure I could even if I wanted to."

"How is it that your parents hold so much sway over your life? You're a grown man, Hunter." My anger and annoyance had returned, relieving some of the ache of sadness and pain. I let it burn, directing it at these people I'd only met twice.

Max's jaw clenched. "You're right. I should go." He hurried for the door.

"Max, wait."

He paused, one hand on the door, poised to open it. He didn't turn.

I sighed. "I'm sorry. I want to be friends, but I need you to be honest with me. I expect that from friends, too."

His shoulders dropped, but he kept his back to me. "I want to be honest with you, but there are things about my family that I can't share with anyone."

In a strange way, I understood him. I had my own secrets now, secrets that weren't mine, that I couldn't share. "How about this, then. Can we promise to be honest with each other about our own stuff? No lies? And if we need to protect someone else's secrets, we just say so? Will that work?"

Max pulled a pen and his notebook from his pocket as he turned around. He opened the small black book and scribbled something on a blank page inside. The lawyer in me wondered if he thought I wanted him to sign a contract or something. I was about to set him at ease when he showed me the page.

"Do you know what this is?" He'd drawn a symbol of some sort on the paper.

"No."

"It's a rune. If you have a certain type of magic, you can use it to get someone to tell the truth, even if they don't want to."

"I thought we already established that I don't have any magic."

He grinned. "I know. I have another idea. It doesn't involve magic, just trust."

"Okay?"

He closed his notebook and slid it back into his pocket but kept his pen gripped in his fist. Then he reached out to take my hand. His fingers hovered in the air above my skin. "May I?"

I nodded.

He pulled my hand toward him, turning it so that the wrist faced up. Then he drew the symbol on the inside of my wrist. When he was done, he drew it on his own wrist as well.

I stared at the ink drying on my skin. "There's no magic in this?"

"None."

"It's just going to come off in the shower."

He held up his pen so that I could see the writing on the side. Waterproof. "It should hold up for at least a few days."

I shook my head. "You're such a geek."

He grinned. "I know."

———

LEAVING ANGIE'S HOTEL ROOM was both harder and easier than I'd expected. My body was drained. I felt like I'd been wrung out like a sponge, and at the same time, every nerve on the surface of my skin felt twitchy and hypersensitive. My hands pulsed with pent-up magic that I needed to release, but the hotel lobby was booming with people coming and going from the popular bar, and the streets were still filled with folks enjoying one of the first pleasant evenings that signaled the coming break from the long, rainy winter.

I pulled out my phone and swiped to call Morgan. She was the only one I could talk to who could understand my current state. Luckily, she picked up on the third ring. By then, I was already out the door and halfway down the block.

Morgan's voice sounded sleepy. "Max?"

"Did I wake you?" I crossed at the corner and headed toward the Silicon Moon office.

"What time is it?"

"About ten. I didn't realize you went to sleep so early. I can call you in the morning."

"No. It's fine. It's just the time difference." She yawned. "We just got home from the airport a few hours ago. I fell asleep on the couch. I needed to get up and go to my actual bed, anyway."

"Where's Brady?" I knew she didn't like to talk about family stuff when her husband was around.

"He may have already crashed. I don't know. Why? Do you need to talk?"

"Yeah. Did you get my text?"

"Hang on." Her voice was replaced by the sound of foot-steps padding down an echoey hallway. Then it returned. "I read it. Just give me one more minute."

I pictured the layout of her modern mansion in Los Angeles and guessed she was heading from the living room with the floor-to-ceiling wall of glass separating the inside from the deck and lap pool outside and city lights in the distance, back through the house to her inner sanctum. A door clicked shut on the other end of the connection.

"All right. Free to talk now." Her office had been padded with sound insulation and fireproofing as well as magical warding to allow her a safe space to release her powers when the pressure built up. It had been my mother's wedding gift to her. "There is only one person I know named Lilium, and she is the head of my sire's demon clan."

"Wait. What? No." I checked around me to see if anyone was close enough to overhear my conversation.

"Yes."

"That's too weird to be a coincidence, right? But there's no way she was married to one of our engineers. We'd know that. And, what would she want with his stuff, anyway?" I remembered the notebook pages that Angie had shown me, the ones she'd been so concerned about.

"Anything is possible. I think it's definitely worth checking out before you send her anything. You haven't sent her anything, yet, have you?" She asked her question in that annoying older sister way that made it sound like I was an idiot who needed saving from himself. At least this time it wasn't true.

"No. I have someone helping me go through his stuff. We've found some strange items. At first, I thought it was just the usual wizard engineer quirk, but now I'm beginning to wonder." I paused outside our office building and looked up the ten floors to find my office windows.

"Someone from Silicon Moon? Or someone Mom sent?"

I grimaced. "Neither, actually. That's one of the reasons I called. It's Angie. She happened to be in town, and I asked her to help because her specialization in law school was intellectual property rights. She's an IP lawyer now, and I thought this was just a straightforward project."

Morgan sighed. "Nothing is straightforward with Silly Moon. When are you going to learn that?"

"Yeah. I know." I started to get my badge out so I could cut through the building to the parking garage.

"So, Angie, huh? I suppose at least she's non-magical enough that those Moon engineer 'quirks,' as you call them, will go right over her head."

I slid my badge back into my pocket. It was a nice evening, and if we were going to talk about Angie, I'd be better off walking. "You'd be surprised. She's oddly good at uncovering them, even if she has no idea what she's looking at."

"Huh."

"Yeah. But, it also turns out she's in the know." I chose my words carefully as I started down the long blocks that led to the base of the hill where I lived.

"In the know?"

"She confronted me about it. She overheard me talking with Varun and Jayden and apparently has this friend who filled her in on some things. I should have asked her for a name, then I would at least know if this friend of hers was one of us." If Angie had been talking to a wizard who had left the Society, she might have gotten the wrong idea about my family.

"One of us? Really, Maxie? You're starting to sound like

Mom.'"

I turned left at the corner and walked past a packed bar blasting techno music that pulsed through the walls and out onto the sidewalk. "Give me half a break, please? I'm walking home from dropping Angie off at her hotel, and I just told her the short version of why we couldn't be together, and I'm feeling a little raw at the moment, okay?"

"Short version being that you were too selfish to break up with her even though you knew you wouldn't be able to marry her because you are a good little mama's boy?"

"Ouch. Really?" I'd called her for empathy, and all I was getting was tough love.

"Let me guess... She didn't swoon at your confession."

"You're mean."

Morgan sighed, again. "Maxie, you know I love you and would do anything for you. And I appreciate what you've done for me, I really do. But when are you going to learn? You are the one in control here. Mom needs you. You don't need her permission to live your life."

"She thinks I can't handle this. She wanted you, and she got stuck with me. If I don't prove to her that I can handle it, she might put this back on you. I can't let her do that. I promised you."

"Is that what you're worried about?"

"You haven't seen her at the Council meetings. She's worried. The Barringtons are pushing, angling to take over. This is exactly the sort of thing that could win them favor." I paused at the street corner to wait for the light to change. "Callie is dating Grace now. Did I tell you that?"

"Grace Shin? The one with the Fae sire?"

Grace's mother wasn't on the Council, but she was powerful enough to lure one of the Fae. The story spread like a legend through the hushed whispers of the Society and followed Grace everywhere. According to the gossips, Grace's mother had sought out a Fae lover on purpose, then later decided that she hated the idea of aging while Grace's Fae sire would remain youthful and lovely for centuries. So she had her brief affair, then parted ways with her Fae lover before he discovered that she was pregnant with Grace.

"Yep."

"Ooooh. That must have pissed Mom off. I'm surprised Hannah didn't mention something to me."

"It's pretty new, but it seems serious. Grace is awesome, and marrying Callie would catapult her from the outer circle directly to the inner Council."

Grace had inherited a strong affinity for air from her Fae sire, as well as some other odd abilities that came in handy from time to time, but she didn't fully know how to control them. She blamed her mother for letting her grow up without a father, but we all knew that Fae were fickle creatures and couldn't be trusted. As our friend and part of our group, we had taken on the role of helping her learn as much as she could.

"You think that's the only reason Grace is dating Callie?" Her voice took on a little bit of an edge.

I backpedaled. "No. Of course not. But it certainly doesn't hurt."

"Gods and runes, you sound like Mom. Seriously. Do I need to pop over there and shake some sense into you? Do I need to remind you that Brady was an outsider before marrying me? Should I ask him if that's why he wanted to get married? So he could get a seat on the damned Wizard Council?" She was pissed, and rightfully so.

"I'm sorry. You're right. I'm sorry. It's been a rough night, okay? I didn't call to fight with you."

"I know you didn't. Just try not to be an insensitive jerk, okay? You're better than that."

"So what do I do about Angie and that Lilium woman, and the mysterious stuff that this engineer left behind? There are files and notebooks and paper like you would not believe, and some of it is completely new stuff."

"You really want my advice?"

"Why else would I call you?"

"I just don't think you're going to want to hear what I have to say."

"Lay it on me, then." I started the long slog up the hill to my house, so I wasn't going to have enough breath to argue with her, anyway. I could just be quiet and listen.

"Fine. I don't think you should push Angie away, not if she's helping you on this project, and definitely not if you still have feelings for her. If you love her, you should fight for her. Forget Mom. And I know about the key. Hannah told me. Don't be mad at her. She doesn't know why you're chasing down old wizards and trying to steal their secrets, but I do, and I don't need it. Mom may think a little demon blood in the family shows weakness, but I'm strong, and I'm figuring out how to deal with this on my own, thanks to you. Thanks to the fact that you put a buffer between me and Mom. But you don't need to find me some magical cure. I'm good. Okay?"

"You make it sound like it's so easy."

"Because it is that easy." She inhaled and exhaled in a sigh. "Just look at your friends, okay? Grace, Varun, even Hannah. Do they care who's in charge of the stupid Society? No. They do not. All this drama that Mom stirs up about the families and the heritage and magical bloodlines and secrets and all that, it's not more important than making sure wizards get the training they need and not just what the Society thinks is appropriate. Take your friend Jayden, for example."

"You mean my assistant? The one who is more loyal to our mother than he is to me?" I paused to wait for a car to turn and took a moment to admire the view.

"Yeah. That one. Why do you think that is?"

I hadn't really thought about it. "I don't know."

"He's an 'outsider,' as you put it, right? His family doesn't have a seat on the Council, but he has still managed to make a name for himself. And he's a self-taught wizard who doesn't come from some illustrious family who can trace their ancestry back to some sordid encounter with a faerie in the woods, right?"

"Yeah." I kept my response short because I was breathing hard as I neared the top of the hill.

"He sees winning Mom over as his ticket into the Council. Why he wants in is anyone's guess. Maybe he thinks it will give him validation. Maybe he wants to blow the whole thing up from the inside. Who knows? But that's his goal, and babysitting you is what he thinks is going to get him there."

"Ouch."

"I mean, I'm sure he likes you, but ambitious wizards got goals, you know?"

"Now who sounds like our mother, huh?" I grinned as I turned down my street.

"When did I ever claim not to be ambitious?"

"You're scary."

"I'm older and wiser, and you would do well to remember that. Now stop listening to Mom and be your own leader."

"Thanks for the pep talk."

"That's what I'm here for. Oh, and Maxie?"

"Yeah?" I pushed my key into the lock on my front door.

She started to sing. "Go on and kiss the girl..."

I set my head against the wood with a thump. "I'm hanging up now."

She kept singing, ignoring me. "You better do it soon—"

I spoke over her again. "You're the worst, but thanks. Love you."

"Tell that to Angie."

I groaned and hung up. She was right. I hated that she was always right. I stepped inside and shut the door behind me. Turning my wrist up until I could see the rune I'd drawn there, I thought back to my conversation with Angie. She'd broken up with me, but I had been a selfish chicken. Then I'd gone and messed it up worse tonight.

I traced the lines of the rune with the edge of my house key. Truth. There wasn't any magic in these lines, but we didn't need magic. I had enough for both of us, if she'd let me have a second chance to prove it.

9

THERE were seven messages on my phone when I woke up in the morning. I hadn't bothered to check it before going to sleep. After Max left, I could barely manage enough energy to wash my face and brush my teeth before falling into bed. I wasn't looking forward to facing him, but I had a mission to complete, and I wasn't about to leave without the information I came here for.

I showered, taking care not to scrub off the rune he'd drawn on my wrist. I stared at it as I let the hot water beat down on my neck and shoulders. Truth, huh? Even if he was only honor bound to be honest with me, it might make getting information about the boxes easier. The faster I got what I came for, the faster I could leave all this behind me and put him out of my mind for good.

The scramble I'd ordered from room service arrived just as I finished getting dressed. So, I sat down to eat while I read my messages. Willow had confirmed what Eve and I already guessed. Grace, Hannah, Varun, Callie, Jayden, and even Kyle were all wizards. The interesting thing was that they weren't all members of the Wizard Society.

Willow offered to give me a primer on the rift between the Society and the outsiders, those who quit or never joined in the first place. She suggested I call her. I waited until after I finished my breakfast. Then I set myself down in front of a mirror and settled in to do my makeup while she talked.

She started her lesson with a question. "You're familiar with the game of rock paper scissors, right?"

"You mean where you go one, two, three, shoot, and then make a shape with your hand?" I responded as I searched in my makeup bag for my powder brush.

"Exactly."

"Sure, but what does that have to do with this Wizard Society?"

"Think of it like this: demons are like rocks, the Fae are like paper, and the wizards are like scissors."

"This is not helping." I screwed the lid shut on my powder and reached for a light blush.

"The point is, there are three categories of magical creatures in the word, but they all have a natural dominance over one of the others. Just like paper covers rock, the Fae control demon magic. And just like scissors cut paper, the humans with magic have the ability to capture and control the Fae."

I considered her analogy for a minute. "That would mean that those same magical humans can be beat somehow by the demons."

"You got it. In this case, the demons prey on the humans. All humans, but especially magical humans because they can use them like a battery when they're not getting enough magic from the Fae. The Fae don't mind because they would be happy if there were fewer magical humans in the world."

"What a mess." I stared at my face in the mirror, wondering how long it would be before the demons figured out what I was up to and came after me.

"Yep. And that's where the Society comes in."

"Saviors of humanity with a mission to keep magic a secret from the·non-wizards." I searched my tote for the lip gloss samples that Hannah had given me.

"Precisely."

"So why wouldn't all the wizards want to be part of this exclusive secret club?"

"Not everyone agrees with the rules made by the Council, and seats on the Council are hard to come by. There are twelve. They're all inherited, and families like the Hunters keep a tight hold on who gets one whenever Council families merge and are forced to give up one of their precious seats."

"Merge like marry?" Max had made it sound like his parents wanted him to marry someone from one of the other families on the Council, but that didn't make any sense based on what Willow was saying.

"Yep. Except they don't have to give up the seat when they marry. That's why both of Max's parents can sit on the Council. When they retire, they'll only get to pass one seat on to one of their kids. The other will go to someone new."

"Why would any of the families on the Council marry each other if it meant giving up a seat?" Since I'd opted for the shimmery lip gloss, I decided to keep my eye makeup minimal.

"They do it when the desire to strengthen their magic is stronger than the need to control votes on the Council. And, since the family giving up their seat gets to nominate a candidate to take over, they can still influence those votes by carefully selecting their replacement."

"But replacements would still have to be voted on by the Council, right?" I finished lining my eyes and reached for my mascara.

"That's where things get a bit fuzzy. No one except the Council members really know how that process works."

"This all sounds very sketchy." I scowled as I packed away my makeup and tidied up the countertop.

"You can see why not all wizards want to be part of it, then?"

"Yeah. But what I don't understand is, if the demons are the natural predators of the humans, then why would the wizards help the demons by building these boxes that can drain and trap magic?"

"The wizards may not be. We only know for sure that it was a wizard who designed the boxes. Emilio. But we don't know why, or if he was doing this on his own or with the help of others." She paused to take a breath. "See, roughly speaking, there are two types of wizards."

"The kind that join the Society and the kind that don't?"

"Close. The kind that side with the Fae and the kind that side with the demons."

"Why would any wizards side with the demons if the demons are trying to drain their magic and kill them?"

"The enemy of my enemy is my friend, I guess. Or something like that." She sighed. "It's complicated, but most wizards hate the Fae."

I shook my head. "I don't get it. Did your parents care when they found out Arabella is Fae?"

"We haven't told them."

"Oh."

"Yeah. It's complicated, and you're going to have to watch your step and keep your eyes open. Use what you know to get to the bottom of this thing with the boxes, and then get out of there."

"Got it." We hung up after I promised her again that I wouldn't go anywhere without Salty and those nasty blood coins she'd given me.

One last check in the mirror confirmed that I was ready to make Max regret his decision not to stand up to his meddling parents. I collected my things, apologized to Salty as I clipped on her leash, and headed out the door to meet up with Jayden.

When I arrived, he was already in line. I secured Salty's leash to the bike rack and headed inside. He didn't turn his head to look when the bell over the door announced my entrance. So I slid past the couple in line behind him and tapped Jayden on the shoulder.

"Morning." I gave him my friendliest smile.

He looked up from his phone. "Hey."

I glanced at his screen as he clicked it off. "Busy morning?"

He frowned. "Boyfriend trouble."

"I'm sorry."

He waved a hand. "It's not a big deal."

I scanned the pastry display as we waited in silence. This wasn't going well. I needed to say something, but I had no idea what.

"So I think I forgot to pack extra ink cartridges for my fountain pen. Is there a good stationery supply store around here somewhere?"

Jayden looked at me sideways, like I'd asked the single dumbest question possible. "If you tell me what you need, I can pick something up for you while you and Max are working."

"This may sound silly, but I like to browse. Stationery stores make me happy, and sometimes I can pick out a color of ink that reminds me of a place I've visited... I don't know. It's a little thing. I can just look it up. I only asked in case you had a recommendation." As I talked, Jayden stared straight ahead, making me feel like a fool for even trying.

We were both silent for a moment. Then he surprised me. "I know the perfect place to send you."

The guy in front of us moved toward the pickup end of the counter, and Jayden stepped forward to place his order. "Two cappuccinos and one large regular coffee." He extracted three thermal mugs from his bag and handed them over the counter. He glanced over at me. "And, uh, two chocolate croissants?"

I shook my head. "If one of those is for me, thanks, but I ate breakfast at the hotel."

"Got it. Scratch the croissants. I'll just take one of those sunrise muffins instead."

I tried to give him some money, but he waved my cash away. So I slipped a few dollars into the tip jar, instead. As I did, the sleeve of my rain jacket shifted up, revealing the drawing on my wrist. Jayden's eyes were instantly drawn to it. They narrowed as his mouth shifted into a scowl.

I tugged my sleeve down and followed him toward the group waiting to pick up their coffees. "Thanks."

"It's just coffee. Don't get too excited." He pointed to my wrist. "Where did you get that?"

"A friend." It wasn't exactly a lie. Max wanted to be friends. I just wasn't sure if that was something I wanted. At least, not after last night.

"A tall, brooding, dark-haired, and annoyingly handsome friend?" He crossed his arms.

I nodded.

"Interesting." He stared at the baristas and continued

scowling.

They didn't deserve his wrath, so I drew his attention back to me. "What did I do to make you hate me so much?"

Jayden's scowl softened into an annoyed frown. "I don't hate you."

"Then what?"

He released an exasperated sigh and turned to face me. "In case you hadn't noticed, our friend has one major weakness, and I am looking at her."

"And that is my fault, how?"

"It's not. You just keep showing up."

The barista called Jayden's name, giving me time to form a witty response, but I was coming up with nothing. On the one hand, it was nice to know that Jayden thought I had some influence over Max, but I knew better. It didn't matter how much he cared about me, he wasn't willing to make it work against the wishes of his parents and their all-important Wizard Society. So that was that. I almost wanted to explain that to Jayden, but it would mean letting him know that I knew what they were up to.

I held the door for Jayden, then I untied Salty's leash. She watched Jayden while I loosened the knot, but she didn't move to greet him. I waited until we started walking to respond to his comments.

"It wasn't my idea to come here." That much was the truth. "I'm here on business. I have no intention of trying to get back together with Max, especially since he's made it very clear that he has no intention of trying to get back together with me."

Jayden snorted.

"What?"

"I'm not blind." He paused to glare at me out of the corner

of his eyes. "He was definitely flirting with you last night, and you were definitely letting him."

He scanned his card on the electronic pad outside the building, and I opened the door for him, then followed him inside. I opened my mouth to respond, then I spotted Max waiting for us by the elevator. His hair was a mess, and there were dark shadows under his eyes. It looked like he hadn't slept.

"Oh, good." He walked toward us. "Coffee. Which of these is mine?"

Jayden pointed to one of the mugs. "You look like you went toe to toe with a tumble of trolls and got your ass handed to you."

"Thanks." Max closed his eyes and took a long sip from his cappuccino. He sighed and opened his eyes. "Much better. I think I'm going to need about three of these to remain functional this morning."

Jayden glanced at me, then back at Max.

I held my hands up and shook my head. "Don't look at me. I had nothing to do with this."

Max laughed, but in a dark sort of way that I'd never heard from him. "In a way, you did, but not in the way he's thinking." He turned his back on us, then stalked over to the elevator to jab the up button with his finger.

Jayden and I were left staring at each other with equally baffled looks.

"Come on," Max called. "We have a lot to discuss, and we're not going to do it standing around down here."

———

I STARED AT MY DISTORTED REFLECTION in the chrome panels that lined the interior of the elevator and wondered if I really looked as sleep deprived as I felt. If Jayden was to be believed, the answer was a definite yes. I hadn't bothered to spend much time in front of a mirror before heading into the office. I'd had other things on my mind.

Neither Angie nor Jayden said a word on the ride up to the tenth floor. When the elevator chime announced we had arrived and the doors slid open, I was the first one out. Salty chased after me, pulling Angie along. Jayden started to turn away, heading for his cube.

"Everyone in the conference room. That means you, too, Jayden." I would have preferred to deal with Jayden alone, but I didn't want to let Angie out of my sight in case she decided to disappear before I could say what I wanted to say to her.

Jayden paused. He flashed me a questioning look but pivoted to follow us. Once he'd crossed the threshold, I flicked my wrist and shut the door with my air magic.

Jayden's mouth dropped open. "What the hell, Hunter?"

"Stop gaping and take a seat. She knows." I was done hiding my magic from Angie.

"You told her?"

"I guessed." Angie sat in one of the chairs and folded her arms across her chest.

"How the hell did she know enough to guess, Max?" Jayden gripped the edge of the table as he leaned toward me.

"I have a friend who is an earth wizard. Her name is Willow Heathman." This was the first time Angie had mentioned her friend's last name. It sounded familiar.

Jayden glared at her. "You're friends with the Heathmans' daughter? Well, that explains a lot. Is she the one who lent you her familiar?" He pointed at Salty, who was circling my feet, trying to get my attention.

"Her familiar?" Angie clearly had no idea what Jayden

was talking about, and I had questions that needed answers. The details of Angie's friend, her dog, and what Jayden knew about her family could wait.

I bent to pick Salty up and settled down into a chair at the head of the table with Salty in my lap. "Drop it, Jay. We have more important things to discuss."

"I'm not sure what's more important than the fact that you are exposing secrets to an ex-girlfriend who shouldn't even be here, and who also happens to be the friend of someone whose mother worked with Emilio Cortez. The Heathmans left the Society right around the same time that Emilio disappeared." He sighed. "Seriously, Max. Her entire presence here is highly suspicious. Tell her to get out."

I remembered the one woman in the picture Varun had found. The caption beneath had named her as Bethany Heathman. No wonder the name sounded familiar. Still, I'd been the one to push Angie into helping me, and she seemed just as surprised by her friend's family's association with our deceased engineer as I.

"Sit down, Jayden. Angie is not going anywhere. Neither of you are until we've had a nice long chat."

Now it was Angie's turn to gape at me. At least she'd already taken a seat at the table.

Jayden shook his head. "I've given you enough rope, man. I think it's time for me to do what I should have done from the beginning." He took out his phone and headed for the door.

I waved my hand, and flames shot up from the carpet, blocking his path.

He jumped backward, then turned to glare at me. "Now I know you've completely lost it."

I gestured again and sent one of the chairs rolling in his

direction on a current of air. "Sit. Down."

The chair hit Jayden in the back of his knees, and he sank into it. "Fine, but I'm calling Marcella as soon as we're done here."

"If you want to call someone, call the rest of the group and get them over here. We have work to do." I needed to talk with them as well, but first, I had to settle the questions about Jayden that Morgan had planted in my head.

"With her here?" Jayden pointed to Angie.

I shot Angie a pained look that hopefully also conveyed an unspoken apology. "I told you. Angie isn't leaving. I think we're going to need her help."

Jayden crossed his arms. "She's not one of us."

Angie shifted in her chair. "No. I'm not. But that doesn't mean I can't be helpful. Maybe we should hear Max out before deciding who stays and who goes." Angie turned her attention to me. "I'm guessing this has something to do with Emilio's papers?"

"It does. I've been up all night thinking about those plans that you showed me." I'd also been thinking about everything Morgan had said, but I didn't want to get into that yet. "Something about them was bothering me. I wasn't sure exactly what it was, but I kept coming back to the sequence of symbols on the pages, and it got me thinking. Can you find those pages while I get Jayden up to speed?"

"Sure." Angie stood and made her way over to the stack of notebooks.

I focused my attention on my assistant. "I made a deal with Angie last night, and I'd like to make the same deal with you."

"Does this have something to do with that rune on her wrist?"

"You noticed?" I couldn't help wondering how he'd seen

Angie's wrist when she was wearing a long-sleeved shirt and a rain jacket.

Jayden sighed. "You're just making this harder on yourself, man."

I needed to focus on one thing at a time. "You're probably right, but that's my problem. What I need to know is if I can trust you."

"Of course you can trust me."

That wasn't quite what I'd had in mind. "I need you to promise to tell me the truth."

Jayden's eyes narrowed. "I wouldn't lie to you."

"Then prove it. Make it so that you can't."

Jayden glanced at Angie, who was standing there waiting with the notebook I'd asked her to get. Then he looked at me. "I promise. You can trust me."

I drew a handful of ash up, off the carpet, sucking it into a tiny whirlwind. Then I deposited it in a heap on the table in front of him. "Draw the rune."

We stared at each other for a full minute while Jayden waited for me to back down. Morgan had planted the seed about Jayden's loyalty, and once I'd realized what the plans in that notebook might mean, I needed to be sure. This was the only way. If he refused, then I had at least part of my answer.

Jayden set down his coffee and pushed up his sleeves. He flexed his wrists, then he dragged one finger through the pile of ash, spreading it into the familiar shape of the rune for truth. He kept the symbol small enough to be pressed against the inside of his forearm. Once it was done, he looked up at me again.

I stared at him, waiting, preparing myself in case he decided to run.

He didn't run. He sighed and shook his head. Then he

waved one palm over the rune. The ashes glowed golden for a moment before he smothered the light with his bare forearm, pressing it down into the table as his face scrunched in recognition of the discomfort.

He held his arm up to show me the mark on his skin. "It's done."

Everyone in our group had done this. Once when we'd sworn our loyalty to the Society, and again when we'd sworn to have each other's backs. It took earth magic to make the marks, and they would only last for a few hours—just long enough to swear an oath or testify. Then the magic preventing the marked person from lying would fade.

"Thank you."

Jayden rolled down his sleeve. "Now what is all this about?"

"Are you, or is anyone you know, working with the demons?"

"What? No." Jayden's face scrunched up in disgust.

I released a breath, and some of my tension drained away, replaced by relief. Then I remembered I'd mentioned demons in front of Angie. Jayden must have realized at the same time, because both our heads turned to look at her.

"What?" she asked. "I'm not working with the demons, if that's what you think."

I choked out a laugh. "No. I just... You know about demons?"

She shrugged. "In theory. I've never seen one in person." She paused and held up one finger. "Wait. I take that back. I do know a half demon, but not very well."

"Half human and half demon?" I was becoming more and more curious about these friends of hers and how she'd fallen in with them. Maybe she was one of those people who just gravitated to magic, even though she lacked powers of her own. That would explain how she'd ended up immersed in my friend group, only to leave me and be drawn into another group of magical humans.

"Half wizard, technically, but yeah."

Jayden's eyes narrowed. "There aren't many of those around. Who is it? Someone else we know?"

Angie shook her head. "The deal was personal truths. I'd rather not be revealing all my friends' secrets."

She was right, that had been our deal, but now I was curious, too. I'd never heard of anyone besides Morgan who was half wizard and half demon. I had questions, but my time was running out on Jayden's truth rune. My questions for him were going to have to take priority.

"Fair enough, but it may be relevant later. For now, can you show Jayden the pages you showed me yesterday?"

Angie took a step toward Jayden, eyeing the bit of table where the ashes had been and were no longer. She laid the notebook down, open to the page with the drawings of cubes. Jayden pulled it toward him so he could study the pages.

"What is this?" he asked.

"Angie found it in Emilio's things. Have you ever seen anything like this before?" The question, so similar to the one Angie had asked when she'd shown the pages to me, sparked another thought. I glanced at her, realizing that I'd never asked her if she knew what this was, even though she'd known enough to question me about it, just like I was questioning Jayden.

"Never." Jayden's fingers traced the notes that filled the spaces between the cubes. "But these are formulas or...theories. I could be wrong, but it seems like you would need control of all four elements to do this. Whatever this is."

"To do what?" I wanted to know if he'd come to the same

conclusion.

"I'm not sure. It's like..." He scanned the pages, scrutinizing the details. "It's like he was trying to build a container... for magic...but that's impossible."

"This isn't a Silicon Moon project, then?" I asked because Jayden had been working in this branch of my family's business longer than I had, and I wanted to be sure I was right.

"Not one that I've ever seen or heard of."

I stood, shifting Salty to the ground so I could pace. "What I can't figure out is why a wizard would build something like this—something that would allow the demons to torture and control wizards more easily."

Jayden snorted.

I stopped pacing and looked at him. "What?"

He rolled his eyes. "Of course you wouldn't know why."

"What's that supposed to mean?"

"What do you think happens to all those wizards that don't want to be part of your oh-so-exclusive Society?" Angie sounded as annoyed as Jayden looked.

"Exactly." Jayden's finger stabbed at the pages. "This is exactly the sort of thing a desperate outsider would do if they thought they could trade it for knowledge. Training. Security. All the things the Society offers, but only to those who agree to abide by their rules."

"But Emilio was part of the Society." I suddenly remembered what Morgan had told me about his widow. I slapped the table with my palm. "Shit. Of course. He was married to a demon."

10

MENTIONING Willow by name had been a mistake. I had forgotten that her parents had been friends with Emilio. They thought that was why he might have gone to their lodge after Lilium had attempted to wipe all his memories. But I didn't realize that Betty had worked with Emilio at Hunter Works. If that was true, my presence here was even more suspicious. I was going to have to be more careful about what I said and did.

At least Max already knew about Lilium, even though he didn't know even half of what I knew about Emilio. It didn't matter that he thought the boxes were meant to drain and trap human magic. Maybe they had initially been intended for that, but that wasn't the demons' current plan for them.

"The widow is a demon? How do you know that?" Jayden asked.

Max scowled. "I can't say. You're just going to have to trust me, like I'm going to have to trust you. But before I do, I have one more question."

"Just one?" Jayden smirked.

"I can keep doing this all morning, but I didn't get much sleep, and we have a mountain of paperwork to go through that we clearly can't be sending off to Emilio's widow."

Jayden's fingers gripped the armrests. "I'm not a demon, if that's what you want to know."

"It wasn't, but thanks. I want to know if you're planning on destroying the Society from the inside. Is that why you want to be appointed to the Council so badly?" Max looked hurt, like he didn't want to believe that it could possibly be true.

The way Jayden shifted in his chair, though, made me think Max might be on to something. "Not...exactly." Jayden's face twisted like he'd been hit in the stomach.

"You're lying."

"I don't expect you to understand. Your father controls the Council, and the Council makes the rules, and none of the members, not even you, would dare vote to change a thing. You're too worried about protecting yourselves. You don't care about the rest of us."

"Do you have a plan?"

Jayden's fists clenched. He pressed his lips closed to prevent himself from responding.

Max shook his head. The shadows under his eyes were darker, somehow. "It's fine. Don't tell me. I don't deserve to know. But, you're wrong about me. I do want the Society to change. Will you give me a chance to prove that to you?"

Jayden looked skeptical, but he nodded.

"Thank you. Now can you go round up the rest of the group and get them here as quickly as possible? I have something I want to tell them, and then we have work to do."

Jayden stood. "Max..."

Max waved his words away. "It's fine. Just don't call my mother. At least not yet. Okay? Give me a chance, first."

Jayden nodded, then started for the door. He hesitated at the spot where Max's magic had left the carpet scorched. Then he flicked his wrist as he stepped over it. By the time he'd reached the door, the carpet had repaired itself.

I'd been so busy watching Jayden's magic work that I hadn't noticed Max approach. He stopped next to me and set one hand on my shoulder.

"Hey." He looked so fragile and raw.

I wanted to comfort him, but I tucked my hands into my pockets instead. "That was...interesting."

"I'm sorry you had to be here for all that, but I didn't want to send you away." He paused. "I don't want to send you away, Angie. Ever. You were right. I've been a fool, and I'm so sorry." His hand lifted from my shoulder so his fingers could skim my cheek.

The sensation radiated through my skin all the way down to my toes. "What are you saying?"

His fingers drifted down, away from my face, until they wrapped around my hand. "I'm saying that I love you. I've always loved you. I never stopped loving you, and I was wrong to push you away. I won't do it again. If you'll give me another chance."

"What about the Society? What about your parents, and your magic?" My heart slammed against my rib cage, beating faster and faster with every hopeful breath I took.

He shrugged. "My plan is to use my position to change what I can, but if that doesn't work, we'll start something new."

I wanted to believe him. "You're asking me to trust that you aren't going to eventually decide that magic and your family's rules are more important than me."

"I am." He took a half step closer.

"I don't know, Max." I wanted to trust him, but he was sleep deprived and probably not thinking straight. Did he really think he could walk away from everything that was important to him? For me? It had taken me years to recover from our breakup. I couldn't handle opening my heart to him again only to have him crush it.

The corners of his mouth pulled down. "Will you at least give me a chance to prove it to you?"

I considered his words, the sadness in his face, and his sincerity. "What happened to make you change your mind?"

The left corner of his mouth tilted up. "I talked to someone older and wiser than me."

"You told your parents you wanted to get back together with me?"

He laughed. "Not yet. I wanted to talk with you, to make sure there was still a chance for us, first. But I'll call them and tell them right now if that's what you want." He slid his phone out of his pocket.

"You're serious."

Max pressed a button and the screen lit up. "I'm serious."

I swallowed as I stared into his brown eyes. Then I snatched his phone away and leaned past him to set it on the table. "You can call them later."

He set his hands on my hips as I straightened and tugged me closer. I was hyperaware of every single one of his fingers where they pressed into the denim fabric. My chest rose and fell, causing my blouse to rub against his rumpled cotton T-shirt.

I gripped his shoulders. "Don't break my heart, Hunter."

"I won't." He whispered the words, and then his mouth

was on mine. Our lips pressed together and parted, wet and hungry and urgent. He crushed his hips against me as his hands slid up to skim my waist.

My fingernails scraped up the back of his neck until they met the close-cropped hair at the nape. I shifted until our bodies aligned. Every piece fitting together, exactly where it was meant to be. Then I melted against him, unable to resist his pull. I had to trust that this was going to work, because if it didn't, losing this connection might break me.

"I knew it was only a matter of time." Jayden's voice broke through the haze of bliss.

Max smiled against my lips. He pulled away just far enough to speak, but didn't release his hold on me. "Get used to it, man. I told you, Angie isn't going anywhere."

I stared into his eyes, still locked with mine, and scowled. "Um, actually? Angie does have to leave at some point."

Max caught one of my hands in his as he took a step back. "We'll see."

Jayden just shook his head. "I knew this was going to happen."

"Did you get everyone? Are they coming?" Max kept his eyes on me, even though I knew his questions were for Jayden.

"They're on their way. I was going to head down to the lobby to intercept them. I was thinking I might get some more coffee for you, but you seem to have brightened up considerably in the few minutes I left you two alone." Jayden made a face and crossed his arms.

"I promise I'll explain everything when the others get here."

"It's pretty obvious what's going on here. I don't think I need an explanation. I'll honor your request to hold off on calling this in to the higher-ups, but let it be known, I still think this is a very bad idea."

"Thanks for that vote of confidence." I muttered the words as the heady rush from Max's kiss left me and reality, in the form of his grumpy assistant, stared me in the face.

Max squeezed my hand. "This is an excellent idea. It's going to change everything."

"You're freaking me out a little, man." Jayden pulled out his phone and started typing something.

"Everything will make sense soon. I'm good on the coffee front, so just get the others. Angie and I will get to work while you're gone."

After the whoosh of a sent message, Jayden slid his phone back into his pocket. "Yeah, right. More like, the minute I leave, you'll be practically horizontal on this table. I let them know that they should text me when they're all here, and I'll go down and get them."

"Great. Then let's get to work." Max gestured to the stacks of notebooks and papers. "What do you think, Angie?"

"Everything that's left is the stuff that looked like legitimate notes or plans for projects. I don't know what's worth keeping, but I recommend that we go through all of it, keep what you want, and shred the rest. If what you said about the widow is true, then it sounds like we shouldn't give any of this to her, just to be on the safe side."

"Good point. So, we're looking for more weird magic stuff or anything that looks like we should pass it on to one of the project teams to make sure they don't need it before we toss it out." Max released my hand and took a seat. He pulled a stack of notebooks in front of him, and Jayden did the same.

I lingered a moment longer, pretending to check on Salty but actually eyeing the boxes at the far end of the table. The boxes that contained all the items that we'd assumed were personal effects. Things Max was planning on sending to Lilium. I tried to think of a way to smuggle out the metal cube without them knowing, and considered how I could tell them what little I knew about Emilio without revealing anything about the Fae.

I'd already mentioned that I knew someone who was half demon and half wizard. But, if I explained that Nigel was Lilium and Emilio's son, my presence would look even more suspicious. Max would assume I was working for the demons. And if I couldn't tell them about the Fae, then I would have no way to convince him otherwise.

I decided that what little I knew about Emilio's history was irrelevant. It was entirely possible that what Max believed was correct, and Emilio had been working with Lilium on a plot to overthrow the Wizard Society. I had nothing helpful to add, and if I spoke up, I risked losing Max's trust. I had to believe that he would understand those were other people's secrets and not mine to tell.

MY LEG BOUNCED under the table, and I had a difficult time concentrating on the papers in front of me. I kept wanting to get up and pace, or grab Angie's hand just to reassure myself that she was really still there. I settled for quick glances at her every few minutes, but even that didn't do much to calm my nerves. I wouldn't be able to relax until everyone was here and I'd said everything I wanted to say. At least I'd managed to reassure myself that Jayden wasn't teaming up with the demons to destroy the Society. Morgan wasn't wrong, though. He was planning something.

Jayden's phone buzzed, interrupting my thoughts. He

pushed his chair back and stood. "They're here. Do you want me to bring them to the conference room?"

"Yeah. Let's meet here."

Jayden gestured to the papers he'd been going through. "Not much of interest here. Hopefully, you're having better luck."

I shook my head. "Not really. Angie?"

Angie had twisted a piece of her short purple-striped hair around one finger. She was chewing on her bottom lip, fully absorbed by whatever she was reading. "Hm?"

"Found anything?"

"Maybe?" She turned the large sheet of paper she had been studying and pushed it toward me.

I rolled my chair closer to her, and Jayden moved around the table so he could look over our shoulders at the drawings. There were more boxes, but these didn't look like sketches. These looked like engineering plans. Sure enough, Emilio's signature emblem had been stamped in the bottom corner.

Jayden pointed at the design on one of the sides of the box. "I recognize that."

I nodded. "That is a standard sort of protection spell, but I can't tell what it's meant to protect."

"Let me go get the others. Grace has spent more time than any of us in the archives. Maybe she has an idea." Jayden patted me on the shoulder, then headed for the door.

"Jay?"

He stopped and turned to face me.

"Do any of them know about your plans?"

His mouth twisted as he considered my question, then he shook his head.

I nodded. "I won't say anything. For now."

"Thanks."

"I'm still hoping I can change your mind."

Jayden frowned but didn't respond.

I waited until he was gone before turning to Angie. "Hey."

"Hey." She grimaced.

"Everything okay?"

She shifted in her chair and glanced over at Salty curled up near her tote before returning her attention to me. "I could ask you the same thing. What's going on? Can I get a preview, or should I wait to find out with everyone else?"

There wasn't enough time to try to explain everything to her before the others arrived. "I thought a lot about what you said last night. You were right. It's time I stood up to my parents, and not just about how I feel about you."

She rested her hand on my knee and leaned closer. "Your friends are going to support you."

"I hope you're right." Out of the corner of my eye, I caught a glimpse of movement. I turned to look just in time to see a group walking toward the conference room. I counted. "Only four."

Varun was the first to enter the conference room. Grace and Hannah followed close behind him, and Jayden trailed after them.

"Hey, man, what's going on?" Varun flopped down in one of the chairs and stretched out his legs. If he was surprised to see Angie sitting next to me, he hid it well.

"Where's everyone else?" I asked.

"Callie couldn't make it." Grace leaned against the wall. "She's working."

"Kyle is at a family thing." Jayden sat in one of the chairs, across from Varun. "I'll fill him in later."

I'd wanted to tell everyone at the same time so I could see their reaction and judge it for myself. Especially Callie, since my mother thought the Barringtons were somehow out to get us. But the rest of the group was waiting for me to say something. I'd called them here to make an announcement. I had no choice but to start talking.

I stood up. It seemed like the right thing to do. "First off, Angie's here, and I'm including her in this for a few reasons, but the most relevant at the moment is that she knows."

"You told her?" Hannah grabbed a chair and sat down. "Wow. I did not see that coming."

Angie responded before I could. "Don't be mad at Max. He didn't tell me. I guessed because I already knew about magic. I have a friend who is a wizard."

"She's friends with Willow Heathman." Even though Jayden was whispering to Hannah, he spoke loud enough that we all heard him.

"No joke?" Hannah's eyes bounced between Jayden and Angie.

"I didn't even know the Heathmans had a daughter. Huh." Grace set her elbows on the back of Hannah's chair and propped her chin in her hands.

Varun tilted his head to one side. He crossed the ankle of one long outstretched leg over the other as he studied my face. "You said first thing. That implies a second thing. Interesting as it is, I'm assuming you didn't call a meeting just to announce that Angie is friends with the daughter of the only wizards to have quit the Council in more than a hundred years."

When he put it that way, something clicked in my brain. It almost seemed like a warning, but I was so focused on that second thing I wanted to talk about with them that I ignored it. The pieces of the puzzle that were so close to falling into place.

I took a breath and dove into the speech I'd planned. "You all know about the fact that the Council thinks there is a wizard, or a group of wizards, who are working with the demons to take over control of the Society. And you know that we found evidence that Emilio Cortez may have been involved in some way."

I paused, waiting for nods or some sort of acknowledgment.

"Because Kyle connected Emilio with that key of yours?" Grace asked.

"That, plus what we've found going through his notebooks and papers." I gestured to the mess spread out on the table. According to that old wizard, the key was supposed to lead me to something that was going to help my sister. I'd never guessed that the key would actually lead me to evidence of a wizard working with the demons against the Society.

"What sort of evidence did you find?" Hannah asked.

"There are plans here for a device that I believe would drain someone of their magic. I'm not sure that it works, or if the device ever got past the planning stages. I need your help to put the pieces together, but I also need to know that I can trust you never to breathe a word of this to anyone outside our group."

Grace and Hannah pushed their sleeves up to their elbows and exposed their forearms. Hannah dug a tube of lipstick out of her purse and drew one truth rune on the inside of her arm and another on Grace's arm. She held the lipstick out to Varun, but his arms were crossed as he stared at me.

"Yes, Varun?" I asked, wondering why he was waiting for an invitation to speak.

"Okay, Hunter, here's the thing, I'm going to speak bluntly. I like Angie, I really do. Under any other circumstances,

I'd be thrilled that you're finally being honest with her and including her."

"So what's the problem?" I leaned forward and pressed my palms against the top of the table.

"I think you're letting your feelings blind you to the facts." He ticked them off on his fingers as he spoke. "One, you find this key just before Angie suddenly returns to town on some mysterious business assignment—sorry, Angie, but I warned you I was going to be blunt."

Angie tensed next to me, but she nodded. "It's fine. Go ahead."

Varun grimaced, then continued. "Two, we find out that she just happens to be friends with the Heathmans' daughter. Three, you saw the picture I sent you of the engineering team, Bethany Heathman was one of those engineers. If you're looking for wizards who might want to get their hands on whatever tech Emilio developed, the person you should be asking if you can trust is sitting right next to you."

The warning I'd ignored earlier began to make sense. I studied my friends' faces and saw the same pained look written on each. Morgan had told me to stand up to my parents and be a leader. In the process of trying to follow her advice, I'd let my feelings cloud my judgment. Varun was right to be suspicious of Angie.

Next to me, she'd gone still. When I turned toward her, she stared at me with wide eyes.

Across the table, Hannah stood and offered Angie the tube of lipstick. "Care to prove Varun wrong?"

Angie swallowed. She pushed up her sleeve, revealing the truth rune I'd drawn on the inside of her wrist.

Hannah stepped back and plopped down into her chair. "See, Varun? Max already questioned her."

"He didn't." Up to that point, Jayden had kept quiet, even though I could tell he agreed with Varun. "He would have had to ask me or Grace to do the binding spell to activate the rune. We're the only two in the group with earth magic. He didn't ask me. Did he ask you, Grace?"

"No." Grace's voice was almost apologetic. "But I'll do it now if it will end this nonsense. What do you think? That she came up with a scheme to take down the Society as some sort of revenge on Max?"

Grace left her position behind Hannah's chair and paced around the table to where Angie sat. When she reached her, she held her hand out, palm up. "Give me your wrist, and let's get this over with."

Angie laid her wrist in Grace's palm, rune facing up, without a word. Her other hand gripped the arm of her chair so tight that her knuckles turned white.

Grace must have noticed. "Don't worry. It won't hurt unless you lie."

Without waiting for Angie to respond, Grace swirled a finger in the air above the rune I'd drawn. It glowed blood red for a moment as the spell activated.

Angie spoke without prompting. "I'm not trying to destroy the Wizard Society, Willow isn't trying to destroy the Society, and neither of us is working with the demons or anyone who is trying to destroy the wizards, as far as we know."

She glanced briefly at the others before turning her gaze up to meet mine. "Is that sufficient?"

I reached over and set my hand on top of the one that was still clutching the arm of her chair. Wrapping my fingers around hers, I pried her hand off the arm and rubbed the pad of my thumb against her skin.

Then I turned my attention to my friends. "Does anyone

have any questions for Angie? Or are you ready to take your oaths and get to work?"

Grace activated the rune Hannah had drawn on her arm. "I swear to keep whatever we find here secret."

Hannah and Varun followed with their oaths.

Once it was done, I breathed a sigh of relief. "Hannah, why don't you and Angie go through everything in those boxes, just to make sure we didn't miss anything. The rest of us will go through this paperwork and see if we can make any connections. Okay?"

11

I WASN'T mad about the truth spell. I would have done the same thing in his position. But I was a little annoyed that he hadn't told everyone that we were back together. Then again, did one kiss and a promise to tell his parents that he wasn't going to do what they wanted him to do mean that we were back together? The more that I thought about it, the more I worried that I'd just bought a one-way ticket to another broken heart.

Max snuck up behind me and slid his hands around my waist. He rested his chin on my shoulder and pressed his chest against my back. "Hey."

"Hey."

His fingers pressed into my hips as he placed a lingering kiss on the side of my neck. "I think we made some progress."

"Oh?" I set the lid on the box I'd been searching through. My eyes fluttered closed, and I reveled in the feel of his body against mine. I'd missed it more than I'd realized.

"Yeah. I think this guy actually built a few of these boxes

and then hid them. We're not sure why, but we think that the key that I have might unlock wherever it is that he kept the map. So if you come across anything with a keyhole, let me know. Okay?"

They were making progress. This was exactly the sort of information I'd been sent to find. If I was going to end up with my carefully pieced-together heart broken again, I could at least have something to show for it.

When I turned to face Max, he kept his hands on my hips. Behind him, on the other side of the conference room, I noticed almost everyone was filing out the door and heading toward the elevator. "Where is everyone going?"

"Varun has a flight to catch, and Grace is going to drop him off at the airport. Hannah and Jayden are grabbing lunch."

"Oh." My eyes followed them, and my stomach grumbled a complaint, but my mind was distracted by the rush of warmth that spread through my body, radiating out from the point where Max was touching me.

Max's head tilted to one side. "Are you okay?"

I blinked at him, realizing I hadn't been paying much attention to his words. "Did you say something about a key?"

"Yeah." Max let me go so he could pull the little black notebook he always carried with him out of his pocket. He flipped to the back and slipped a small silver key out of the pocket.

The key looked a bit like the ones that came with the diaries I saved up to buy at the stationery store in the mall in middle school. This one was a little larger, and the teeth appeared to be somewhat more complicated than the simple design that was supposed to keep my childhood secrets safe from spying eyes.

"I suppose I never told you about this. I probably should have." He held the key up, and I took it from him to examine it.

"What is it for?" I remembered he'd mentioned a key, but I hadn't wanted to interrupt and ask when he was talking about it with his friends.

"That's what we've been trying to figure out. I got this from an old wizard who said it would help me find something I was looking for, but he disappeared before telling me what it opened or what I was supposed to do with it."

I met his eyes and raised an eyebrow. "You realize how weird that sounds, right?"

He ran his hand through his hair, messing it up as he grinned at me. "Yeah. I'm aware."

"He didn't also have a long white beard and a pointy hat, did he? Maybe some tiny spectacles on the end of his nose and a long staff? Tell me he wasn't wearing robes."

Max started laughing. He shook his head. "We don't wear robes."

"Not even at those swanky Society meetings?"

He tossed his notebook on the table to free up his hands so he could pull me closer. Our noses bumped as he lowered his forehead to rest against mine. "Not even then."

"What about bathrobes?"

He grinned. "I prefer to walk around naked."

"I remember."

"You do, huh?" He traced a line from my earlobe to my collarbone with the tip of his finger.

I caught my bottom lip between my teeth. "Uh-huh."

His arm wrapped around my waist as his other hand reached the collar of my blouse and followed it down. His fingers traced the edge of the fabric and skimmed across the bare skin beneath. "Want to know what I remember?"

"Hmm?" My body was so focused on the sensation of his

teasing fingers that my tongue refused to form words.

His head dipped down until his lips found the spot right below my ear that drove me wild. I pressed my body closer to his, wanting more. He responded by tracking kisses down my neck to the hollow at the base of my throat.

I slid the key into my pocket so I wouldn't drop it. Then I slipped my hands under the hem of his shirt and hooked my fingers into his waistband. He pressed his front teeth against the skin at the base of my neck, then lifted his head until our lips met.

He kissed my mouth with a hunger that echoed mine. When we finally broke apart to catch our breaths, I sighed.

"Tell me the truth," I said. "You kicked them all out just so you could do that."

He grinned. "I will always tell you the truth. And you are absolutely correct."

"I thought so." I rested my hands on his shoulders. "Do you know what else I've been thinking about?"

"No." His hands clutched my hips, and his thumbs pressed into the soft spot just inside my hip bone as he kissed the tip of my nose. "What?"

The key I'd put into my pocket got trapped between Max's thumb and my skin. I shifted a little to avoid the discomfort and suddenly remembered seeing a box with a lock on it that might fit that key. As much as I was enjoying catching up on everything I'd missed in the few months I'd been away, and the four years that we'd been apart before that, kissing Max erased all thoughts from my head. If we started making out again, I'd forget all about that little wooden box.

"Hang on. I just thought of something."

"Yeah. You were just going to tell me what it was."

"No, this is a different something." I twisted out of his arms and hurried over to the stack of boxes I'd been going through with Hannah.

I threw the lid off the one on top but didn't see what I was looking for, so I moved that one to the floor and pulled the top off of the next one down.

"What are you looking for?"

"There was a little wooden box. It was in one of these, but I don't remember which."

"And it is suddenly very important that you find it?"

The rounded corner of a polished wood grain peeked out at me from beneath three brightly colored juggling balls. The box was rectangular and small enough to fit in my palm. It was plain but polished to a shine with a scrolling inlay of wood in the center of the lid. From the outside, it looked like a jewelry box, and that's what I'd assumed it was. I held it in one hand and extracted the key from my pocket with the other.

That got Max's attention. "Oh."

I slid the key into the lock. It fit, but nothing happened.

"Turn it over."

I took the key out, flipped it over, and tried again. A click signaled success. As I tilted the lid back on its hinges, a small wooden globe lifted up to hover in the opening. A tinny music box played "It's a Small World" as we stared at the sphere, which was painted to look like a miniature Earth.

"Does this make any sense to you?" I asked.

"None."

When Salty started barking, I assumed she was trying to let us know that something about this was important, like the other objects she'd sniffed out. Or maybe she didn't like the music. But it wasn't either of those things. She was trying to tell us we had company.

"Maxwell Hunter, what in the name of the elements is she doing here?"

Max and I both turned our heads toward the conference room door. An older woman stood glaring at us in a pencil skirt and suit jacket, her gray-streaked hair pulled back from her face, highlighting her dark eyes, sharp cheekbones, and full lips. I bent down and picked up Salty to quiet her and keep her from running at the woman who I recognized as Max's mother.

"I thought he agreed not to call you." Max's muttered comment confirmed that he was as surprised as me to see who had graced us with her presence.

"Who agreed not to call me?" She tugged at the hem of her jacket to straighten it.

"Never mind." Max took a step toward her, putting a little more distance between us. "Hello, Mother. I didn't know you were in town."

"I am, and you still haven't answered my question." She set her hands on her hips.

Max turned to me, first. "Angie, you remember my mother, Marcella Hunter."

We had met briefly at a university event back when Max and I were dating, then again at Max's graduation. I got a glimpse of her at Morgan's wedding, but I had spent most of the evening avoiding her. "Nice to see you again, Mrs. Hunter."

Marcella raised an eyebrow in acknowledgment but kept her lips pinched shut.

"Mother, you may not remember, but Angie is an intellectual property lawyer. She was in town for work, and I asked her to help me with the Cortez project."

"The Cortez project?" Marcella's mouth softened a bit as

she glanced around at the cardboard cartons stacked in the corners of the conference room, and notebooks and papers spread across the conference table. "Is that what's going on here?"

"Jayden didn't tell you?"

"Your assistant? That nice Reyes boy? So sad to hear about his parents." She made a noise that was something between a sigh and a scolding tsk. "I believe he mentioned something in his weekly report about Emilio's widow asking for his things. But that should be a fairly straightforward assignment for some secretary or mail clerk, no? I don't understand why you are here, up to your eyeballs in dusty old junk, making a pig-sty of your best conference room, and employing an intellectual property lawyer to assist you."

"I wanted to be sure we didn't accidentally send any corporate secrets to an outsider." Max folded his arms across his chest.

Now that I knew what to listen for, I could understand the subtext in Max's explanation. Silicon Moon may not exclusively employ wizards, but there were likely enough of them working here that more than a little bit of magic seeped into their product designs, and before he'd realized that Lilium was a demon, he'd thought Emilio had been married to a human without magic, or at least one who was not in their Society.

The fact that he'd chosen to communicate that to his mother without stating his concerns outright made me think that he was trying to hide the fact that I knew exactly what was going on here. It was probably best that she didn't know, but it made me doubt that he was going to have the nerve to tell her that we were getting back together.

"I SUPPOSE IT IS a good idea for us to keep a close eye on our secrets." My mother's eyes focused on Angie, who was standing slightly behind me. "I came to extend my condolences to Jayden, in person, but it sounds like there are a few things we should discuss. Alone."

Whatever my mother knew about Jayden was news to me. The fact that I didn't know what she was talking about bothered me. I decided to believe that whatever she'd heard, she'd discovered through Society gossip and not because Jayden had shared information with her and not with me. When he returned, I would ask him, but first, I needed to convince my mother to leave.

Angie moved away from me, circling around the far side of the table to where she'd left her tote. "I need to take Salty for a walk, anyway. I'll just leave you two to chat."

I hurried after her and pressed my badge into her hand. "Here. Take this so you can get back into the building."

She glanced down at the plastic rectangle with my photo and name. "Thanks."

I wasn't sure if she realized the significance of what I'd just given her, and I had no way to check while my mother was standing there glaring at me. Since I was in charge of Silicon Moon, that badge opened everything. I never let it out of my possession, and I'd just handed it to her. All I could do was squeeze her hand and hope that she understood.

Angie had barely made it to the elevator when my mother started in on me. "Honestly, Maxwell. I thought we'd had this discussion and agreed. There is no place in your life for that girl."

"We did talk about this, but we don't agree. Angie knows

about magic." I held up one hand. "And before you ask, she didn't find out from me. It turns out that she has friends who are wizards. Outsiders."

My mother scoffed. "What difference does that make? Just because the girl is hanging around with the riffraff of the wizard world doesn't change the fact that there isn't a magical bone in her body. You need an heiress by your side, not some regular human."

"First of all, she is a woman, not a girl. And second, I wouldn't be so sure about the bones in her body. She appears to have a natural affinity for magic."

"A natural affinity for gold digging is what I would call it."

"Enough. I will choose my partner. Not you."

"You will do as your father and I say, or I won't name you as heir."

"And who will you name in my place? Morgan? Are you finally ready to explain her unique qualities to Father and make her your heir, Mother?"

"Are you attempting to threaten me?"

"I'm telling you that you made your choices, and I will make mine."

"I didn't make that choice. That choice was taken from me, and that's why I'm here." She dusted off one of the chairs and perched on the edge of it. "Did you see the name of Emilio's widow on that letter from her lawyer?"

"I did, and I talked to Morgan. I know who she is."

When she caught me staring at her trembling hands, she interlaced them and set them in her lap. "She trained the incubus who seduced me. She is more than powerful enough to have seduced Emilio. I don't believe for a minute that they were in love. I knew Emilio. He had a family. A daughter, if I remember correctly. I never met them because one moment he was happy and in love and the next he was gone. Disappeared." She lifted one hand and snapped her fingers.

"You think he was seduced?" I should have realized that was a possibility once Morgan reminded me who Lilium was.

"Have you found any family photos among his things?"

I stared at the cartons we'd packed full of what we'd assumed were his personal possessions. "Huh. No. None."

"I don't know what she wants with all this, but whatever it is, it isn't good. I didn't want to say anything in front of your little friend, but you were right to scrutinize everything before sending it to her."

"I think I know what she wants. At first, I thought maybe Emilio had been plotting with the demons against the Wizard Society, but your explanation makes more sense."

"What did you find?"

"Plans for some sort of magic trap."

My mother paled. "Show me."

With the help of the others, there was more than just the notebook to show her. I gathered the papers and notebooks in my arms and carried them down to her end of the table. Then I spread them out in front of her.

She studied the pages and plans, then lifted her head to look at me. "We need to destroy these. Immediately."

"I plan to, but first, I want to figure out if Emilio was truly working alone, or if there are other wizards who may have known about his plans, or had plans of their own to help the demons destroy the Society. I know there are plenty of outsiders who hate us, and with good reason."

"Good reason? We're the ones with a good reason. They can't be trusted, and we can't risk angering the demons." She clenched her fists and pressed them against the table. "Destroy all this or I will."

"Give me time to figure out what's going on here, first." I tensed, preparing to counter if she decided to use her water magic to ruin everything. At least she could only control one element. Her options for attack were limited.

"If Lilium finds out that you're keeping things from her, she will send her minions after us. We can't risk drawing her attention."

"We need to know if anyone else was involved in this. So long as there is division among the wizards, the demons will be able to exploit it."

"No wizard would be stupid enough to act against the Society. We would destroy them."

"Jayden confirmed that there are wizards plotting to take over the Society." I didn't want her to know that Jayden was involved, at least not until I'd had a chance to win him over and change his mind.

"Impossible." Mother waved my words away.

"I asked him, under the pain of a truth rune. I needed to be sure I could trust him with all this. He confirmed that he's not working with the demons—"

She scoffed and interrupted me. "Of course he's not working with the demons. His parents were both just killed by them. Haven't you heard? It was horrible."

"What? When?"

"Your father is working with some of the other Council members to figure out exactly what happened. But it looks like they were dabbling with something they shouldn't have been, and got caught."

"Does he know?"

"I would assume so. Everyone knows." She tilted her head to one side. "Except you, it seems."

"Grace and Hannah and Varun? They all know?"

She waved a hand in the air. "Well, I can't be certain about your friends, dear. But, isn't Grace dating the Barringtons' daughter? She must know. Her parents are working the case with your father and Kyle's family. Of course, the Barringtons both insisted on participating, even though neither of them has anything useful to add to the investigation. I swear they're just waiting for us to take one false step so they can pounce."

"You're paranoid. Callie is perfectly nice, and her parents aren't out to get you and Father." We'd had this conversation before, when I'd told her that I'd been spending more time with Callie because of Grace.

"I am merely paying attention, and it would behoove you to do the same. If you want to inherit your father's position as head wizard, you should know what's going on."

"I know what's going on. The Society is forcing more and more wizards out for dabbling in experimental magic. If this continues, there will be more wizards outside of the Society than in it. These archaic rules about training need to be abolished."

"Destroy all this, and I'll think about it." She waved a hand in the direction of the pile of paperwork at the center of the table, and I cast a current of air to deflect an attack that never came.

"There isn't time to think about it. We need to reach out to them now, before it's too late. My friends and I are going to figure out what Emilio was trying to build and why, but you need to talk to Father and convince the Council to change the rules. Magic is magic, and we need to protect it, or we'll lose it."

Behind me, someone clapped once, then again. Another pair of hands joined in. I turned to find Jayden and Hannah standing in the doorway, paper lunch sacks tucked under their arms to free their hands. They were both grinning.

Hannah stopped clapping first and shoved her bag at Jayden. "Hi, Mama-ella. I didn't know you were in town." She leaned over and kissed my mother, once on each cheek. "It's nice to see you again."

My mother stood and smoothed her hands over her jacket and skirt. "It's lovely to see you as well, my dear. I'm afraid that I can't stay. I wanted to come offer my condolences to Jayden in person." She moved closer to Jayden and rested her hands on his. "I am sorry to hear about your parents. They were excellent people and valuable members of the Society. They will be missed."

"Thank you." Jayden met my mother's sympathetic gaze with his chin held high.

I wanted to kick him for not saying something to me. Instead, I glanced at Hannah to see if she was just as surprised by this news as I was. If she was, her expression didn't show it.

"I've instructed Maxwell to burn all this. Destroy it. Make sure no one is able to reconstruct any of it." My mother turned to meet my gaze. "Send only the trinkets to Lilium, and make sure she never finds out there was more. Once it is done, then we'll talk."

As she moved to leave, Jayden stepped back to allow her to pass. "Marcella, if you meant what you said about my parents, then honor their memory by listening to your son."

She paused just outside the conference room door and twisted her head to look over her shoulder at Jayden.

He didn't wait for her to respond. "Until you agree to stop punishing wizards for pushing the boundaries of magic outside of the Hunter-sanctioned corporations, I refuse to take orders from you."

"I appreciate that you are grieving, young man, but you have no right to speak to me so directly about such things. That is Council business, and you would do well to remember your place."

Jayden set the lunch bags on the ground and stepped forward. He flicked his wrist up, then in a half circle, and the floor surrounding my mother curled back, leaving her standing on an island of carpet, perched on a beam, with nothing but an open-air drop around her. One step and she'd go plummeting down to the floor beneath us.

12

S ALTY and I circled the block at a slow walk as I debated how much time was enough time to leave Max alone with his mother. My heart was still racing from my encounter with her. She'd surprised us enough that I'd forgotten I was still holding on to Max's key, but I'd left the little box with the globe in the conference room. I couldn't remember closing the lid, but I also didn't remember hearing one note of that song after Marcella arrived. I could barely hear my own thoughts after she walked in.

One lap didn't seem long enough, so I started us on another. Salty tried to pull me back toward the office entrance, but I made her keep going.

I gave her a pep talk. "One more time around. You can do it. Maybe she'll be gone by the time we get back."

It wasn't until the words were out of my mouth that I realized that they were probably more for my own benefit than to reassure my guard dog. I pulled my phone out and bent down to snap a photo of Salty, then I sent it to Eve and Willow on our AWEsome chat.

Who's available to talk? Anyone?

Evie's response came almost immediately. Me!

Three dots bounced next to Willow's icon. Calling now.

My phone rang a moment later.

"Angie?"

"Yep."

"Hang on, let me get Eve on."

The phone went silent for a moment, then Evie's voice spoke up. "How are you?"

Willow asked another question before I could respond to the first. "How did it go with Max?"

"I can't talk about all of it right now because I'm walking around the block with Salty, but this morning has been intense."

"Intense bad?" Evie sounded concerned, like there might have been demons involved.

I clarified a bit. "Intense like: truth runes, questions about loyalty, and a surprise visit from Max's mother."

"Okay, then." Willow released a sort of shocked laugh.

Evie groaned. "I'd say that's pretty intense."

"The good news is that we made a little bit of progress. Maybe." Because I'd been going through trinkets with Hannah, I still wasn't sure if the rest of the group had figured out the location of the boxes, or if they had only finally figured out that Emilio had made and hid them for some unknown reason. "It's a lot more complicated because everyone is involved now."

"Everyone?" Willow asked.

"Almost everyone. Kyle and Callie were busy, but I'm sure they'll be involved soon enough."

"How did that happen and why?"

I considered how I could tell them and have it still make sense without saying anything specific about magic or demons. "Max thinks Emilio was working with Lilium and her... friends? He thinks that the devices are meant to be used on people like them."

"Wizards?" Willow asked. "Huh. I suppose that would be a logical explanation if you didn't know what's been going on between the demons and the Fae."

"Would they? Know that, I mean?"

"No." Evie didn't hesitate. "The Fae want nothing to do with the humans, present company excluded."

"And the demons prey on the wizards. They probably aren't going to be sharing a lot of inside information with them."

"Got it." I rounded the last corner, and the front door of the building came back into sight.

"Listen." Willow's voice sounded far away but urgent. "Be careful with Marcella. My parents are convinced that she's hiding something."

I stared up at the glass windows on the top floor of the Silicon Moon building as Salty and I walked toward the entrance. "I am such an idiot. She wanted to talk with Max, alone, and I actually left them up there to talk. I should have found a way to spy on them." I groaned. "I'm sorry. I'm really not good at this sneaky stuff."

"It's okay." Evie spoke in her best soothing tones. "You're doing great. Just figure out if she knows about the boxes. Then get whatever information you can about them, and get out of there. Okay?"

I realized that I hadn't said anything to them about Max and me. "Yeah...about that."

"Angie. No." Evie's voice held the warning of a scolding, already anticipating with her best friend intuition that I'd done the thing that we'd agreed I would not do.

"He said he loved me, and that he was going to tell his parents that he wasn't going to follow their rules."

"Did he tell Marcella?" Willow asked.

"Not before I left them alone, but he might have been waiting until I left."

"Listen, Angie, I don't know you as well as Evie does, and I didn't even know about this Wizard Society until Arabella told me, but based on everything I've heard, Max's parents are not going to just let him go off and do as he pleases, especially not if they plan to name him as their heir on the Council."

"Why does he have to be the heir? He has an older sister. Is this some sort of patriarchy thing?"

"You'd think so with this group, but no. Rumor has it that there is something wonky with Morgan's powers. The gossips say she's weak or something. That's why they let her marry a wizard with no pedigree to speak of and essentially disappear from the Society."

"Wait. Brady Killigan is really a wizard?" Evie asked the question that had been on the tip of my tongue.

"The irony, right? I know. I'm not sure if that makes his acting better or worse." Willow sighed.

"Better. To be able to hide the real stuff and fake it in episode after episode? I have so much more respect for him now. I'm feeling bad about thinking he was just a pretty face." I started to walk past the entrance to Max's building, thinking we would do one more lap while I finished my conversation, but Salty planted her butt down and refused to budge.

"He still has a very pretty face, though." Evie laughed.

"I hate to cut this short, but Salty seems to think it's time we went back up."

"Listen to your guard dog." Willow's comment was more reminder than warning.

"And, Angie, please be careful?" Evie was worried, and that made me nervous.

"I will. I'll let you know whatever I find out, and I'll do my best to steer clear of Max's mother." I fished Max's badge out of my pocket. Staring down at his picture jogged my memory. "Oh, there was one other thing before I go. Max's mother made it sound like something bad happened to Jayden's parents."

"What sort of bad?" Willow asked.

"She didn't say. But it sounded curious. I thought you should know."

"Thanks. I'll look into it."

"Okay. Time to put my game face on and get back in there." Salty pulled me toward the door as if she understood what I'd said. I hung up with Evie and Willow so I could swipe Max's badge. The lock on the glass door clicked, signaling I was clear to open it, and then I was inside.

As I stood there, alone in the lobby, I wondered what else his badge might unlock. He'd given me the key to his castle. I could go anywhere. But Salty insisted on heading for the elevator, and Willow had instructed me to listen to the guard dog, so I followed her lead. She seemed to be in a hurry to get back.

The elevator wouldn't let me up to the top floor without another swipe of Max's badge. Once it was finally moving, I took another long look at Max's picture, then slid the plastic card back into my pocket. I needed to put my feelings for Max out of my head until I dealt with the issue of the magic traps and got that information back to Fiona. I closed my eyes and tried to focus.

When the elevator chimed and the doors slid open, the first thing I heard was yelling. Salty took off running so fast that her leash slid out of my hand and dragged along the carpet behind her. I broke into a jog and hoped that she wasn't leading me into a fight.

I turned the corner and a gust of air hit me in the face. I stumbled to a stop and put my hands up so I could squint through them. Max and Hannah stood on either side of Jayden, and all three of them stood facing Max's mother, who appeared to be saying something that I couldn't decipher over the wind whistling past my ears.

It wasn't until Salty veered to the right to avoid some obstruction that I realized there was a gaping hole in the floor surrounding Max's mother.

"Woah. What is going on?" The gust of air disappeared as I started speaking, allowing the others to hear me.

All four looked in my direction.

"You careless fool. Look what you've done." Max's mother directed her words at the others, but I couldn't tell which of them she was calling a fool.

"I told you, Mother, Angie knows about magic." Max beckoned to me.

I realized I'd stopped walking when I noticed the floor. I continued my approach, keeping well away from the edge of the gap.

"Knowing and seeing are two different things, Maxwell. You shouldn't even be talking about magic with her, but you certainly shouldn't be giving her demonstrations." Once she'd finished lecturing Max, she turned her attention to Jayden. "You have broken our rules about doing magic in front of regular humans, and you will pay the price. Now release me."

"No."

"You irresponsible, disagreeable, common wizard. I had hoped to avoid using this in front of you, but you are leaving me no choice." She slid a flat metal rectangle out of her purse. It was about the size of a phone but narrower and pointed on one end.

"Agree to speak to the Council as your son asked, and I'll let you go."

"I do not negotiate with terrorists." She pricked her finger on the pointed end of the object, then pressed it against a divot on one side. A moment later, she disappeared.

"What in the name of gods and demons was that?" Hannah asked.

"I thought those were still in beta." Max looked at Jayden.

"It looks like I need to have another talk with the engineers about who is allowed to test their tech." Jayden lifted one hand and twisted his wrist.

The floor reappeared, inch by inch, until the island in the middle was indistinguishable from the rest and the seams were no longer visible.

"That is some of the best earthworks I've seen outside of the Council, Jay. I'm impressed." Hannah held her palm up, and Jayden slapped it with his own.

"Thanks."

Max put an arm around Jayden's shoulder. "I'm really sorry to hear about your parents. I wish you would have told me. I feel like an ass for questioning your loyalty."

"Don't. I would have done the same in your place. I'm glad you told your mother where to shove it."

"Yeah, well, you saw how well that worked." Max shrugged and ran his hand through his hair.

"Do I dare ask what happened here?" I stepped closer, keeping well away from the former hole in the floor. "And where did my dog run off to?"

———

WE SPLIT UP to look for Salty, but it didn't take long to realize Angie's dog had rushed into the conference room and was standing watch over Emilio's papers. When Angie walked into the room, Salty barked once, turned in a circle, and pranced over to the little wooden box that we'd been looking at before my mother interrupted us.

"Is it me, or is it weird how that dog always knows exactly which objects have magic associated with them and which don't?" Hannah stared at Salty with her arms crossed.

I shrugged and walked over to pick up the box. At least it had finally stopped playing that annoying song. "Jayden thinks Salty is a familiar."

"That would explain it, but Angie doesn't have any magic." Hannah turned to Angie. "No offense."

"None taken. What's a familiar?" Angie asked.

"Ah. Something she doesn't know." Jayden rubbed his hands together.

"Some wizards—" I started to explain.

"Earth wizards." Jayden interrupted, eager to point out how those who could wield earth magic were unique and potentially superior to other wizards.

I shot him a look. "Usually wizards with an affinity for earth magic, but sometimes other wizards, find they have a unique connection with a specific animal that may or may not help them with their work."

"Oh. And you think Salty is one of those?"

"You said your friend Willow is an earth wizard, didn't you?"

"Sure, but she only recently learned about her powers.

They were sort of dormant for a while, I guess? I don't know how all this works. Anyway, Salty was more of a gift from Willow's girlfriend. She thought Salty would be good for me." Angie scratched behind Salty's ears as she explained.

"Is Willow's girlfriend also a wizard?" Hannah asked.

Jayden spoke at the same time. "Willow didn't know she had magic?"

I had been thinking something similar. "But her parents were on the Council before they quit."

"That was before we were born," Hannah added.

"True. It's still odd, though."

"It makes sense to me." Jayden rolled up his sleeves to reveal the edge of a tattoo on his forearm. "They probably didn't want the Society to know they had a daughter, let alone one with magic. If her powers stayed hidden, then the Council wouldn't come for her. You know how it is."

"That's not a thing the Council does, is it?" I asked.

"Oh, you sweet innocent child." Hannah patted my shoulder.

Jayden laughed. "It's a thing."

"But why?" I searched their faces for any hint that they might be kidding.

Salty barked once. When we all turned to look at her, she stood and wagged her tail. Her mouth dropped open and her tongue curled out, and it really looked like she was smiling. Angie bent down in front of her, but Salty ignored Angie and poked at the box with her nose.

"What is your deal with this box?" Angie picked it up and lifted the lid.

A few notes of the song drifted out, then stopped.

"Is that a music box?" Hannah asked.

"It turns out that is the thing our mystery key opens." I

reached for my notebook, only to remember that I'd given the key to Angie. "Do you still have it?"

Angie sat back on her heels. She cradled the box in one hand and dug into her pocket with the other. "Here you go."

I plucked it from her fingers and tucked it back into the pocket of my notebook. Then I secured the strap that held the notebook closed and put it back into my pocket.

"Why this?" Jayden moved closer to Angie and bent down to study the globe. "And what does it have to do with the plans?"

"Could this be one of those magic traps?" Hannah crouched down next to Angie. She held her hand over the globe and wiggled her fingers. A single drop of water dripped from her fingertip onto the top of the little wooden world. When it made contact with what would have been the Arctic circle, it split into a dozen rivulets that streamed down the sides like longitudinal lines on a globe.

"Woah." Angie sucked in a breath. "Weird."

The water disappeared at the base of the sphere without dripping into the bottom of the box.

"Hang on. I want to try something." Jayden hurried out of the room, and I knew he was going to his desk to retrieve his box of herbs and potions.

"Didn't you say that you thought that key would lead to a map?" Hannah took the box from Angie and stood up. "This is a map."

"Sort of." I scowled. The thing looked like a child's toy. The accuracy of the size and shape of the continents, painted as dark-forest-green blobs on top of the bright-blue paint that covered the surface of the sphere, was questionable, at best. "How are we supposed to find anything using this?"

Jayden returned with his little wooden box of supplies. I

suspected that a large number of the items it contained had been declared forbidden for spell casting by Society wizards. Since Jayden had already run afoul of my mother and been threatened with expulsion, I guessed it didn't matter much if I paid closer attention to what he was about to do.

Hannah set the music box globe down on the table next to where Jayden had started laying out his supplies. "What's your plan?"

"I'm going to see if I can get this thing to reveal its secrets." Jayden held a cork-stoppered vial up to the light and tilted the silver liquid inside back and forth. Then he picked up what looked like a spice jar and shook it until the brown powder started to glow.

I cringed. "Do I even want to know what that is?"

Jayden paused in his preparations and met my gaze. "I suppose that depends. Do you plan to report me?"

I slid my hands into my pockets. "I plan to make it so that you don't have to worry about that sort of thing."

Jayden shrugged. "How about this? If it works, I'll explain what I did."

"Fair enough, but you don't have to. If it works, I don't really care about how or why. You're the only one here with earth magic. It probably wouldn't even make any sense to the rest of us."

"Good point."

"How do you guys even know that there's anything hidden on this thing in the first place? It looks like an ordinary trinket you might pick up at a science and space museum or something." Angie pulled one of the chairs closer and sat down on the far side of Jayden.

"Oh. Yeah. You're right. That's exactly what it looks like." Hannah reached for the globe, but Jayden swatted her hand away.

"It isn't giving off any signs of magic, if that's what you mean." I walked around Jayden so I could stand near Angie, just in case anything weird happened. She was the only one of us who hadn't been trained to protect herself with magic.

"But there has to be some sort of magic on this thing—otherwise, when I dropped water on the globe, it wouldn't have reacted like that." Hannah settled herself into a chair on the other side of Jayden, who was busy mixing a drop of the silver liquid into the brown powder that had stopped glowing.

He stirred them together in a little clay bowl that reminded me of a homemade version of the tiny porcelain bowls they gave at my favorite sushi restaurant. The sort of thing you put soy sauce in. His mixture looked more like a paste than a sauce, though.

Jayden lifted his little bowl off the table and turned to me. "I need to borrow your air magic for this next part."

"What do you need me to do?" I stared down at the gray sludge that was starting to dry into a fine white powder.

"It needs to coat the globe evenly and all at once. Can you manage that?" He offered me the bowl.

I pushed up my sleeves. "It will be easier if you hold it. Then I can use both hands."

Behind me, Angie muttered something that sounded a lot like, "That's what she said."

I smirked. Hannah snorted and started laughing. Even the corner of Jayden's mouth twitched up. It was starting to feel like old times, and I was loving every minute of it. I'd love it even more once we knew what the demons were after, but if this trick of Jayden's paid off, we'd be one step closer to figuring that out.

I flexed my wrists and stretched my fingers. Then I focused

on the magic coursing through my veins, directing it down my arms and into my hands. What Jayden wanted me to do required finesse more than power. I hadn't had to exercise that sort of control in a while.

With one hand, I directed a current of air into the bowl, scooping up the white powder.

Jayden reached behind him for the music box, but his eyes remained fixed on me and the powder. His fingers missed by a few inches. Hannah leaned forward and grabbed the box, lifting it up and holding it open next to where the powder was hovering in the air.

"Thanks." Jayden set the bowl down so that he could take the globe from Hannah. She started to step back until Jayden gave her his instructions. "Get ready with your water magic. You're up next."

I waited until Hannah had shifted into position, then I took my focus off the powder long enough to meet Jayden's eyes. "Now?"

Jayden nodded. "Now."

Using both hands, I directed the air current to swirl the powder around the outside of the globe, keeping it well away from the surface until the individual granules spread out to create a thin veil that almost made it look like a mist had surrounded the little sphere. All it took was a tiny flex in my wrist to draw that mist closer and closer. When the powder finally settled on the surface of the globe, it glowed bright.

"Your turn." Jayden looked at Hannah.

Hannah held her hand, palm down, over the top of the glowing sphere, just as she'd done before. When water dripped from her fingers and fell onto the globe, it flowed as it had before. This time, though, it erased all trace of the powder in its wake. At first, it seemed like nothing had changed.

Then I noticed the first red dot pulsing like a beacon near the southern coast of Europe.

13

THERE were a total of four points marked on the globe. I knew Emilio had created six boxes. I knew because Nigel knew, and Nigel knew because Lilium knew. What I didn't understand was why four little pulsing dots appeared when Max, Hannah, and Jayden combined their magic to reveal the information Emilio had hidden. Had Emilio spread the boxes out and left them in four different locations? Were they all in one of those locations and the rest were just decoys?

"Now what?" Hannah's question summarized all the ones that were already swirling through my mind.

"Now we pick a place and go there and see what we find." Max turned the box until the dot closest to Seattle was facing him.

"But this only tells us generally where to look. These boxes aren't that big. How do we narrow it down to an exact location?" Hannah asked another excellent question, this time one I hadn't thought of yet. "See that dot there in South

America? There are, like, three different countries near that point. How do we know which one to look in, let alone which city?"

Jayden leaned over Max's shoulder and pointed at the dot pulsing on the West Coast, approximately near the border between the US and Canada. "Is this one in Seattle? Or nearby? It could be in Portland for all we can tell."

"There has to be another piece to this puzzle." I stared at the mound of paper on the table, thinking through all the pages I'd skimmed, searching for any information about the magic traps, and tried to figure out what I'd missed.

"Do we know what sort of magic this guy had?" Hannah asked.

"It must be in his personnel file. I can look it up." Max set the wooden box down on the table, leaving the lid open.

"Fire." Jayden spoke softly, his eyes still fixed on the globe. "It must have been fire magic."

"Why do you say that?" I asked, even though I already knew he was right.

Jayden plopped down on one of the chairs. He twisted the seat back and forth as he explained. "Think about it. What magic did we use to reveal the locations? Water, air, and earth, right? What element is missing from that?"

"Fire." Max nodded. "But why would he make it so that his own magic wouldn't be able to reveal the secret?"

"Maybe he was hiding the information from himself?" Hannah tilted her head to one side.

"But why would he do that?" Max asked.

"Maybe he wasn't working with the demons. Maybe the demons were using him, and this was the only way he could keep the information from them." It was the scenario I had been hoping was true before Max said that the wizard Council thought there was a wizard, or a group of wizards, working with the demons to take over the Society. He thought Emilio had been working with the demons, but I knew Emilio's loyalty had been to his Fae mate, at least until Lilium got her claws into his mind.

Nigel and Arabella hadn't been able to figure out why Emilio had built the boxes. They'd assumed it was under orders from the Wizard Society, but based on everything I'd seen and heard, I had pretty much ruled that out as a possibility. That left two remaining options. Emilio either started working on this project for his own reasons, before he encountered Lilium, or Lilium forced him to do it.

Max's fingers curled into fists at his sides. "It's definitely possible. Lilium is a succubus."

"You think she seduced Emilio and made him do her bidding?" Hannah's eyes widened.

"That is how that sort of arrangement usually works." Jayden scowled.

Hannah put her hands on her hips. "I know my demon clans just as well as the next wizard, Jayden. No need to be snarky."

Jayden folded his arms across his puffed-out chest. "Know them from a textbook, you mean. You probably have never met one in person, have you?"

Max rested one hand on each of their shoulders. "Enough. Let's all agree that Jayden is our current expert on demons and split all this up so we can search through the documents again. Look for anything that refers to locations, specifically places near these points. Got it?"

Hannah apologized to Jayden, and the three of us took seats around the table. We each took a stack of papers and bent our heads down to get to work.

When I realized Max hadn't joined us, I glanced up and found him staring down at Salty.

"I don't suppose you want to give us any help?" he asked my guard dog.

Salty lifted her head off her front paws and cocked it to one side. Her tail thumped once against the carpet, but she didn't get up.

"You've picked an excellent time to decide to be a regular dog." He shook his head. "I'm going to my office to see what I can find in Emilio's employee record. Who knows, maybe there is some note of him traveling to one or more of these places."

"Good luck." Hannah kept skimming pages and didn't look up.

Once Max left the room, Hannah glanced around. She turned to make sure he was gone, then leaned across the table to whisper to me. "Okay. Spill. What is going on with you two?"

Jayden groaned. "Can we just focus, please?"

"No." Hannah glared at Jayden before refocusing on me. "Are you getting back together or what?"

I flipped the page in the composition notebook I'd selected, thinking whatever we were looking for was most likely going to be hidden in one of these lab notebooks that Emilio had used almost like journals. My eyes flicked up to meet Hannah's, then went back to skimming pages. "Yes. Maybe? I don't know. It's complicated."

Jayden snorted.

Hannah and I both turned our heads to glare at him.

"What?" He shrugged. "You have to admit, that's pretty much the understatement of the month."

"Fine. You're right. The whole thing is hopeless, and I don't even know why I let him try to convince me that it was going to work this time."

Jayden sighed. "Oh, come on. You don't have to be like that. I didn't say it wouldn't work."

"You heard his mother. You really think she's going to cheer when Max tells her that we're getting back together?"

"He said he was going to tell her?" Hannah asked. "That's promising, right?"

Jayden shook his head. "I have to agree with Angie here. Marcella is not a fan."

Hannah wadded up an old memo from the top of the shred pile and threw it at Jayden. "You are not helping."

Jayden flicked his fingers, and the crumpled paper hurtling at his face turned into a handful of confetti that fluttered down to the tabletop before it even reached him. "What do you want me to do? Lie to the poor girl? I mean, it's not like I'm Marcella's favorite wizard at the moment. I'm in no position to put in a good word for her, if that's what you're after."

"You don't have to be so negative. Can't you see they're in love? They're like the perfect couple. They should be together." Hannah leaned back in her chair. "You could at least be supportive."

I smiled but didn't say anything. While I appreciated Hannah's support and enthusiasm, the thing was, they were both at least a little right. Sure, Max and I deserved a chance to be together without all the secrets and the lying getting in the way, but it wasn't going to be easy, and there was nothing that either of them could do to change that.

I flipped to the final page in Emilio's notebook. The scrolling vines he'd doodled in the margin looked familiar. I assumed it was because I'd already looked through this notebook at least once. So, I shut the cover and pushed it to the side. When I reached for another, my eyes drifted over to the wooden music box, still propped open on the table.

The wood inlay in the lid. That's where I'd seen that design before.

I set the notebook I'd been reaching for down and flipped the other one open to the last page. The pattern wasn't an exact match, but it was close.

"What did you find?" Jayden leaned across the table to get a look at the page I was staring at.

Hannah stood and walked over to my side to get a better look. "Is that supposed to be poetry or something?"

There were four blocks of text on the page. Each of them contained three sentences. The vines curved down the left margin with branches extending out into the middle of the page, separating the blocks.

I read the first one out loud. "Throw or hurl. I am good enough. Train schedule."

"Is it a haiku?" Jayden asked. He had left his seat to come over and look at the page with us.

"Or maybe it's just a list of reminders?" Hannah pointed to the right of the sentences where someone had traced the outline of some of the squares on the gridded paper. "Was he bored?"

"There's another group outlined here." I pointed farther down the page. There were outlined squares next to each block of text. None were the same.

Jayden picked up the notebook and held it close to his face. "There isn't anything written inside of these squares."

"I could have told you that." Hannah tugged the notebook away from Jayden.

Jayden released it. "I mean, there isn't even an indentation in the paper from where something was written and then erased."

"Please tell me you found something." Max walked through the door. In one hand, he held a rectangular device like the one his mother had used to disappear from the office. In the other, he held a coffee mug.

Jayden closed his eyes as he inhaled. "Please tell me you brought that coffee for me."

"You can have it if you have something for me." Max walked over and waved the mug closer to Jayden's nose. "What did you find?"

Jayden snatched the mug from Max. "Angie either found some bad poetry or a secret code. You decide. I'll be over here."

Max moved behind me and Hannah so he could look over my shoulder at the notebook page. "Less than a lemon. Sonic noises. Society castings. Why did he outline these squares in the shape of an F. What is this supposed to be?"

"A crossword." A surge of excitement rushed through me. I tugged the notebook closer and pointed to the boxes next to the block of text Max had read. "Look. 'Sonic noises' are 'booms,' right? Five letters that would fit in these boxes here."

"Oh! And 'Society castings' could be 'spells,' right?" Hannah pointed to the boxes that formed the top of that F shape. "That would fit in these six boxes."

Jayden took a sip of his coffee. "So this guy gets bored in a meeting and starts making crossword puzzles. How do we know this has anything to do with the points on the globe?"

I pointed to the vine doodle. "This is the same pattern as on the inlay at the top of that box. Or, it's close enough, anyway. That has to mean something."

"Three words. Each one of these is three words. That reminds me of something." Max pulled out his phone and bent his head over the screen as he started typing. "Here it is. Yes.

We used this at a team-building event in grad school, remember?"

I glanced at Jayden and Hannah, but they looked as baffled as me.

Max groaned. "Ugh. Right. None of you were there. Fine. Grace and Varun would know what I'm talking about."

"Well, they're not here, so maybe you should explain?" Hannah flopped down in a chair and crossed her arms as well as her long legs.

"There's this company that made a tool that uses three words to define each three-meter square of the globe. If we can figure out the three words, then we can translate those into coordinates. Since we have the markers on the globe, we know approximate locations. So if we guess something wrong, we'll know if we're way off track."

"Who's good at crossword puzzles?" Jayden asked.

I looked at Max. Meeting for coffee on Sunday mornings and solving the crossword puzzle had kind of been our thing.

He grinned at me. "We've got this."

———

SITTING SHOULDER TO SHOULDER with Angie, hunched over Emilio's notebook and working together on crossword clues, brought back so many good memories. All we needed were two cappuccinos, a couple of chocolate croissants, and a slightly more private location, and it would be perfect.

Hannah had run out to get more coffee, but Jayden kept walking in and out as he relocated the boxes to the mail room and prepared to ship them off to Lilium. He glared at us every time he walked in, as though he could see my hand on Angie's thigh under the conference table. His icy stare threatened to ruin my increasingly optimistic mood.

The whole thing was taking longer than I would have liked, but we were so close to getting our hands on one of these magic traps. Once we did, I wasn't sure what it would tell us. I still didn't understand why that wizard with the key thought this information might somehow help my sister.

Angie bumped her knee against mine. "'Sublime' fits. Test this one."

I typed the three words from the puzzle we'd started with into my phone. "It's the one in Alaska."

Angie copied down the coordinates under where she'd written the three words. We decided we didn't want to write in Emilio's notebooks. So Angie had copied the boxes onto a scrap of paper and numbered them based on the clues. That was where we were testing out our guesses.

"Should we go, or do another one?" Angie asked.

I wanted to try the transporter with the closest location, first. The information I'd found in the engineering reports said nothing about transport radius when traveling with two humans, and I planned to take Angie with me. The engineers had tested the option of transporting two people, just not as extensively. I was pretty sure we could reach the closest dot on the globe. I just wasn't sure we could make it to any of the others and back without recharging.

Alaska was close, and tempting, but the other dot was closer. The problem was, we had no way of knowing which of the four puzzles aligned with which of the dots on the globe.

"Let's try the next one." I pointed at the puzzle below the one we'd just solved. The one at the bottom of the page.

We read the clues, brainstormed ideas, and tested our guesses. When Jayden returned to collect the last two boxes, I asked him to check on Hannah. After he left, I looked down at the paper where Angie was filling in the final word.

"There." She grinned. "Test it."

I typed in the words and waited. The location was close. Really close, and perfect for a test run with the transport device.

"Got it. Are you ready?" I grabbed for the transporter so that I could enter the coordinates into the display on the side.

Angie's shoulders tensed. "Are you sure this thing works?"

"I promise, it's been thoroughly tested." Based on what I'd read in the reports, I was fairly certain we would be fine. The worst case would be that we wouldn't have enough power to get home, but we'd be close enough that we could spend the night near where we landed and hitch a ride home in the morning.

"Have you tested it?" Angie asked.

"You mean, have I used one of these before?" I stood and pulled her up with me.

"Yeah." Her face paled in anticipation of my response.

"No." I pulled out my phone to text Jayden and let him know where we were going.

"Not exactly helping your case, Hunter." Angie grabbed her raincoat and slid her arms into the sleeves.

I set my free hand on her shoulder. "Do you think my mother would risk transporting herself with one of these if it didn't work?"

Angie frowned. "I really, really don't like this part of the plan."

"Just close your eyes and count to ten. When you open them, it will be over."

Salty hopped up onto Angie's chair and wagged her tail.

Angie scooped Salty up and hugged the dog against her chest. "This is a terrible idea."

"Trust me." When she straightened, I dipped my head

down and captured her pouting lips with mine.

Her eyes closed, and she leaned against me. I slid my hand from her shoulder, up to cradle the nape of her neck. Then I pressed the thumb of my other hand against the needle at the end of the transport device and slid it down until the pad of my thumb pressed against the indentation in the metal before letting myself get lost in the kiss. A moment later, the rattle and hiss of waves lapping against a gravel beach brought me back to reality.

Angie pulled away from me and opened her eyes. "You tricked me."

"I distracted you, and I would happily do it again."

She made a face, half amused and half scolding me for my cheesy line. "Let's get what we came here for, and then maybe, maybe I'll let you try it again."

Salty barked. Angie bent down to let the dog take the lead with her weird little magic sniffing nose, but she kept a tight grip on the end of Salty's leash. The wind whipped her hair into her face. When she stood, she zipped her jacket as high as it would go and shivered.

I turned in a slow circle, taking in our surroundings. We'd appeared at the upper end of a narrow strip of beach on the southern edge of what, according to the map, was a tiny island, nestled into a bay of a much larger island. Judging from the waves lapping around the rocks and threatening to soak our feet, it appeared to be close to high tide.

Salty picked a route up the boulders to the flat, center part of the island. No trespassing signs had been pinned to the trees closest to the beach to discourage exactly what we were doing.

"You said this place is uninhabited, right?" Angie asked.

"According to the satellite photos on the mapping software, there shouldn't be structures or anyone living here."

"Then what's with all the signs?"

"Private land?" I guessed.

Angie shook her head. "If someone tries to kill us for dropping out of nowhere and walking around their island, are you going to defend us? Or is that against your Society rules?"

"Self-defense is allowed." I flexed my hands, readying them and hoping it didn't come to that. "But it's getting dark and there shouldn't be anyone here. I didn't see any boats, and this is a terrible night for camping."

From our vantage point at the top of the rocks, overlooking the beach, I pulled my phone out to check our coordinates. It took a moment for the app to load, then another for the satellites to find us. By the time I had a lock on our location and had figured out the distance and direction to the coordinates we'd calculated, Angie and Salty were nowhere in sight.

"Where'd you go?" I asked, keeping my voice low.

It seemed impossible that they could disappear so quickly, since the tiny island wasn't more than just a pile of rocks with a few scattered gnarly trees sprouting up between them. There was a denser collection of trees, equally twisted and weathered near the north end, blocking the view of the town on the bigger island across the bay, but there was no way they could have made it that far in such a short amount of time.

"Over here." Angie's response was so quiet, I almost didn't hear her. "I think I found something."

Her voice was coming from behind a clump of rocks in the right direction for that to be a distinct possibility. I kept my phone out and tracked my progress as I searched for her red raincoat. I spotted a glimpse of movement ahead, then glanced down to check my phone. It should be only a few more steps.

When I looked up, I found myself staring into the dark eyes of a doe. She stood completely still only an arm's length away from me. My heart pounded, and I sucked in a breath to calm myself.

"What's taking you so long?" Angie's voice came from a rocky ledge off to my right.

The deer bolted at the sound, bouncing off toward the trees at the north end of the island. I exhaled, checked my map, and took a few strides to the right. Angie stood and Salty sat next to a large, mossy rock that was nearly as tall as Angie and probably wider than my arm span. It rose up at an angle, too steep to comfortably recline on. Given the margin for error on the GPS, the rock was a near match for the location coordinates we calculated.

"Salty appears to think something's up with this boulder." Angie gestured to the moss-covered granite lump in front of her. "She walked all around it, sniffing, and then sat down. Now she won't budge."

I glanced down at the dog. She opened her mouth, letting her tongue fall out as she grinned at me.

"But it's a rock. How do you hide a metal box in a rock?"

"Maybe it's underneath?" Angie leaned over the top and poked at the dirt around the base with a stick.

I frowned. "Don't ever tell him I said this, but I kind of wish we had Jayden's earth magic right now."

"You can go back and get him, if you want." Angie looked up at me.

I shook my head. "It would take too long to recharge the transport device." I walked around the rock, searching for a clue as to where Emilio might have hidden the box.

He was a fire wizard, like me. If he came here, alone, he

would only have his own powers to rely on. But there was no evidence of fire anywhere on the stone face or on the ground around the area. I completed my circumnavigation and stopped next to Angie and Salty.

Angie stood up. "I think we're going to have to dig. We should have brought shovels."

"I have a better idea." I took a step back and focused on the rock. Then, spreading my hands out at my sides, I called on the wind, directing it around and under until the boulder shifted.

Angie scurried back, pulling Salty with her.

I refocused and the rock began to lift. Sweat beaded on my upper lip and brow, only to be blown off by the wind whipping across the bay. It was too heavy to raise up, but I managed to rock it back until the angled face lay almost parallel to the earth. When I had moved it enough for us to see what lay underneath, I let my body fall slack and leaned over to press my palms against my thighs. I breathed in and out until I stopped panting and could breathe with ease.

"Woah." Angie gaped at me. "Impressive."

I stood and ran my hand through my hair. "I'm out of shape. Too many hours in the office."

Angie raised an eyebrow. "If you say so."

My cheeks warmed. "Come on, let's see if there's anything down there."

"That's what she said." Angie whispered the words, but I heard them and grinned.

Angie and I crouched down next to the indentation in the earth. I searched for the flashlight setting on my phone, but Angie beat me to it. The bright light flicked on just as Salty bolted forward and started digging with her front paws. Her claws scraped against something hard, and Angie pulled the dog back.

I reached down, careful not to block the light with my arms, and patted the earth until I found the edge of something. I wiggled it to loosen the dirt packed around it. Then I pulled it free.

Angie kept the light pointed on the object. Once it was out from under the rock, I could make out the edges, even though it was caked in dirt.

"It's definitely cube shaped." I directed a gust of air at the clumps of earth clinging to the sides and used it to clear the debris off until we could see the outside edges.

"That has to be it. Let's take it and get out of here before someone finds us." Angie turned off the light and pocketed her phone.

"Hang on a minute. I should put this rock back before we go." I tucked the cube under my arm.

Angie scooped up Salty and stepped back as the rock slid back into place. Once it was done, Angie closed the distance between us. She wrapped her arm around my waist. "Take us home."

"You don't want to stay and watch the sunset?" I grinned at her, giddy that our mission had been a success.

"It's freezing, and we're about to get dumped on by that dark cloud over there." She angled her chin toward the storm clouds looming over the south end of the bay, heading north. "If you get us all back in one piece, I think we can find a better way to celebrate."

14

I GRIPPED the back of Max's jacket with one hand and held on to Salty with the other. It took him a minute to get his transport device out and ready to activate. I pinched my eyes shut and pressed my forehead against his chest.

"Just tell me when it's over."

"That's what she said." Max's chuckle resonated in his chest.

I groaned.

"You walked right into that one, Ang." He kissed the top of my head. "You can open your eyes now."

The wind had stopped, and the briny smell of ocean mixed with the damp earth scent of sun-warmed wet rocks had been replaced with the faint aroma of commercial carpet cleaner.

"Can I see it?" I released Salty so I could get a better look at the metal cube cradled in Max's arm.

Max passed me the box and watched as I turned it to examine the designs etched into each side. It was hard to believe that this thing that I held in my hands was powerful enough to drain the magic from the Fae, leaving them defenseless and at the mercy of the demons and the humans.

The problem was, now that we had one, I didn't know what to do with it. I couldn't take it without Max knowing. The best I could hope for would be if I could convince him to destroy it. And the plans. Max's mother was right about those. We needed to destroy the plans before the demons found out about them.

"So how do we destroy it?" I asked.

"Destroy it?" Max sounded surprised. "Don't you want to figure out how it works, first?"

"If these things are as dangerous as you said they are, don't you think it's better if we find them and destroy them? Why would you want to mess with them? You might end up draining your own powers, and then what would you do?"

Max blinked at me. I knew him well enough to realize that whatever I'd just said had given him an idea that made him more interested in the boxes and not less.

"What are you thinking?" I gripped the metal between my fingers. I had no intention of letting him have it back as long as he had that look on his face.

Max shook his head. "Nothing. Let's lock up the plans, and figure out where the others went. They'll want to see this. We can search for the other boxes tomorrow."

"Tomorrow is Monday."

"Oh. Right." Max started collecting all the papers and notebooks into one neat pile. "You have a new contract that starts tomorrow. You're busy."

I wasn't busy. Finding these boxes and destroying them for the good of the Fae was my job. But I couldn't tell him that. "I might be able to delay for another day."

"No. It's okay. I'm sure Jayden has me scheduled for back-to-back meetings all day tomorrow, anyway. We'll have to wait until tomorrow evening to work on this some more." Disappointment caused his shoulders to sag a bit.

If Max was busy, I could solve the puzzles on my own and send the coordinates to Evie and Willow. Then the Fae could collect the rest of the boxes before Max had a chance. "How long will it take that transport device to recharge?"

Max studied the shiny metal thing that looked like a remote control with a pushpin sticking out one end. "I can't remember. There's a calculation for it. I think it has something to do with distance and load carried? I copied it into my notebook from the engineering reports, but I'm guessing it will at least be a few hours."

"Well, let's get it charging while we work out the coordinates for the rest of the locations. Maybe once we're done there will be time for another trip tonight."

"Good idea. I just need to run down to the lab to grab one of their cradles and some charging fluid." Max kissed my forehead before heading to the door.

I didn't want to ask what sort of fluids were needed to charge a device that was powered by wizard blood. "I'll work on the last two puzzles while you do that."

As soon as Max was gone, I pulled out my phone and snapped a few photos of the box we'd found. Then I posted them in our AWEsome chat and typed a message to Evie and Willow.

Got one.

Their responses were almost immediate, even though it was way too early to be awake in England.

Nice work! Evie added a few confetti cannons to her message.

Destroy it. Willow punctuated her response with a stabbing knife.

How? I asked.

I stared at my phone screen, waiting for a response. There was nothing. Not even a few dots to let me know one of them was typing. I groaned and set my phone down on the table. At least I could work on Emilio's crossword puzzles while I waited.

Figuring out the first clue of the first puzzle wasn't hard. I did a quick thesaurus search on "throw" and "hurl," counted the number of letters needed, and decided it had to be the word "fling." The second and third clues had me stumped, though. So I skipped them and moved on to the next puzzle.

"Breathes fire" had to be the word "dragon." After that, I stared blankly at the second and third clues. My mind didn't want to focus on puzzles. It wanted to figure out what to do with the box sitting on the table next to me.

I checked my phone. I had strong cell and Wi-Fi signals, but still no responses to my question. I set my phone down and leaned over to poke at the box with the end of my pencil. It was nothing like the metal cube that Max had found in Emilio's things. That one had open sides with a labyrinth of steel segments that created a sort of cube-shaped cage. This one had solid sides, also steel, with designs etched into each face.

Wavy horizontal lines covered half of the side facing me. The side facing the ceiling featured a large triangle with smaller triangles nested inside. I didn't know what any of it meant, or if there was a correct orientation. Was I even looking at it right side up?

I nudged it with my pencil, turning it so I could see the other sides. I wasn't sure why, but I didn't want to touch it without Max around. I half expected it to start glowing or spinning or floating, or possibly all three of those things, at any minute.

My phone chimed with a message alert, and I nearly jumped out of my chair.

Can you talk?

I scowled at the screen, then stood and searched the cubicle area for any sign of Max or the others. The office area was dark, lit only by the glow of exit signs and safety lights above the doors, plus the shimmer of the Seattle skyline visible through the rain-splotched windows. I wasn't sure where Jayden and Hannah had run off to, but I was certain Max would be back soon.

I typed a quick response. Not a good idea. What's up?

Three dots appeared, disappeared, reappeared, then pulsed for almost a full minute while I watched and waited.

No one knows how to destroy them. Can you steal it?

My jaw clenched. I wanted to say no. Just the idea of stealing the box from Max seemed wrong. I was fine with telling the Fae where to find the others. I would have been happy to make sure this one couldn't function. But stealing it? Right out from under Max's nose when I was the only one here, and he'd left it with me?

I reminded myself that I'd sworn an Oath to serve Fiona. I cringed. Not easily. Can you come up with anything else? Please?

I'd do it if it was an order, but only as a last resort. There had to be another way. I set my phone down on the table next to the notebook with the puzzles and the scrap paper where I'd been recording the solutions. Then I took a breath and reached for the magic trap.

Nothing happened when I touched it, just like nothing had happened when Max handed it to me. I didn't have magic. I was safe. It couldn't hurt me.

I glanced down at Salty. She was curled up with her head resting on her paws and her eyes closed. I decided that meant she agreed that I was safe.

Returning my attention to the cube, I twisted it around so I could study each side. There were no seams. No way to open it that I could see or feel. I traced each design with my fingertip, searching for a hidden opening. Nothing.

Maybe it was already broken. Nothing had happened when Max had touched it. Maybe it didn't work.

My phone chimed again. I held on to the box with one hand while I checked my messages with the other and sent a silent plea out to the universe that the message wasn't Fiona ordering me to steal the box.

Ok, but don't let it out of your sight. Gwawr is working it. Apparently she has one?!?

Evie's punctuation told me that she was just as surprised as I was to find out that the Fae already had one of the boxes. Maybe that was why there were only four dots on the globe. But, if there really was only one box at each of those locations, who had the sixth box? I texted the question to Willow and Evie.

Willow responded. Nigel thinks that the demons have at least one box.

If that was true, then each of the groups had one box. Tied score?

Evie replied with a laugh-cry emoji.

I'm working on the locations of the other boxes. I'll let you know when I have them figured out.

Willow sent a thumbs-up emoji, and Evie sent a heart.

With a sigh, I put my phone down and stared at the box. "Now what?"

Salty stood up, shook herself, and trotted over to where I'd left my tote bag on the ground next to the wall. She nudged the bag with her nose.

"What's that supposed to mean?" I couldn't tell if she was trying to say that she wanted to go out or if she wanted a treat.

I walked over and bent down to find the little bag of treats, hoping that would be good enough. I couldn't take her out until Max returned. As I tugged the foil bag free and lifted it out of my tote, Salty nudged the magic trap with her nose. It tipped out of my hand and landed in my tote. I stared down at it.

"I suppose that's one way to handle it." I cringed. Evie had said not to take my eyes off the box, and Max had suggested that we find the others so we could show it to them. I convinced myself that if we were going to leave the office, that was the safest place to keep the box. I just had to remember to tell Max so he wouldn't think I was trying to steal it from him.

THE LIGHTS IN THE engineering lab washed the large room in a bright-white glow. Tables were grouped in the center so that the large racks of computers could be pushed up against the walls next to the testing benches. The recharge kit for the transport device was where I'd left it on one of those long tables, next to the locked storage cabinet where I'd found it.

It took me a minute to locate the various solutions needed to create the recharge fluid. I measured everything according to the instructions, set the device into the charging cradle, and attached the cradle to the tray I'd filled with the recharge fluid. Then I pulled out my notebook and ran the calculation to determine how long we had to wait.

When I was done, I called Morgan to share the good news with her.

"I have an update for you," I said when she picked up the phone.

"An update? So soon? Could this have anything to do with why our mother made a sudden appearance at my house this afternoon?" Pots and pans clanged in the background.

"Ugh." I grimaced. "Sorry about that."

Morgan sighed. "It's fine. We had a nice chat, and then I sent her on her way."

"Did she tell you—"

The kitchen noises were silenced by the whoosh of a sliding door. "That you have uncovered a plot to destroy the Wizard Society, and you refuse to obey her commands?"

"Is that what she told you?" I turned out the lights in the lab and closed the door behind me.

"She also mentioned something about how you wanted the Society to abolish all rules governing the use of magic, or something like that."

"Great." I rolled my eyes.

"So, tell me what happened to get her all excited. She was nearly frothing at the mouth when she arrived. And don't forget to tell me exactly which one of your brilliant engineers gave her a device that lets her travel anywhere she wants whenever she wants, in the blink of an eye. I would like to have words with whoever thought that was a good idea."

"I know. Get in line." I'd skimmed the e-mail that Jayden had sent to the head of engineering on my behalf, requesting a meeting first thing Monday morning. "At least the thing can only be used a few times before it needs to be recharged. That should cut back on her zipping around a bit, at least until we can get the device back."

"Get it back. I like being the only one in the family who can disappear and reappear at will."

"Have you managed to get to anyplace besides my house, yet?" Transporting was one of the powers Morgan had inherited from her demon sire. Since she had to keep her demon powers a secret, she had no one to teach her how to use them. I had been hoping that the key would lead me to something that might help her. It still might, but not in the way I'd thought.

"I'm working on it. But I'd rather not bore you with the details. Tell me what you know about the conspiracy."

"There are sort of two things, and I can't figure out if they're connected or not. One is the fact that the outsiders are definitely planning something. Jayden wouldn't admit it, but he also wouldn't deny it when I questioned him under the pain of a truth rune."

"Wow. You made him cast a truth rune on himself. Harsh."

"I maintain that it was necessary, but even with all that honesty, he didn't bother to tell me that some demons killed his parents. Our mother dropped that one on me, making me feel like an insensitive jerk. Tell me you didn't know about that. You didn't, did you?" I paced outside the elevator, not wanting to call it and risk losing my connection with Morgan.

"Should I lie to you?"

I groaned. "You could have said something."

"I didn't know when we last talked. Does that make you feel better?"

"A little." I sighed. "But that sort of rules him out for the 'conspiring with the demons to drain all the power from the wizards' theory that I had going."

Her end of the phone was silent for a moment. "What makes you think anyone is conspiring with the demons?"

"That project that I was telling you about. That wizard who died and the succubus claiming to be his widow that wants all his stuff. Remember that?"

"Sure. Did you find something in his stuff?"

"Yeah. It turns out that he designed these boxes that are meant to work as a sort of trap for magic. It looks like they can be used to drain power from a wizard and store it. Scary stuff. Worse because he actually built some." I leaned up against the wall and slid down until I was seated on the floor next to the elevator.

"Are you sure? How do you know?"

"I just used one of those devices you hate so much to go retrieve one." I tilted my head back and stared up at the ceiling.

"How did you know where to look? Is there a map or something?"

"Kind of. That key that you wanted me to stop messing with? Turns out that it opens this sort of wooden jewelry box. Except the only thing inside was this globe. We had to mess with it a bit, but when we did, it revealed four locations. One was close to Seattle. Another was farther north, somewhere in Alaska. There was one in South America and one in Southern Europe."

"That's not terribly specific. How did you figure out where to look?"

"It's complicated, but we found all these notes and plans and diagrams. There's this puzzle hidden in one of the notebooks. We are using that to decode the coordinates for each location."

"So you have one now? There in the office with you?" She sounded a little more excited than I expected that she would.

"Yeah." I wondered if she was thinking the same thing I'd been thinking. I didn't know enough to suggest it, but I thought maybe it would be possible for one of these boxes to drain her demon powers.

"Are you going to go get the other boxes?"

"Eventually. Why?"

"No reason. I'm just curious. It sounds interesting. More interesting than anything going on around here." Her voice had returned to her usual too-cool-to-be-bothered tone.

I decided to wait to tell her about my idea. I didn't want to get her hopes up. "Well, I should get back upstairs. I left Angie alone."

"Have you kissed her?"

I grinned. "None of your business, but yes. I'm working on patching things up."

"Maybe you should take a break from this project of yours and take her someplace nice. Like a date. You know? I'm sure you're familiar with the concept."

"Ha. Ha." I considered the fact that we had almost an hour until the transport device was ready to use again. It wasn't much time for us to get out of the office and do something fun, but there was a gelato place nearby that was almost as good as the place we'd gone to almost every night when we were in Italy. "Maybe you're right."

"Of course I'm right. Big sisters are always right."

"Okay. Hanging up now." I reached up and pressed the button to call the elevator.

"Bye, Maxie."

I ended the call and stared at my reflection in the silver metal doors until they slid open. My mother had gone to Morgan's after leaving here. Maybe she was seriously considering naming my sister as heir instead of me. I didn't expect to feel disappointed by that, but my stomach sank as the doors closed and the elevator started to rise.

Speaking up was maybe going to backfire on me. If I'd kept my mouth shut, I could have made all the changes I wanted as soon as they transferred power over to me. It would have been a few more years, but it would have been just like I'd always planned with Grace and Hannah and Varun.

The elevator doors slid open. I stepped out onto the top floor and started walking toward the conference room. When I turned the corner, I caught a glimpse of Angie's purple-striped hair. Her head was bent over the notebook laid out on the table in front of her. She tapped the end of her pen against her lips. The tension in my shoulders melted.

If I'd stuck to the plan, she wouldn't be sitting there, finally part of the team, and part of my life again. If I'd waited, there might not be a Wizard Society to lead. Even if Emilio had been working with the demons against his will, there were wizards who were mad enough at the Society to try to destroy it. I had power, and I needed to use it now, before it was too late.

Angie looked up when I walked into the conference room. I crossed the room and knelt down next to her chair, sliding it out from under the table so that she faced me.

"What are you doing?" She set her pen down on the table.

I gripped her thighs with my hands, squeezing them through the denim as I spread her legs so I could slide her chair closer. "Something I've wanted to do since you first walked into this office."

She glanced at the table out of the corner of her eye. "What about the rest of the coordinates?"

I reached over and pushed the papers away, toward the center of the table. "They can wait."

"What about Jayden and Hannah?" She angled her head to look out the door.

I used the opportunity to kiss her cheek. "Jayden is down in the mail room, and I haven't heard from Hannah. She's probably with Jayden."

I closed the conference room door with a gust of wind and locked the door, just in case either of them happened to return. Then I created a downdraft that blew the blinds on the window closed.

Angie grinned at me. "Show-off."

My fingers worked the buttons on the front of her blouse. "I considered asking if you'd like to go out and grab some gelato with me, but I then I saw you sitting here, and I changed my mind."

"Aww. And here I was thinking, 'boy, I could really go for some gelato right now.'" She tugged the hem of my T-shirt up until I was forced to raise my arms so she could pull it over my head. She dropped the shirt on the ground and raked her fingers down my bare chest. "I suppose this will have to do."

I pushed her blouse down her shoulders and watched her pull her arms out of the sleeves. Once it fell onto the seat of the chair, I wrapped my hands around her ass and stood, scooping her up with me so that I could deposit her on the table.

She raised her eyebrows. "Dang, Hunter. Nice moves."

"It has been way too long." I lowered my head to kiss along her bare collarbone as I unfastened her bra.

"It's been three months." Her fingers found the buttons on my jeans. She tugged me closer.

I lowered her down, angling my body over hers so I could kiss her mouth, her chin, her neck. "Promise me you'll stay."

"I'm going to have to leave, eventually." Her nails skimmed

up my back as I continued down.

"Then I'm just going to have to work harder to convince you." My lips closed over one nipple as my fingers found the other.

She arched under me, and her nails dug into my shoulders. Now that I had her back, I was never letting her go again. If it took all night to convince her, the boxes could wait.

15

ONCE we were both dressed again, Max left me to check on the transport device. I paced the conference room, alone. I should have been giddy. This was what I'd wanted. But for some reason, I still couldn't shake the feeling that everything was going to come crashing down again. I still wasn't sure that whatever was between us, as unbreakable as it may be, could stand up against the force of his family and his magic.

Salty watched me walk back and forth, curious and confused by my unrest. Or, perhaps that was just me. My toe collided with the edge of my phone and sent it sliding under the table. It must have fallen off the table at some point. I hadn't noticed and hadn't cared, but once I saw it, I remembered I was still waiting for an update from Evie and Willow.

I crouched down and reached for it, keeping my head low and half crawling underneath the table until I could grab it. Salty barked, and I banged my head trying to turn and see what was going on. She ran toward me and shoved against my legs, nudging me farther under the table.

"What is your problem, dog?" I whispered the question in case Max happened to walk in at that moment. He was already suspicious of Salty, even though all their talk of familiars seemed to reassure them that there was a logical, or at least wizard-approved, explanation for Salty's affinity for magic.

Salty bit the sleeve of my blouse and started tugging.

"Hey. Stop it. You're going to rip that." I leaned toward her to keep her from tearing the fabric and lost my balance, falling onto my butt fully underneath the table.

Voices in the hall kept me frozen there. One of them was definitely too high-pitched to be Max, and it was too soon for him to be back from a trip down to the fifth floor, anyway. I thought maybe it might be Hannah and Jayden. I started to scoot forward, but Salty nudged me back. I stared down at her, and she butted her nose against my shin again. Deciding I'd better obey my guard dog, I slid backward until my spine touched the thick center leg of the table.

"There's a light on in here." The voice sounded female and close, like the speaker was standing just outside the conference room door.

I bent my head to see if I could identify who it was by their footwear or pant legs. I caught a glimpse of black Converse and bare legs. They were joined by someone with larger feet shoved into plain navy flip-flops paired with jeans.

"What a mess." The second voice was deeper, but definitely not Max or Jayden.

"Be quiet and start looking. If the light is on, that means he's still here somewhere." The one in the Converse started walking toward the conference table.

I scrunched farther back. My hand bumped into my phone,

and I scrambled to silence it before it gave them a reason to look under the table. I really hoped Max would return soon.

"I thought you got rid of him." Flip-Flops lingered near the door and didn't sound thrilled to be sneaking around.

"Apparently he didn't take my advice. It happens. Now come on. It has to be here somewhere."

Above me, papers rustled and boxes scraped against the wood.

Flip-Flops took a few tentative steps into the room and stopped. "How do you know he didn't take it with him?"

"Maybe he did, but we'll never know if you don't help me look."

Salty nudged my upper thigh with her nose. I looked down at her, and she did it again. She was trying to tell me something, but I couldn't figure out what. I reached over to scratch her behind her ear, and she nudged my hand down until it brushed against my thigh and the two hard, flat circular lumps in my pocket.

I twisted sideways so I could slide one of the coins out and stared down at it. I had nothing to prick my finger with, and I wasn't sure that inviting Arabella and her Queen's Guard into the Silicon Moon offices was going to turn out well.

"We should go. It's not here." Flip-Flops backtracked toward the door.

"Let me at least get a few photos of these plans, first. Maybe there's something here we can use. The locations have to be around here somewhere. Keep looking."

Flip-Flops ignored Converse and hurried to the door. "I think someone's coming."

I really hoped it was Max. Hurry.

"Come here, then."

One minute, Flip-Flops and Converse were toe to toe, and

the next, they were gone. I shifted onto my hands and knees as Salty bolted for the door. She intercepted Max just as I poked my head out from under the table.

"What are you doing down there?" Max cocked his head to one side.

I crawled out and sat back on my heels so I could meet his gaze. "We had some visitors."

"Under the table?" He held his hand out to help me up.

"No." I slid the blood coin back into my pocket, then wrapped my fingers around his and let him haul me to my feet. "Two people. One wearing Converse and one wearing jeans and flip-flops. That's all I saw."

Max squinted at me. "What were you doing under the table? Why didn't you talk to them? Ask them what they were doing here?"

"I know what they were doing here. They were looking for this." I crossed the room and reached into my tote to pull out the magic trap we'd retrieved from the island.

"What is that doing in your bag?" Max crossed his arms.

I hadn't had a chance to tell him before the kissing started. This wasn't how I'd wanted him to find out what I'd done. "It's not what you think."

"Okay..." The corners of his mouth pulled down as he waited for me to explain myself.

My initial instinct was to change the subject and hope he forgot. "Can we focus on one thing at a time here?"

"I am. I'm asking you why you have Silicon Moon property in your tote." He uncrossed one arm so he could point at my bag. "Is there anything else I need to know about in there? Do I need to search you and take away your phone, too?"

I sighed. "I thought we'd agreed we were going to trust each other."

"I thought so, too." His arms dropped to his sides, fists clenched. "So, tell me, why is that in your bag?"

If I had just stuck to the plan and not allowed myself to fall for him, again, then I wouldn't have this problem. I also wouldn't have ended up half naked on the Silicon Moon conference table. So there was that. I trusted Max and wanted him back in my life, so I told him what I'd planned to tell him.

"You said you wanted to find the others so you could show them the box. I thought that was what we were going to do while the transport thing charged. So, I put it in my bag. Then you came back and started kissing me, and I forgot about it." I paused for a breath. "Now can we talk about the fact that two people just came in here searching for this box and then took a bunch of photos of those papers?"

Max ran his hand through his hair. "Tell me again what you saw and heard."

"Two people. They walked in from somewhere out there." I pointed to the room full of cubicles just outside the conference room. "They came in here, searched through all that, took some photos, and disappeared."

"Disappeared?"

"Yes. Poof. Vanished." I pointed to where I'd seen them standing. "They were standing right there when they disappeared."

"That would explain why I didn't see them, but only demons have the ability to transport themselves that way." His head tilted to one side. "And any of the engineers who were approved for testing our transport device."

"Do demons wear flip-flops?" I asked. The one I'd met wouldn't have been caught dead in them, but I didn't know if that was a demon thing or a Nigel thing.

"You think they were engineers?" He must have assumed

that I thought engineers were more the flip-flop type.

I shrugged. "They definitely knew you. One of them said that they thought you'd gone home."

"Are you sure? Did they mention me by name?"

"No, but I'm not sure who else they could have been talking about. Jayden, maybe?"

"You think there are people on my own team that know about this." His gesture encompassed all the cardboard boxes and papers and the magic trap still in my hand. "And that they are working with the demons?"

"I don't know. Is it possible?"

He didn't answer. Instead, he paced over to the table and studied the papers that were spread out there as he rubbed his chin. "You think they took photos of this?"

I nodded. "I heard one of them say something about pictures, and then I heard that camera app sound a few times."

He grimaced and pointed at the piece of scrap paper I'd been using to guess the three-word codes for the other locations. "Are you sure about these?"

I walked around the table to stand next to him. "You still need to look up the coordinates, but yeah. We figured out the Alaska one, and I managed to finish the second one. I'm still working on the first one. I'm stuck on that second clue, 'I am good enough.'"

"Well, this thing is charged." He held up the transport device. "Maybe we should go grab the one in Alaska, since the coordinates are written right there. Then we can figure out the other two when we get back."

I checked Max's outfit. He had on his usual faded denim with a charcoal-gray T-shirt. I was pretty sure he'd been wearing a sweatshirt at some point, but I didn't remember taking it off him.

I gestured to my thin blouse and skinny jeans. "I don't think either of us is dressed for a trip to Alaska right now."

He shrugged. "We'll be fast. Grab your rain jacket."

"What if they come back while we're gone?"

"You can stay if you want."

"I'm not staying here by myself."

"Then come on. Let's go. We could have been there and back by now."

I called Salty.

"You could leave the dog." He bent over the dials on the side of the device, checking coordinates as he rotated the number wheels to the correct alignment.

"I can't." I ducked my head to look under the table, but she wasn't there.

"She'll be fine here. We'll be right back." He'd found his sweater and was sliding it over his arms when I stood.

I didn't answer him. Instead, I tried calling Salty again and walked over to the conference room door to see if she'd wandered out into the hallway.

"Last chance." Max tapped the transport device against the table.

A flash of tan fur caught my eye. I turned my head to follow the movement and spotted Salty running straight for me like she was being chased. I didn't want to wait around to see if anything or anyone was following her. I tucked the magic trap under one arm and bent to scoop her up with the other. Then I hurried over to Max.

"Let's go."

———

ANGIE'S BEHAVIOR was starting to worry me. She hadn't let go of the box since she'd pulled it out of her tote. I tried not to let it bother me. I was more worried about whoever had been here taking pictures. The only demons I knew of with humanlike forms, at least enough to pass as a human with only a slight glamour, were the incubi and succubi. They tended to be a bit particular about their appearance, though. I didn't think it was likely that any would be caught wearing the sort of footwear Angie had described.

That left me suspecting my engineers and my friends, because they would have to be working together if they had a transport device and knowledge of Emilio's secret project. My thoughts strayed to Jayden as I finished setting the coordinates into the transport device. He had no reason to work with the demons...unless he wasn't doing so willingly. Perhaps they were blackmailing him in some way or threatening to kill him if he didn't agree to help them.

I pushed that thought out of my head. Angie would have recognized Jayden's voice. I looked over at her in time to see her scoop up Salty. There was a crease between her eyebrows as she walked toward me.

She stopped next to me with the box cradled in one arm and her dog in the other. "Let's go."

"What about your jacket?"

She shrugged. "You said we weren't going to be gone long."

"You're taking that with you?" I gestured at the box.

Her eyes narrowed. "Do you have someplace else where we can keep it safe while we're gone?"

"You think it's safer with us?"

Her face softened, and her lower lip pouted as she stepped closer and studied my face. "Maybe it's just that I have a personal investment in the safety of one particular wizard, but I'm not about to let this fall into the wrong hands." She pressed up on her toes until her lips met mine.

Her explanation reassured me enough that I leaned into the kiss. Wrapping one arm around her to keep her close, I pricked the index finger of my other hand and set it against the activation pad, sending us north.

The cold air cut through my cotton hoodie, making me think maybe Angie had been right. We weren't dressed for this. Alaska in May felt a lot more like Seattle in December than I'd expected.

Angie shivered and pressed her body closer to mine. "Damn, that's cold."

"Maybe we should go back." I rubbed between her shoulder blades, trying to create some warmth from friction.

She shook her head. "We're here. Let's just get this over with."

We were surrounded by trees, and close to a collection of houses. There were at least six of them, possibly more in the distance. The nearest of them was still five or six yards away. Aside from the houses, nothing jumped out at me as an obvious location for hiding a metal cube.

While I hesitated, Angie released Salty. The dog landed on the ground between melting patches of snow and shook herself from ears to tail. She sniffed the air but didn't run off.

I was so focused on Salty that I didn't realize we weren't alone until the crack of a branch alerted me to another presence. Angie and I both turned our heads to look. I spotted someone or something moving in the shadow of the house closest to us. Whatever it was, I couldn't make out any details in the low light.

"We should go." Angie tugged on my sleeve and pointed down at her dog.

Salty was nipping at the cuff of Angie's jeans, trying to get enough of a grip that she could tug her away from whatever was moving in the shadows.

I wasn't going anywhere. If someone had beat us to the box, it had to have been one of the people Angie had seen in the conference room. I wanted to know who it was. I pressed the transport device into her hand and curled her fingers around it.

"If anything happens, leave me and get out of here," I whispered.

Her eyes went wide. "What are you doing?"

Before she could stop me, I crept toward the houses. Behind me, she whispered my name, but I didn't stop. I was halfway to the house closest to us when I remembered that Angie couldn't leave without me. The mechanism in the transport device worked by tapping into the Fae blood that gave wizards their magic. The blood in our veins was too weak to allow us to transport ourselves the way the Fae and the demons could, but with a boost from Silicon Moon technology, we could manage something similar enough.

There was nothing to do about it except go back, and I wasn't about to do that until I knew who had betrayed me. So I kept my eyes focused on the spot where I'd seen movement and moved forward as quietly as I could without looking down at the ground.

The closer I got, the more I thought my eyes were playing tricks on me. I searched the shadows, but there was nothing there. I stopped a few feet from the house, near where I thought I'd seen something moving.

The windows in the house were all dark. No one was home, or no one lived here. It was the same in all the houses nearby. No lights on. No one lurking in the dusky twilight.

But there were footprints in the dirt. I stepped closer and bent to get a better look. They were about the length of my hand, and the tread was striped and crisscrossed in a pattern that appeared to be more sneaker than work boot. The rounded toe of the print pointed in my direction and then vanished near where I stood.

I followed the indentations in the opposite direction of travel, keeping close to the tracks as they curved around the back of the house to a cluster of confusing marks. I stopped and crouched down and was trying to figure them out when Salty jogged up and nudged my thigh with her nose.

"What?" I leaned back on my heels and stared at Angie's dog.

She ran in a circle around the tangle of prints, then took off toward the far corner of the house. When she realized I wasn't following, she ran back and nudged me again. Then she trotted off, but this time, she stopped to wait for me.

Angie intercepted me when I stood and started to follow. "Did you see anything?"

I motioned to the ground, noting that Salty was following the tracks as they continued off in this direction. "Just these footprints."

Angie reached into her pocket and pulled out her phone. She had managed to hug the metal cube against her body, pinning it between her forearm and her chest, so that she could tuck her bare fingertips under her other arm to keep them warm. With her free hand, she found the flashlight setting on her phone and angled the light down to illuminate the footprints.

"Converse." She said the words with a sigh, like she'd expected as much.

"How can you be sure?" I squinted at the prints.

She paused and pointed, making a swirl in the air with her fingertip. "She how the tread in the center has a sort of diamond shape to it?"

Ahead of us, Salty had stopped and sat down next to a mound of dirt.

"Sure, but how do you know that's Converse?"

"Let's just say that I had several pairs in middle and high school and spent a lot of time writing on the bottoms of them."

"Why would you write on the bottom of your shoe?"

Angie shrugged. "Why do teenagers do anything?" She shivered, then scanned the light from her phone over the area around Salty. "What did you find, girl?"

I pointed toward the corner of the house, near the foundation. "There. Shine the light on that corner."

I crossed the beam of light to get onto the far side so that my body wouldn't block the light. Two bricks lay on the ground next to the concrete foundation. The sides of the house were wood, and it took me a minute to figure out where the bricks had come from. One end of the chimney was just a few feet away from where I stood.

"Up here." I pointed to a gap in the silhouette as it stretched up to meet the roofline. The missing bricks had come from a spot at about eye level for me. "Give me that box."

Angie put the metal cube into my hand. It was still warm from her body heat. I held it up to the opening to confirm what I'd already suspected.

"Someone got here first." Angie said what I was thinking.

I handed the cube back to her and reached my hand inside, feeling around the empty cavity, just to be sure. "It's gone."

"Can we go directly from here to the next location?"

I considered the possibility. "Do you have the three words?"

"Not with me."

It wouldn't take that long to go back and get the paper with the words from the puzzle, but that extra trip would probably use up too much of the remaining power for us to travel again without charging the device. My numb fingers fumbled with the controls, trying to get a glimpse of the power gauge, but it was too dark, and I was too cold to make sense of it.

"Let's go." I bent down to pick up Salty and handed her to Angie. "We'll let the transport device charge while we sort out the coordinates for the other two locations. Then we'll hit both of them at once."

"But what if they get there first?" Angie shivered.

"We cross our fingers and hope they don't know how to convert the words into locations." I put my arm around her and tucked her body against my side. "I don't like it any more than you do, but we can't transport without proper coordinates or we'll risk ending up in the middle of an ocean or colliding with something on the other end."

She grimaced. "I didn't need to know that."

I kissed the tip of her nose. "Just close your eyes and hold on."

16

THE second that the cold wind stopped blowing, I knew we were back and opened my eyes. Max released me and started pacing. I fiddled with the blood coins in my pocket and wondered if it was time to call in the reinforcements.

"Damn it. I wish I knew who snuck in here. They could be taking that box to the demons right now." Max shoved his hand into his hair. "Or maybe they already have, and they're on their way to the next location."

I picked up the piece of paper I'd been using to test out solutions to the puzzles. "They would have to know that the three words convert into coordinates. They may not realize that. We have time."

"Where's the notebook with the riddles?" Max searched the table.

I set the paper with the coordinates down and leaned over to help him look. "It was right here."

Max paused. He placed both hands flat on the table and

turned his head toward me. "You didn't put it in your bag, did you?"

I stepped back from the table. His accusation stung. "No."

"I'm just asking."

My eyes narrowed and my jaw clenched. I pushed the cuff of my blouse back to reveal the mark he'd made on my wrist. "I didn't take it."

"Fine." He stared down at his hands and exhaled. "Someone did."

My phone started ringing. I pulled it out to silence it as Max watched. "It's Evie. I'll...um...I'll call her back."

Max swallowed and stood. "Let's get this cleaned up and put away. I want to keep the designs but get rid of anything we don't absolutely need."

My phone chimed once and then again, but I ignored it. "If we figure out the coordinates first, then maybe there's a way for us to get to the boxes before they do."

Max glared at my pocket, then at me. "We can't transport ourselves like they can. It's over. The demons know where the boxes are. They didn't even know that this technology existed, and now they do, and it's my fault. Someone on my team told them, and now I need to figure out who I can even trust."

"But if you let them get the boxes, then you won't be able to destroy them." I started scribbling the puzzle clues for the first puzzle onto the back of the paper in case we couldn't find the notebook.

"Destroy them? I'm not going to destroy them."

"You're not?" My phone chimed again.

Max scowled. "Maybe you should check that."

"I'm sure it's nothing." I couldn't believe he seriously planned to keep the boxes and the plans. Whatever Evie and

Willow wanted, it could wait. If Max wasn't already convinced that this technology was dangerous, I needed to make sure he understood and did the right thing.

"It's okay. Check your phone. I'll take the engineering designs to my office and be right back." He rolled up Emilio's design documents and stalked out the door.

When he was gone, I took out my phone and checked my messages. Gwawr was still working on a way to destroy the boxes, but she had figured out how to lock down the magic so that it couldn't be used against anyone. I skipped over the details and started typing a message of my own.

Demons got one of the boxes. Need help. Can I tell him?

Max returned but paused in the doorway. "I'm going to go and charge the transporter in case we find that notebook and can finish figuring out the coordinates."

I glanced up from my phone screen. "I remember the clues for the last puzzle. We can figure it out even without the notebook, and I have some friends who might be able to help us, if you want."

"Did you tell someone about this project?" Max tensed.

"No." I cringed and bit my lip. "I mean, not really. These friends of mine...and I know this is going to sound really bad, but...they already knew about the boxes."

"What?" Max took a step forward, then paused and took a breath. When he spoke again, it was in a much calmer voice. "What, exactly, are you saying, Angie?"

"I should have told you before, but I thought it didn't matter. My friends are in danger. I promised them that I wouldn't tell anyone about them. I didn't say anything because I was keeping their secrets, and I didn't think it was relevant, but now that the demons are involved..." I let my voice trail off.

His face showed no hint of emotion. There was none of the

HUNTER OF THE FAE

softness and joy that had been there earlier, but he hadn't yet closed me out. "Who are these friends? Wizards?"

"Yes. Some, but that's not all." My phone chimed again, and I glanced at the screen.

Evie's reply was one word and all I needed to see. Yes.

The words tumbled from my lips on a sigh of relief. "The demons want these boxes so they can use them to destroy the Fae. There is no plan to use them on the wizards, at least not one that we know about."

"The Fae. Why would the demons care about destroying the Fae? That makes no sense."

"It's a really long story, but that half demon I mentioned earlier? He's Lilium and Emilio's son. Emilio also had a daughter with the sister of the Faerie Queen. She's the one who gave me Salty, to protect me."

"To protect you from what?" Max's hands curled around the back of a chair.

I swallowed. "From the demons. In case I encountered any."

"And why did she think you were going to encounter demons, Angie?" Max was gripping the chair so tightly that his knuckles turned white.

My lips had gone dry. I wet them before forcing out the final piece of information. The one that was going to end everything between us. "Because the Faerie Queen sent me to talk with you and see what you knew about the boxes. She thought maybe the wizards were working with the demons, but I told her you weren't."

"And you told her that we'd figured out where the boxes were."

I cringed. "They weren't the ones who took that box."

"I trusted you, Angie." He crossed his arms and shook his head. "I have no choice. Bring me your bag."

"Max. They want to help. They can help us. They can take us—you—to retrieve the other boxes. You don't have to wait for that transport device to charge. You can beat the demons."

"Bring me your bag."

I slid my phone into my pocket and retrieved my tote from where I left it on the floor of the conference room. Salty followed me, tail wagging. I picked up my bag and held it above the table, pausing to meet Max's eyes before I dumped out the contents.

Max stepped forward and scanned the items now spread across the only bit of table that hadn't been covered in papers. The bit of table that had supported our truly excellent bout of make-up sex and now displayed the proof that I'd lost Max forever.

"Thank you." He swept the contents up on a current of air and deposited them back into my bag. "You should go."

"Max. Please. The agreement was that we wouldn't reveal other people's secrets. You know how the Fae are. I'm on your side. They're on your side. They want to help you."

Max laughed. "You're right. I know how the Fae are. That's why I find it hard to believe that the Fae want to help the wizards. Want to help me. What is it going to cost me? My firstborn child? My sanity? My memories? Come on, Angie. You can't trust the Fae."

"They can't lie, Max."

"They don't need to lie. They're charming tricksters. And if that's not bad enough, they made us who we are and then abandoned us. Every bit of magic known to us, we had to teach ourselves. Why do you think the Society is so important? It's the Society that exists to help the wizards. The Fae don't care."

"They care about this."

"They care now that they are threatened. Well, that's not my problem." He sighed. "I'm sorry it had to end like this. I'll see you out."

"That's it? You'll 'see me out.' Max, why? Let my friends help you."

"Angie, I can't expect you to understand. This secret you kept from me, you may believe that it's only about helping the Fae hide from the humans who might harm them, but it's more than that. How can I trust you when I can't even be sure that they haven't charmed you? The Fae are just as bad as the demons. They may not be actively trying to kill us, but they left us to survive in a world of humans who fear us and have been trying to kill us for thousands of years."

When he put it like that, it made sense to me why he'd hate them so much. "Don't you have some sort of rune to prove I'm not being charmed?" I pushed up my sleeves and offered him my forearms. "Test me. Go ahead."

He shook his head. With a flick of his wrist, my raincoat floated across the room to rest on my tote. "Come on. Let's go."

He walked to the door, then he turned to wait as I slid my arms into my jacket. I retrieved Salty's leash from my bag and bent to clip it onto her collar. She sat with her head cocked, watching me. Once her leash was secure, I scratched her between the ears, then stood and squared my shoulders. I had no choice but to follow him to the elevator.

I'd tried my best, and in the process, I'd lost Max forever and failed Fiona. Pausing at the door, I took one last look at the room. My eyes landed on the paper with the words from the puzzles. Max was waiting for me. Watching me. There was no way I could grab it.

I slid my hand into my pocket. My fingers closed around one of Arabella's blood coins. I tried to remember Willow's instructions. If I sent a message to her now, would it bring her to this location? Or would it bring her to me, wherever I was?

Either way, I needed blood to activate the coin. I slowed my pace and reached a hand into my tote, feeling around inside for something sharp. I tried to remember the contents as they had been laying out on the conference table.

Something poked at me from the bottom of the bag. I was only a few feet from the elevator. Max had already reached it and pressed the button. I fumbled with the object, realizing it was that oddly bent and twisted paper clip. Before I could think about it, I scratched the pad of my thumb across the end. Then I pressed my lips together to keep from crying out.

I pulled my hand out of my tote and jammed it into my pocket before Max had a chance to turn and see what I was doing. Just before I reached him, I pulled the coin out and whispered to it.

"Hurry. Get the coordinates before he comes back."

Max turned at the sound of my voice, but the blood coin had already disappeared. I held up my hand so he could see the blood smeared on my thumb.

"I seem to have cut myself. No big deal."

———

As MAD AS I WAS, I reacted before I had a chance to think about it, taking her hand in mine to study the injury. "What did you do?"

Angie shrugged and tried to pull her hand out of my grip. "Something sharp in my bag. I don't know. It's fine. Really. Don't worry about it."

The elevator doors opened behind me. I led her inside, keeping a firm grip on her injured finger. There wasn't anything I could do except clean it and apply pressure until the bleeding stopped, like any other regular human would. Wizards didn't have healing powers, and we bled like anyone else.

I pressed the button for the lobby and took a closer look at her thumb. It was a shallow cut, but long and jagged. "You can wash it out when we get to the lobby."

She twisted her hand, and slid it out of my grasp. "It's fine. I'll take care of it back at the hotel."

"Don't be stubborn. It could get infected. Just take a minute and wash it off before you go, okay?"

Her eyes narrowed. "I'm not stubborn. My hand is my problem, not yours. I think you made that clear when you kicked me out of your office."

My heart ached. Angie was the one person I'd thought I could always trust. I didn't want this. I wished she could see that, but every word from her mouth made me more convinced that she'd been enchanted. Why else would the Fae have chosen to reveal themselves to her? They were using her to get to me. Her suspicious behavior made so much more sense now.

"You really were going to take that box, weren't you? That's why you put it into your tote. So you could give it to the Fae."

Angie looked away from me. "I told you. I was just trying to keep it safe."

The elevator doors opened, and I stepped out into the dimly lit lobby. Without looking back, I walked toward the restrooms, assuming Angie would follow. Our footsteps and the clicking of Salty's nails against the marble floor were the only sounds that broke the silence between us.

My hands clenched into fists at my sides. I used one to push open the door to the lobby restroom. The motion-activated light clicked on, illuminating the small room. Angie slid past me and held her hands under the faucet to activate the sensor. Water flowed into the sink and over her hands. I watched her face in the mirror as she scrubbed her cut and rinsed it off.

"Is there anything I can say to convince you that the Fae are dangerous, and you should stay as far away from them as you possibly can?" I crossed my arms and leaned against the doorjamb.

Angie glanced up and met my eyes in the mirror. Tears welled in her lower lids, threatening to spill over and splash down her cheeks. She swallowed and raised her chin. "No."

We stared at each other a moment longer. Then she dried her hands on a towel and turned to face me. "Is there anything that I can say to convince you that the Queen of the Fae is willing to support you?"

I tilted my head to one side. "No strings attached? She wants nothing in return? She's just going to support me and the rest of the wizards?"

Angie grimaced. "You'd have to let her have the boxes and also destroy all of Emilio's notes and plans."

I shook my head. "That doesn't sound like unconditional support. That sounds like a trade. One I'm not willing to make. I told you. I don't trust them."

Angie stepped closer to me, angling her body into the door opening so that we stood face-to-face. "Trust me, then. Trust that I never stopped loving you, and I would never do anything to hurt you."

I couldn't tear my eyes away from her face and the truth

that I could see there, but I couldn't bring myself to close the distance and reach for her, either. "I love you, too. I always have. But I have a duty to protect the wizards. All of them. And I can't turn my back on them or put them at risk. Especially not now."

"You're choosing them over me, again." Her lips trembled, and she pressed them together. Then she slid past me and marched toward the building entrance with Salty at her heels.

I followed, but she didn't pause or look back until she reached the door. "If you change your mind, you know where I am. I'll be there until tomorrow at noon. Then I'm leaving."

She didn't wait for me to respond before stepping out into the rain. She tugged her hood up to cover her head, tucked her tote tight against her waist, and walked away with Salty trotting along at her side, down the sidewalk, in the direction of her hotel.

Without realizing it, I moved toward the door and pressed my forehead against the glass. I was so fixated on watching her disappear into the darkness that I didn't see Grace approaching from the other direction. She knocked on the glass next to my face, and I turned my head.

"Hey. Good timing. Let me in." Her voice was muffled by the glass.

Callie jogged up, hunched against the rain and holding her hood up so it wouldn't fall back, just in time to tumble through the door when I opened it to let Grace in.

"Phew." Callie let her hood fall back and shook some of the beaded-up rain off her jacket's waterproof fabric. "Wind's picking up out there. Gonna be a stormy one tonight."

"You found a place to park the car pretty fast." Grace narrowed her eyes at Callie.

Callie's already-pink cheeks shaded a bit darker. "I got one of those thirty-minute spots."

"I thought you were staying." Grace put her hands on her hips.

I glanced down at their feet while they argued. Grace was wearing a version of the same black lace-up boots she'd been wearing since college. Today she wore them with leggings and thick socks. Callie still wore her scrubs. The shiny toes of her comfortable burgundy leather clogs poked out from beneath the navy-blue hem. They couldn't have been the ones that Angie had seen.

Their voices quieted, and I looked up to find them both staring at me. "What?"

"Didn't you hear me?"

"No. Sorry. My mind was on something else."

"Clearly. I asked what you were doing down here. You didn't answer my text message. I thought I was going to have to call you to let you know we were here."

"Oh. Sorry. Angie just left. I've been a little distracted."

"Distracted?" She raised an eyebrow.

I shook my head. "Not like that. We broke up. For real, this time. I think."

"All right. This doesn't sound like a lobby conversation. Let's get you upstairs, and then you can tell us what happened, from the beginning, and we'll figure out how to fix it." Grace slung her arm across my shoulder and led me to the elevator.

I shrugged away from the comfort she offered and crossed my arms. "It's done, and I don't want to talk about it. We have bigger things to worry about than the fact that I was forced to kick Angie out because she's probably been enchanted by the Fae."

Callie jabbed the up button with her finger as Grace turned

on me. "The Fae? And Angie? What could possibly be bigger than that? Spill it. What's going on, Hunter?"

We filed into the elevator, and I hit the button for the top floor. "Before I tell you about that, someone in our group is working with the demons. I'm really hoping that it's not one of you."

"Didn't we already go over this, earlier?" Grace glared at me.

I held up both hands. "I know. I know. But someone broke into the office. They transported in. So, they either have access to one of our transport devices, or they hitched a ride with a demon."

"Could it have been your mother?" Callie asked. "Grace said she was here earlier and she had one of those devices."

"How do you know someone broke in?" Grace asked.

The elevator chime alerted us that we'd arrived at our destination, and the doors slid open. I stepped out, and they followed me to the conference room as I explained. "Angie saw two people, but she only saw them from the knees down. She hid under the table when she heard them coming. She would have recognized my mother's voice if it was her."

"Could your mother have lent her transport device to someone?"

The idea hadn't occurred to me, but it was possible. "Who would she have lent it to that would have been wearing Converse or flip-flops?"

"Flip-flops?" Callie shook her head. "If that's true, then at least one of them is not from around here. This is not flip-flop weather." She gestured to the rain dotting the windows.

The other elevator opened, revealing Jayden and Kyle.

"What's all this about flip-flops?" Jayden asked.

Grace put her hands on her hips. "Apparently, someone

wearing inappropriate footwear broke into the conference room, and Max broke up with Angie because she's been enchanted by the Fae. Where have you been while all this was going on?"

"I was down in the mail room packing boxes to ship to Lilium. When I came up to the conference room, everyone was gone, so I left to pick up Kyle and get dinner. Did you find a box?"

I shoved my fists into my pockets. "We got the one near Seattle. But the demons, or whoever is working with them, beat us to the second location."

"Which one?" Jayden asked.

"The one in Alaska."

"Where's Angie?" Kyle glanced around.

"Max kicked her out." Callie shrugged.

All eyes turned to me. "She said she's been working with the Fae this whole time. They seem to think that the demons want the boxes so that they can destroy the Fae and that this has nothing to do with the wizards aside from the fact that one of us created these things."

Kyle tapped his finger against his bottom lip. "Huh. That kind of makes sense, if you think about it."

I curled my fingers into my hair, ready to pull it out in frustration. "Look. It doesn't matter. The point is that she wanted me to let them help."

"The Fae wanted to help you, and you turned them down?" Grace leaned toward me, but Callie put a hand on Grace's shoulder to hold her back. "Do you know what I would give to make contact with the Fae, and you had this opportunity and turned it down? Why would you do that?"

"Angie lied to me, and we can't trust the Fae. You, more than anyone, should know that."

"Do not go there, Hunter." Grace's fists clenched and her face flushed.

"She put the box we retrieved into her tote and then attempted to convince me that it was because she was trying to keep it safe."

Kyle leaned back so he could see around Jayden and into the conference room. "Where is it now?"

I ignored him. "And then the notebook with the puzzles we were using to figure out the location coordinates went missing."

Jayden dug around in his messenger bag and pulled out a composition notebook that looked like the ones Emilio preferred. "You mean this notebook?"

"You have the notebook?"

"I took it with me when I went to meet Kyle for dinner because I thought we might be able to figure out that last puzzle. I didn't know where you went, but wherever you were, you weren't using it."

"Maybe we should all calm down and talk this through." Callie rubbed Grace's back and spoke in a soothing voice. "Who else besides us—and Angie—knows about Emilio's stuff?"

Jayden looked around. "Where's Hannah?"

"Besides Hannah," Callie said.

"No, really." Jayden met my eyes. "Did she ever come back from that coffee run?"

"That was hours ago." In all the excitement of chasing down the boxes with Angie, I'd forgotten all about the coffee and Hannah.

Kyle took out his phone. His fingers flew across the screen, and a moment later, he looked up. "She hasn't posted anything since this morning."

Grace shook her head. "It can't be Hannah. She wouldn't wear flip-flops unless she was going to the beach or a pool or something."

"Who else knows besides Hannah?" Callie asked.

I scanned my friends' faces. "Varun, who's on a plane. My mother. Maybe my father, if she told him. And Morgan."

17

WILLOW and Arabella were waiting for me in my hotel room when I got back. I stood inside the door dripping wet, and all I wanted to do was cry, but I couldn't. There would be time for that later, after the Fae had secured all the boxes.

"Did you get in?" I asked.

Arabella's eyes swept over me from head to toe. She waved a hand, and I found myself enveloped in a hot desert wind that instantly dried and warmed me to my core.

"We got in. He had some pretty basic wards. Not bad for a wizard, but nothing that Arabella couldn't take care of. We didn't touch anything, but I got pictures of whatever was lying around." Willow passed me her phone.

I flipped through the images until I found the one with my scratch paper. "This is the one we need right now."

She took the phone from me and studied the photo. "What is it?"

"Emilio encoded the coordinates for all the locations. The

globe provided the general location for four of the boxes. His notebook had four puzzles. Each puzzle had three sentences. The sentences were clues for a word. The three words translated to the location coordinates."

"Transport locations, or box locations?" Arabella asked.

"Transport, I guess? But both times, the box has been hidden very close to the transport location, and both times, Salty has been able to lead us right to the box."

"So Max has the box you found?" Willow asked.

"Yes, but just one. It should have been there, on the conference table. Did you see it?"

Arabella nodded. "I didn't dare touch it, but I did manage to lock it down using Gwawr's instructions. And I made sure none of my sire's things will be leaving that building."

"What did you do?"

"I fixed his wards." Arabella paced over to the windows and pulled the curtains shut.

I turned to Willow and raised an eyebrow.

Willow shrugged. "Can you finish figuring out the last two locations without the notebook?"

I pulled out my phone and scrolled back through our group chat to find the pictures I'd sent, not quite believing it possible that it could have been earlier in the same day. "There."

Willow looked at the image over my shoulder. "How in the world did you figure out that was anything important?" She pointed at the screen. "It looks like a collection of random thoughts of someone stuck in a boring meeting or class. I think some of my old college notebooks have pages like this in them."

"That may have been the point. I think he was trying to hide this information from himself, if that makes any sense."

"Of course. If Lilium could get into his brain, he couldn't

keep that information there."

Arabella interrupted us. "What happened to the second box?"

"We got there too late. Whoever broke into the office must have used the coordinates we scribbled onto that scrap paper and found it. When we got there, it was already gone."

"Then enough of this talking. Give me the next set of co-ordinates." Arabella guided me to the desk chair, and Willow handed me her phone. The image of the paper with the partially completed puzzles was already on the screen.

"This one is done. Let me just..." I entered the three words into the website Max had been using. The location was in Argentina, close enough to the point on the globe that I knew I'd figured out the puzzle correctly. I copied the coordinates for the location onto the scratch pad on the desk and handed it to Arabella.

She took the pad of paper and ripped off the top sheet with the coordinates. "Thank you."

Willow reached for her before she could disappear. "Be careful."

Arabella met Willow's eyes. Some silent understanding passed between them, and Arabella nodded. "I'll get Nigel to provide backup. If there are demons lurking around, I'll let him deal with them."

Willow leaned closer and kissed Arabella lightly on the mouth. Then stepped back. I blinked, and Arabella disappeared. Salty circled the spot where Arabella had been standing. She sniffed the ground, then walked toward the door and curled up next to my tote bag.

"So what happened with Max?" Willow's question hung in the air between us as I considered what to say. "If you don't want to talk about it, that's okay. We can just work on sorting these coordinates out."

I sighed. "No. It's fine. There's not much to talk about. I told him that I was friends with the Fae and they wanted to help find the boxes. He freaked out, got pissed because I'd lied to him, and then told me he wanted nothing to do with the Fae. He warned me repeatedly that they were dangerous and told me to stay away from them."

"Wow." Willow's eyes went wide. "I've heard of wizards hating the Fae, but that's a lot."

"You have? Other wizards hate the Fae? It's not just a Max thing?"

Willow shook her head. "It's definitely not just a Max thing. Though, I'm sure it doesn't help that his parents lead the Council, and the Council is very anti-Fae."

"He said the Fae abandoned them."

Willow nodded. "Yeah. That's the general argument. And I can't say that I blame them. But, I had wizards for parents, and they didn't teach me a damn thing. I didn't even know I had powers. And let me tell you, Arabella was pissed when she found out that my parents hadn't bothered to teach me. She called it irresponsible."

"This is so messed up."

"Yep. Just a bunch of magical weirdos who can't seem to get along. Makes you kind of glad you don't have magic, huh?"

I didn't need to think about it before I responded. "No way. It makes me wish I had magic even more. If I did, then maybe, just maybe, someone would listen to me and take me seriously and I would have an actual shot at getting people to work together."

"Somebody like Max?"

I sighed. "Yeah. I suppose."

"Come on. Help me figure out this last puzzle. It will help take your mind off him."

I showed Willow the words I thought I'd figured out already and the clue I was stuck on. She sketched out a copy of the puzzle boxes and plugged in the words I'd guessed on her paper. Then we set to work bouncing ideas around and trying to figure out the final clue. Every so often, I caught Willow glancing over at the clock as we worked.

"Are you worried?" I asked.

Willow scowled. "She should be back by now."

As if summoned, Arabella reappeared. My heart sank when I realized she was empty-handed.

Willow jumped up and hurried over. "What happened?"

I understood the disappointment in not retrieving a box, but I didn't understand the worry in Willow's voice. To me, Arabella looked exactly the same as she had when she'd left.

Arabella pressed her palm to Willow's cheek and smiled. "Everything's fine. We got the box."

"Where is it?" I asked.

"Nigel took it back to the Fae. I thought that was best given the circumstances."

"I knew something happened." Willow reached for Arabella's hand and pressed her fingers against the inside of Arabella's wrist.

Arabella ignored Willow's fussing and continued to explain. "We weren't the only ones there. Nigel identified another half demon prowling around. He didn't recognize her, but she knew him. He distracted her while I got the box, but she spotted me and tried to get Nigel to help corner me so they could attack. Nigel 'helped' by stepping in, taking the box from me, and disappearing. Once he was gone, I disappeared as well. When the half demon figures out that Nigel is not bringing that box to his mother, then Nigel's cover will be blown. It had to happen sooner or later. I only wish we'd had a little more time to get a few additional details about the demons' attack plans."

"But you're okay?" Willow's eyes traveled over Arabella, taking in every detail.

Arabella grinned. "I'm fine. She couldn't do much. We were in a public place. She's powerful, but not as well trained as Nigel, and she thought he was on her side."

"What did she look like?" I didn't think it very likely that I'd be able to identify this half demon, but it was worth asking, just in case. "Did you at least catch what kind of shoes she was wearing?"

"Oh, I can do better than that." Arabella slid a hand into a fold of the wide fabric belt around her waist and extracted a flat rectangular device that looked completely out of place in her long Fae fingers. "Nigel got a picture of her before she noticed him. I believe one of you will know what to do with this."

Willow took Nigel's phone from Arabella. I stepped closer so I could look over her shoulder. The first thing I noticed about the woman who appeared on the screen was that she had the same hair color as Max, and it was cut almost as short. But I didn't spend much time looking at her face. My eyes skimmed straight past her short jean skirt and bare legs and stopped at her feet.

I sighed. "Converse."

Willow spoke at the same time. "Morgan Hunter is a demon?"

I stopped staring at her shoes and refocused on the woman's face. "No way. That's impossible."

Willow looked at me. "Do you think Max knows?"

"Are you serious? There's no way that Morgan Hunter is half demon. I mean, look at her." I gestured to the image.

Willow turned her gaze to Arabella. "Aren't demons supposed to have horns?"

Arabella nodded. "All demons have horns. Size depends on the species. Hers are glamoured, but I saw them. They're tiny, but you can sort of make them out here and here."

Willow zoomed in on the photo to get a closer look at the spots Arabella had indicated. "Hmm. Interesting. Looks like her hair is a bit messed up there, but that's all."

I shook my head. "If this is true...which half is supposed to be demon? I just saw Max's mother earlier. Max told her all about the boxes. If their mother is a demon..." My voice trailed off as my mind tried to fit everything I knew into this new reality.

Willow tapped her finger against the side of Nigel's phone. "I don't think Max knows. If he did, then he would have realized that his own sister wouldn't need a transport device to appear and disappear wherever she wants."

"We need to warn him." I didn't want to believe that Morgan was working against the Society—and Max—but whatever she was up to, she definitely seemed to be the one who'd broken into the office.

Arabella took the phone from Willow and made it disappear. "Have you two figured out the location of the final box?"

I reached for the paper. "Almost. We just need a few more minutes."

———

JAYDEN AND KYLE RETURNED to the conference room to work on the coordinates for the last two locations while Grace called Hannah and I called Morgan. Neither of them answered their phones.

Callie waited until Grace hung up, then tugged on Grace's sleeve. "I have to go." She kept her voice low, but the office was quiet, and I heard her.

"Really? Right now?" Grace whispered back. When she turned to face her girlfriend, I walked away and headed for the conference room.

Jayden and Kyle didn't look up when I walked into the room. I waited, but they kept their heads bent over their work.

"How's it going in here? Please tell me you have good news."

"Simon responded to my e-mail about the transport device that somehow ended up in Marcella's possession. I got him to relinquish the one that his team has been testing. I picked it up on my way back to the office." Jayden dug around in his bag and pulled out a small plastic equipment storage box.

I clicked open the lid. Inside was another transport device nestled in packing materials. "Is it charged?"

"I believe so."

"Good. Can one of you go down to engineering, get the other device, and bring it up?"

"Sure. I'll go." Jayden stood up. "Did you get in touch with Hannah?"

I shook my head. "Nothing from Hannah or Morgan."

Somewhere, out in the cubicles, someone screamed. I rushed out the door, running toward the sound, with Jayden and Kyle close behind me.

"Grace? Callie?" I called out, hoping one of them would answer me.

"Over here." Grace appeared at the end of one of the rows and waved us toward her.

We caught up and followed her to where Callie was

crouched over Hannah, who appeared to have collapsed and was lying unconscious on the floor.

"She's breathing, and I don't feel any broken bones or see any evidence of bleeding." Callie glanced over her shoulder at me. "I'm going to lay her on her back."

"What are you looking at me for? You're the doctor." I waved my hand for her to continue.

Callie used one hand to protect Hannah's head as she rolled her over. "Hannah, can you hear me? Hannah, it's Callie."

Grace knelt next to Callie, and I stood behind them. Jayden and Kyle stepped carefully over Hannah's feet so they could stand on her other side.

"Hang on." Jayden reached into his pocket and pulled out a small glass vial. He pulled the stopper out of the opening and handed it to Callie.

She took one whiff and her face scrunched up. "Smelling salts? What are you, some sort of Victorian-era lady?"

"Please." Kyle rolled his eyes. "Don't encourage him."

Callie lowered the vial until it was even with Hannah's chin. Then she moved it back and forth, wafting the aroma toward Hannah's nose. We all watched and waited, barely remembering to breathe. As soon as Hannah winced and coughed and tried to curl up on her side again to get away from the smell, we all exhaled in relief.

Grace squeezed Hannah's shoulder. "Hannah, sweetie, what happened?"

Hannah pressed her hand to her head and moaned. "I don't know. I heard a noise. I went to check it out. What is that awful smell?"

"Did you see anyone?" Callie rubbed Hannah's back with one hand. With the other, she held up the vial of smelling salts so Jayden could take it away.

Hannah shook her head, then cringed. She pressed her palms against her forehead and moaned. "Hurts."

I turned to Jayden and Kyle. "Kyle, go back to the conference room and figure out those coordinates. Jayden, go get the other transport device, then help Kyle. We'll join you in a few minutes. Be ready."

Callie checked Hannah's eyes and felt around her skull to make sure that she didn't need to go to the hospital. "Your pupils seem fine, and nothing is tender to the touch. It doesn't seem like you were hit on the head or like you banged it up when you fell. Do you remember anything about what happened?"

Hannah started to shake her head, then winced. "It's like I have a really bad headache."

"Can we give her an aspirin or something?" I asked.

Callie glared at me, and I took a step back. While Callie wasn't looking, Hannah started to stand.

"Hold on." Grace grabbed Hannah's elbow when Hannah swayed a bit. "Where do you think you're going?"

"Thirsty." Hannah tried to swallow and scowled.

I grabbed a chair from a nearby desk. Grace and Callie helped guide Hannah into it. Then Grace ran off to get some water.

I knelt down next to Hannah so that she wouldn't have to look up at me. "What's the last thing you remember?"

Hannah frowned. "The elevator?"

"Coming back with the coffee?" I asked.

"No. After that."

I glanced at Callie, who was monitoring Hannah's pulse. "So whatever happened to you, happened after you came back with the coffee?"

"No one was here when I came back. I left a note on

Jayden's desk. Didn't you see it?"

I hadn't been anywhere near Jayden's desk, and I'd sent him down to engineering, so I couldn't ask him about a note. "I didn't see your note. What did it say?"

Hannah rubbed her forehead. "I got a text from my agent. I needed to meet up with her to sign some papers. When I was done, I came back."

Callie stood. "I think she's going to be okay. I have to run before I get a ticket. If anything changes, have Grace call me. She knows how to reach me in an emergency."

I nodded. "Thanks, Callie."

"No problem. Good luck." She waved and took off at a jog toward the elevators.

Grace returned a moment later with a mug of water for Hannah. "Where's Callie?"

"She had to go." I stood. "Can you stay with Hannah while I go check on something?"

"Sure."

I was moving before she finished responding. We were on the opposite side of the room from my office and Jayden's cube. I wove through the aisles, trying to cut the most direct path to his desk. My heart pounded, and my palms had started sweating. I rubbed them on my jeans.

Two more turns, and the clump of cubes closest to Jayden's desk came into view. I picked up my pace. The way his desk was positioned, I couldn't see it until I reached his cube opening. When I got there, I exhaled with relief. Four thermal mugs jammed into a cardboard carry container had been left on his desktop. Tucked underneath the container was a piece of paper. I recognized Hannah's loopy handwriting from where I stood, but I stepped closer to read her note, anyway. Then I picked up one of the mugs and took a sip.

The insulated mug had kept the coffee warm, but it was no longer hot. I stuffed Hannah's note into my pocket and grabbed the cardboard container. Then I yelled across the office. "Grace, bring Hannah to the conference room!"

"Okay," she called back.

Jayden and I reached the conference room at the same time.

"What's that?" he asked.

I held up the container. "Hannah got the coffee. She left it on your desk because none of us was around when she got back."

Jayden's forehead wrinkled. "Why didn't she just leave it in the conference room?"

"I don't know." If she'd returned while Angie and I were in there with the door shut, I had an idea why she might have left the coffee on Jayden's desk instead. But that wasn't something I wanted to explain to my friends.

Grace arrived with her arm wrapped around Hannah's waist. She gripped the mug of water with her other hand. "Who got coffee?"

Hannah's eyes focused on the cardboard container. "You found it."

"It's still sort of warm, too."

Kyle called out from inside the conference room. "I've got it!"

We all filed inside. I set the coffee down on the table. Jayden and Grace grabbed two of the mugs as Hannah sank into one of the chairs.

I leaned over Kyle and entered the three-word combinations into my phone, then I copied the coordinates onto the paper. When I finished, I stared at my friends. It was time to make some decisions about who to trust with what.

I didn't want to send Jayden off by himself, and I definitely didn't want to send him with Kyle, but Jayden was the only one besides me who knew how to use the transport device. It wasn't that I didn't trust them together. I did. Or, at least, I wanted to. I'd just made enough mistakes for one day and didn't want to risk another.

"Jayden, you take Grace and go to the location in South America." I tore off the bottom half of the scrap of paper and handed it to him. "Here are the coordinates. Find the box and return as quickly as possible."

I tugged the second transport device out of the case and turned it so the display faced up. "I'll go after the other box and meet you back here."

"What about us?" Kyle asked.

"You stay here with Hannah."

"What if you encounter the demons?" Grace asked. "You shouldn't go by yourself."

"Grace is right. Take Kyle with you." Jayden finished entering the coordinates into his device and looked up.

"No." Hannah's voice was weak but urgent. "Don't leave me here by myself."

I scowled, trying to come up with some way to make this work. I couldn't take two people with me. It was too far. And if we wasted any more time, the demons were going to beat us to these boxes as well. It was possible that they already had.

"Jayden, take Grace and go. Kyle, you stay here. Hannah, you come with me." I paced over to Hannah and helped her stand.

"She's too weak—"

I cut Jayden off. "Go! Let me worry about this."

Jayden pressed a button on the side of his transport device, and an amber light started blinking.

"What's that? What are you doing?" My eyes flicked between Jayden's face and the device.

Jayden squinted at me and tilted his head to one side. "Testing the coordinates?"

I stared down at my transport device. There, to the right of the display where I'd entered the coordinates, was a small button. A clear label with the word "test" in a white block print had been applied above the button. "There's a test button? I thought that sticker was just a warning that these were beta versions of the device."

"You mean you didn't test the coordinates before you went to either of the other locations?" Jayden asked. The little amber light on his device stopped blinking and glowed a solid green. "Didn't you read the engineering reports I sent you?"

"I read them." I'd mostly been focused on reassuring myself that the things worked and were safe. I hadn't paid as much attention to the detailed instructions on how to operate the devices. I pressed the button to test the coordinates I'd entered.

"Try not to get yourself killed, Hunter." Jayden shook his head, pricked his finger, linked arms with Grace, and disappeared.

"We could all go." Kyle's suggestion was half-hearted. After Jayden explained how close I'd come to getting myself and Angie killed by almost transporting us into some solid object located at the other end of the coordinates, Kyle was probably in no hurry to join me.

"Three is too many for this trip." I put my arm around Hannah's waist and flashed what I hoped was an encouraging smile at her. "Hannah and I will be fine. Right?"

She leaned against me. "Let's do this."

I could tell she was faking her usual confidence. She could barely stand on her own. I met Kyle's concerned gaze. "Don't worry."

He raised an eyebrow as I pricked my finger and transported us to Italy. The location coordinates weren't far from the apartment where Angie and I had spent part of our last vacation together, the summer before her senior year and my final year of graduate school. The vacation where I'd meant to propose to her. Instead of the romantic dinner I had planned for our final night, we ended up taking a starlit walk that ended with me licking gelato off her nose. The memory stung. I didn't want to remember, and I couldn't possibly forget, how happy we'd been.

Hannah and I materialized in the town square just as dawn was breaking over the little Italian village. I forced myself to focus on the task at hand and realized there was a small group of people nearby. Their backs were to us, so I didn't think they'd noticed our sudden appearance. At first glance, I thought they were villagers out for a morning walk. Then one of them stepped to the side, and I saw her.

Hannah took one step toward them, keeping her hand on my shoulder for support. "Isn't that Angie?"

18

ARABELLA tapped me on the shoulder and directed my attention to something hidden by the broad shoulders of the guard she'd brought with us. But Brianne was already moving, positioning herself to block Arabella and turning toward the potential danger.

When she shifted, I caught a glimpse of the two figures huddled together in the gray early-morning light. "It's Max. And...is that Hannah?"

Something about Hannah's slumped posture, combined with the way she was leaning on Max, made me think she might be injured. I was moving toward them before Willow or Arabella could stop me. Brianne lifted one sculpted arm to hold me back. Her biceps were insane.

"Leave the box," she said, not taking her eyes off Max and Hannah, who hadn't moved since appearing.

I'd forgotten all about the metal cube I was holding. I started to pass it to Arabella, but Willow intervened and snatched it away before Arabella could touch it. She glared at her Fae mate. "You have no idea what that thing can do."

Arabella lifted her eyebrows and sighed like it wasn't worth the effort to argue. "If you're going to warn him, hurry up. We should get out of here before the half demon appears."

Brianne's arm dropped, and I rushed forward, breaking into a jog so I could close the distance between us before Max decided to transport away. I stumbled to a stop in front of them.

Up close, Hannah looked worse than I'd guessed. Her skin was pale, and her eyes were half closed. When she spoke, her voice came out airy and slow, like she was drunk or high. "Angie. What are you doing here?"

"What happened?" I asked, my eyes shifting between Hannah and Max.

"It's a long story." Max adjusted his hold on Hannah. He looked past my shoulder. His eyes focused on Willow and the two Fae across the plaza. "Who are your friends?"

"I'd introduce you, but there isn't time. There's something I need to warn you about." I caught my lower lip between my front teeth as I realized I hadn't considered how best to break it to him that his beloved older sister was half demon.

Max glared at me. He spoke in a threatening rumble. "Did you take the box?"

Hannah shoved at Max with the hand that wasn't holding on to his shoulders for support. "Why are you being so mean? Apologize to Angie. She's on our side, remember?"

I stared at Hannah, shocked that he hadn't told her about our argument.

"Angie's not on our side." Max scowled.

"I am." I put my hands on my hips and focused on him. Whatever was going on with Hannah, there wasn't time to figure it out. "It's your sister who's not."

Max tensed. "What do you know about Morgan?"

I glanced at Hannah. I had no choice but to say what I needed to say in front of her. There wasn't time. "Morgan is working with the demons. She's half demon, Max."

"Morgan would never work with the demons."

I squinted at him. Interesting that that was the part he chose not to believe. "You knew?"

Hannah swayed on her feet. "Don't be silly. Morgan isn't half demon."

I grabbed Hannah's waving arm and slung it over my shoulder to help support her as I questioned Max. "What happened to her? And why did you bring her with you? It's dangerous, and she's clearly injured or drunk or something."

"I don't feel great." Hannah's head dropped to her chest. Her body went limp between us.

"Shit." Max cupped Hannah's chin in his palm and lifted her face up.

Her eyes fluttered like they might open. Then they stilled. Her head tilted to one side.

"Angie!" Willow's voice called out a warning.

I turned my head to look and saw Max's sister had arrived. She'd landed about halfway between me and Willow. Next to her was a man I mostly recognized from television, even though I'd been in the same room with him when he married Morgan. Behind them stood a burly demon with thick horns arcing out of the sides of his head.

Across the plaza, Brianne crouched, ready to fight, her body blocking Arabella, who, in turn, was attempting to protect Willow. My friend was tugging on Arabella's sleeve and yelling at me that it was time to go.

Morgan stepped forward. "No one is going anywhere until I have what I came for."

Arabella whispered something to Brianne, then grabbed Willow and disappeared. As soon as they were gone, Brianne threw one of her knives at the demon. It landed in the meaty hollow between his shoulder and chest. The creature roared and surged toward Brianne.

I nearly jumped when a hand closed around my upper arm.

"Let's go." Arabella had transported herself and Willow over to me. Her grip on my arm made it clear that she wanted me to let go of Hannah so that she could transport us away from here.

I took my eyes off the fight between Brianne and the demon long enough to glance at Arabella and Willow. "I can't just leave them here."

"She's his sister. She won't hurt him." Willow hugged the box against her chest. "Come on."

Behind me, Max had finally noticed my friends. "I knew it. Is this the one who enchanted you?"

Arabella bared her teeth. "Watch it, human."

"Maxie," Morgan called to her brother as she approached. "Thanks for the help, but I can take it from here. Give me the box."

"I don't have it," Max yelled back.

"Come on, Angie. We have to leave. Now." Willow shifted closer to me.

At the same time, Morgan must have caught a glimpse of the metal object Willow was holding. She flicked her wrist in Willow's direction and sent a wisp of magic whipping toward us. "I'll take that."

Arabella released me to counter the attack. In the process, I lost my balance and fell toward Willow, pulling Hannah and Max with me. Whatever magic Morgan had directed at Willow got absorbed by Hannah, instead. She slumped onto the cobblestones in a heap between Max and me.

Morgan froze, then ran a few steps forward before stopping. She fell to her hands and knees a few feet away from her best friend. "Hannah? Hannah?"

Willow tightened her grip on my shoulder, then shoved the box into my arms. "Hold this and distract her if she tries to attack me."

Before I could respond, Willow was kneeling on the other side of Hannah, feeling for her pulse. I took a step back and crashed into Arabella.

She steadied me and yelled to Brianne. "To me. Now."

Brianne lunged at the demon, then kicked out to bring it crashing to the ground before disappearing. She reappeared at Arabella's side. "Should I take the half demon out?"

Arabella spoke in a low voice. "Not if you can help it. You cover Angela and her wizard mate. I'm taking Willow and the injured one back to the Fae."

"Yes, Commander."

I offered the box to Arabella, but she pushed it back against my chest.

"You need to keep that. Use it to distract the half-demon so she doesn't attempt to follow us." She squeezed my arm. "Trust your instincts about your wizard. Leave him or not. It's up to you."

Arabella released me. In one smooth motion, she lunged forward, wrapped one arm around Willow, and scooped up Hannah with the other. In a blink, they were gone.

Morgan leaned back on her heels. She looked up at her brother. "Where did they go? Where did they take Hannah?"

Max didn't say anything. He just looked at me.

Morgan's eyes followed her brother's gaze. They focused on me and narrowed. "Angie. It is nice to see you again. Too bad it had to be under these stressful circumstances."

"Morgan." I hugged the magic cube tight against my belly and wished Arabella hadn't trusted me to keep it safe. I didn't have any magic to defend myself, let alone something as important as what I held in my arms. As for trusting my instincts, I couldn't feel anything beyond the fear churning in my gut.

Morgan stood and dusted herself off. "Why don't you give me that box?"

Brianne shifted her body, angling it between me and Morgan.

Max spoke up before I could tell his sister exactly where she could shove that request. "What are you doing, Morg? What's with the demon?"

I took my eyes off Morgan long enough to catch a glimpse of Morgan's husband, Brady, arguing with the demon and trying to keep it from limping toward us to start another fight. I couldn't hear what he was saying, but the demon didn't appear to be willing to take orders from Morgan's husband.

"I could ask you the same thing. It appears we both have some new friends, little brother." Morgan kept her eyes on me and Brianne, even as Max stepped closer to her.

At first, I thought maybe he had finally come to his senses and was going to knock her out before she could attack. But he disappointed me by stopping next to her and folding his arms.

He matched Morgan's glare with one of his own. "They're not my friends."

"What happened, Maxie? I thought you and Angie were getting back together. Should we take down the pointy-eared bitch and snap your girlfriend out of whatever spell they have her under?" Morgan flexed her hands and cracked her knuckles.

"I'd like to see you try." Brianne crouched, ready to pounce.

Max put a hand on Morgan's shoulder. "I don't think that's necessary. I think Angie will be reasonable. Won't you, Ang?"

Max raised his eyebrows and gave me a look that I couldn't quite interpret. I wanted to think it meant he was on our side, but he was standing shoulder to shoulder with his sister. The reflection of sunlight on something metal glinted off the hand he held at his side. If he was planning something, I didn't dare look down and give him away. Not with Morgan watching my every move.

"What do you want?" I asked.

"Give me the box, and I'll let you and your Fae friend go." He held up his hands so I could see the transport device hidden in his palm. He kept that hand angled away from Morgan as he crept closer. The trust rune he'd drawn on the inside of his wrist peeked out from beneath is sleeve.

Brianne shifted to block him from approaching.

"It's okay. Let him through," I whispered to her.

She stepped back until we were almost side by side. From her new position, she could watch both Max and Morgan and be within reach if she needed to grab me and go.

Max stopped in front of me. Behind him, something shimmered in the air between him and Morgan. "Don't speak. There's a current of air blocking her from hearing what I'm saying. If she sees your mouth move, she'll know what I've done. We don't have much time. You were right. I'm sorry."

Morgan said something, but I couldn't hear her through Max's barrier.

He noticed my eyes flick to her. "I'm going to drop the air shield. Trust me, please?"

He didn't wait for me to respond. I couldn't anyway. Not

without giving him away. The air behind him shimmered again. "Give me the box."

My gut wanted me to grab Max and run, but I could tell he had a plan. I wanted to trust him. Whatever he was planning, it didn't seem like he was going to hand the box over to his sister. If he took the box back to the Silicon Moon office, it would be safe there, at least until the Fae could retrieve it. Arabella had said that she'd warded their office so none of Emilio's things could be removed.

Beside me, Brianne tensed. There wasn't time to explain what I was about to do. I held the box out, and Max's hands closed around it just as Brianne grabbed me from the other side. For a moment, I couldn't breathe, then Brianne and I were standing in my hotel room. Max and the box were gone.

Salty greeted us by running in happy circles around our feet. I bent down so I could rub her head.

"What happened? Where did he go?" Brianne asked. "I was sure I had you both."

"He has a transport device. My guess is that he's back at the Silicon Moon office."

"He has the box," Brianne added.

I nodded. "He has two of them, now."

Brianne took a few steps toward the window, then glanced around the hotel room. "Pack your things. We should go."

"It's late. Arabella warded the Silicon Moon office. We can get the boxes tomorrow morning before the office opens." I ran my hand down Salty's back, and she leaned her weight against my thigh.

Brianne frowned. "We should get you back to England. It's safer for you at Lydbury with the other humans."

I plopped down on the floor and pressed my back against the end of the bed, crossing my legs so Salty could climb up into my lap. "I want to stay in case he tries to contact me. I told him I would be here until noon tomorrow. If we don't hear from him, we'll grab the boxes and zip back to England in the morning."

Brianne fiddled with the folds of her woven Fae armor belt and extracted a coin that looked like the ones Willow had given me. She paced over to the armchair and sat down. Then she rolled the coin between her long fingers and stared at me.

"You can go back, if you want. You don't need to stay with me. I'll be fine." I didn't want to think about what it would mean if he didn't at least call. He'd apologized. He'd asked me to trust him, and I had. I wanted to believe that meant something.

Brianne drew her knife and pricked her finger. She pressed a drop of blood against the face of the coin, then spoke. "At the hotel. Wizards have the box. Returning tomorrow."

The coin disappeared.

I sighed and took my phone out of my pocket to text Max. Where are you? Then I set it on the floor next to me, willing him to reply.

EVERYONE WAS YELLING. They didn't even notice me standing there when I appeared in the conference room. Grace was pointing at Jayden and lecturing him about something while Jayden sat with his arms folded, purposely not looking at her. Kyle was waving Emilio's notebook around and telling Grace if she didn't like it, she could do it herself.

"Hey." When no one responded to me, I spoke again, louder. "Hey!"

Grace and Kyle stopped shouting, and all three of them turned to stare at me.

"Where's Hannah?" Grace asked.

I cringed. Even though my fingers were wrapped around one of the metal cubes, I didn't feel in the least bit victorious. I set the cube and the transport device down on the table, next to the metal box Angie and I had retrieved earlier.

"We have a problem." I focused on Jayden. "What sorts of wards do we have in place here? Can anyone transfer in and out of the office? Or just my mother?"

Jayden's eyes narrowed. "We've never considered transport as a security risk before."

"Well, it is now. How do we keep the demons out?"

Kyle sat up. "There's a ward I know. My parents' house is covered in them now, after what happened..." He glanced at Jayden and reached over to capture his boyfriend's hand in his.

"How long does it take to get them in place? What do you need?" It wouldn't take long for Morgan to guess where I'd gone. I just hoped that I'd managed to make it appear like the Fae who had disappeared with Angie had captured me, too. If Morgan thought that, it might buy me some time before she realized I wasn't taking her side.

"Not much. My parents are air and earth, like me and Jayden." He smiled. "Between the two of us, we can get this place shielded in no time. Faster if you and Grace help."

Grace's power was earth magic, like Jayden's. She rubbed her hands together. "Just show me what to do."

Kyle gave us our instructions, then we paired off and split up, heading toward opposite corners of the office. Grace and I combined our magic to set one pillar of protection that went up through the roof and down into the earth. Then we proceeded to the next corner and repeated the process. When we were done, Kyle activated the walls, ceiling, and floor, connecting them to the pillars and making the entire floor a demon-free zone.

"Now can you tell us what happened? Do we need to go back for Hannah?" Grace asked.

"I think you all better sit down for this."

The truth was, I didn't know what had happened to Hannah. I didn't even know if she was okay. What I did know was that my sister was working with the enemy. An enemy worse than the one I'd accused Angie of working with. Nothing made sense.

Everyone found a seat around the table.

I waited until they were settled, then I started at the beginning. "Angie was there when I arrived. Two of the Fae and one human were with her. They had the box."

"But you got the box." Kyle pointed to where it sat next to its twin on the table.

"I'm getting to that part." I paused. "Angie had the box when I arrived. She tried to warn me that the demons were coming. She said my sister was working with the demons, but I didn't listen to her. Then Morgan arrived. With a demon. Looking for the box."

"Morgan?" Grace looked as confused as I felt. "But why would she be working with the demons? Are you sure that she hadn't been captured or something?"

I shook my head. For a moment, I considered not telling them Morgan's secret. I scrambled for a way to explain things without destroying my family in the process, but there wasn't one. Morgan had chosen her side, and by now, she probably knew that I'd chosen mine. Even if it meant my parents losing their seats on the Council, I had to warn the others before Morgan destroyed the Society.

"Morgan is half demon."

Grace and Kyle recoiled in shock.

Jayden slapped the table with his palm. "I knew it."

Grace shoved Jayden's shoulder. "You did not."

"Not this again." Kyle crossed his arms and rolled his eyes.

"No. Really." Jayden pushed his chair back and started pacing. "This is what I didn't want to tell you before, Max. There's this group of folks—some are still in the Society, some have left for various reasons. They've been suspicious of Morgan's strategic absence from the Wizard Society for a while now. No offense to you, but they assumed—correctly, it appears—that there was no way your parents would name you as heir unless something was seriously off with Morgan. This whole 'her powers are weak' thing didn't make sense."

"And this group is trying to overthrow the Society?" I asked.

Jayden shook his head. "They want your parents off the Council. That's all. They want those seats to go to new families. There's a whole list of demands, but that doesn't matter right now. We can talk about that later. What happened with Morgan?"

"Wait." Grace waved her hand in the air. "You're serious, Max? How long have you known?"

"Who else knows?" Kyle asked.

"I've known nearly as long as Morgan has. I thought I was the only one besides my mother who knew." I looked at Jayden. "But apparently that's not the case."

Jayden sat down and scooted his chair in so he could rest his elbows on the table. "Technically, we didn't know. We just suspected."

"Whatever. Fine." I sighed. "Morgan tried to get the box from Angie, but Hannah got hit with the blast. One of the Fae disappeared with Hannah and the other human. The other one stayed to guard Angie."

"Where did they take Hannah?" Grace asked.

Jayden propped his chin on his knuckles. "How did you get the box from Angie?"

I answered Jayden's question first, because it was the easier one. "I asked."

"And she gave it to you? After everything you've done? Dang." Kyle shook his head. "That girl is too good for you."

I stared at Kyle, suddenly seeing things from Angie's perspective and realizing that he wasn't wrong. "Ouch."

"Truth hurts, man."

"Um, hello?" Grace waved her hand in the air. "Can we get back to the part where one of the Fae disappeared with Hannah?"

Before I could respond, there was a crash in the cubical area outside the conference room. We all froze. For a moment, everything was silent. Then something started thumping. It sounded like someone pounding on a cube wall.

I hurried out of the conference room and headed toward the sound. Grace, Jayden, and Kyle followed me. The thumping stopped, but I kept going.

"At least we know it's not a demon," Jayden whispered.

"Assuming Kyle's wards worked," Grace responded.

"Shh." I signaled them to be quiet so I could listen.

The thumping had started up again. I turned down one row of cubes, then another. Finally, I saw it. Someone was lying on the ground, hands tied behind their back and ankles bound together, kicking at the nearest cube wall. When the feet stopped to rest, the muffled cries began.

We weren't close enough to see the person's face, but I recognized the pencil skirt and suit jacket.

"Is that who I think it is?" Jayden asked.

I broke into a jog. "Oh, shit."

Kyle untied the rope binding my mother's ankles while I worked on the one at her wrists. Grace went for the knot at the back of her head that was holding the bandana gag in place.

Jayden knelt down in front of her and tilted his head to one side. "Hello, Marcella."

My mother bucked, trying to kick Jayden.

Kyle lifted his hands and backed away. I was still working on the knot in the rope around her wrists, but I paused as well. Grace hadn't bothered to untie the bandana. She used her earth magic to dissolve it, instead. As soon as my mother had her voice back, she used it to lay into Jayden.

He ignored her and reached for whatever had been jammed into the pocket of her suit jacket.

"What's that?" I asked, redirecting my mother's tirade using my air magic. It took her a moment to realize what I'd done. Then she focused her angry ranting on me, even though I couldn't hear her.

Jayden held up the first item as he unfolded the second. "Transport device and a letter."

"Read it." I turned my attention to freeing my mother's wrists. When Jayden didn't start speaking, I glanced up. "Out loud?"

Grace was leaning over Jayden's shoulder, reading along with him. "Ooh. That's bad."

"What's bad?" The knot came undone, and I unwound the cord. Then I helped my mother to sit up.

"Your sister wants the boxes." Jayden handed me the paper.

"We knew that already." I bent my head and skimmed the page.

Morgan was pissed. Really pissed. She planned to go to

the Council unless I gave her both the boxes. She'd given me twenty-four hours to hand them over. But that wasn't all. She threatened to hunt down Angie and take her hostage. Then she'd take each of my friends, one per day, until she had proof that Hannah was safe.

I turned to my mother and released the magic keeping her voice silent. "Are you okay?"

She massaged her wrists. "Your sister is an ungrateful, spoiled brat. Give her nothing."

I held up the letter. "If I don't give her the boxes, she said she's going to the Council."

My mother scoffed. "Let her. They won't believe a word she says."

"They will." Jayden tapped the transport device against his palm. "Does Mr. Hunter know?"

I shook my head.

"Why are we even discussing this?" Kyle asked. "If we give Morgan the boxes, the demons will have the power to eliminate wizard magic. They'll suck us dry, and we'll be lucky if they don't kill us."

"If we don't give her the boxes, the Council as we know it crumbles, and maybe takes the Society with it." Grace rubbed her hand against her chin. "Come to think of it. That does seem like the better option."

"Maybe there's another way." I stared past Jayden at the upholstered cube wall behind him. "An option that would help the Society, even if we can't manage to save the Council, at least as it currently exists."

"What do you have in mind?" Jayden asked.

"Something I should have considered when Angie suggested it the first time."

19

MAX never called. I fell asleep in my clothing, curled up on top of the bed, with Salty nestled at my feet and my phone next to my head. When I woke, my mouth was dry and tasted like something had crawled in and died there.

As soon as I moved, Brianne spoke. "Time to pack."

I groaned and hauled myself up, toward the bathroom. "Shower first."

Alone in the bathroom, I let the disappointment hit me. Tears streamed down my face alongside the hot water raining down on me. I let them flow until I couldn't cry anymore. Then I shut off the water, dried myself off, and swore that was the end.

I'd spent too much time crying over Max. I'd tried. I'd trusted him. I'd given him the box. Now I had to go back to England to face Fiona and explain how I'd failed. I'd failed in so many ways. I considered starting a list on the airplane.

When I left the bathroom, I found my suitcase on the bed

with my tote bag next to it. Both were packed. A single pair of jeans, a T-shirt, and my favorite black cashmere sweater were stacked on the bed. My red bra and matching underwear had been left out on top of the pile. Brianne had picked out the perfect "my ex-boyfriend never called, I'm a wreck, and I'm flying back to England" outfit. She'd also packed for me.

"Thanks." I picked up the stack of clothes, hugged it to my chest, and returned to the bathroom.

When I emerged a second time, Brianne handed me my phone. "Arabella wants us both to report back. Our flight departs at eleven thirty. Evelyn arranged everything."

"You're going with me?" I broke out of my self-obsessed funk long enough to realize that Brianne wasn't wearing her usual tunic, leggings, and Fae armor belt.

"I'm your guard." Brianne had kept her boots, but must have used her earth magic to transform her leggings into skinny jeans and her tunic into a gray cable-knit sweater. Once she glamoured her ears and hands, she would easily pass for a human.

"What about Salty?" I glanced around and started to worry when I didn't see any sign of the little fur ball anywhere. "Salty?"

Brianne rested her hand on my arm. "The dog is fine. I sent her home. She'll be waiting for you at Lydbury when you get there."

My heart sank. I'd gotten used to my little guard dog. I realized I was actually looking forward to snuggling with her on the flight back. Rather than complain, I checked my phone for messages. Still nothing from he-who-I-refused-to-think-about.

Evie had sent a series of heart emojis. I knew that was her way of saying, "Call me when you're ready—otherwise, we'll talk when you get back."

There was nothing from Willow. That worried me a little bit. Not because I needed her sympathy or anything. I was concerned because the last I'd seen her, she'd been helping save Hannah from Max's half-demon sister. I'd been so absorbed in my own drama that I'd forgotten to check on my friends.

"Arabella and Willow got back okay, right?" I put my phone away and looked up so I could catch Brianne's reaction. "And Hannah? Is Hannah okay?"

Brianne nodded once. "The Hands are working on healing your wizard friend."

Her carefully worded response didn't escape me. "But Willow and Arabella are okay, right?"

Brianne's jaw muscles flexed. "They're meeting with Fiona."

"Oh." I guessed the Faerie Queen was probably pretty mad that we had a box and lost it to the wizards. Rather, I gave it to a wizard. And not just any wizard. I gave it to the brother of the half demon who had been hunting them down. "She's probably not particularly thrilled with me right now, huh?"

Brianne lifted my suitcase off the bed and walked with it to the door. "She'll get over it."

"Before or after she punishes me for failing her?" I lifted my tote off the bed and slung it over my shoulder.

When I turned toward the door, Brianne was standing there with her hands on her hips, glaring at me. "You didn't fail, and she's not going to punish you."

I wanted to believe her, but her Oath had been to the Queen's Guard. Arabella and Willow were sworn to serve the queen, like me. If they were in trouble, I was going to be in trouble, too. I wondered if she'd wipe my memories of the

Fae and send me home to California. I'd go back to thinking that my best friend had abandoned me and moved to England because she'd fallen for some shaggy-haired guy with an English accent.

Since it was pointless to argue with Brianne, I nodded. I could tell from the way she pursed her lips that she knew I didn't believe her, but she picked up my suitcase and checked the hall through the peephole in the door.

"Stay here while I make sure it's clear." She cracked the door and slipped out into the hallway.

I caught the handle to keep the door from slamming shut. I wanted to hear if she encountered anyone out there.

Aside from my breathing, the room and the hall were both silent. The demons hadn't found me. Brianne pushed against the outside of the door, and I pulled it open.

"Let's go." She waved me forward, and I led the way to the elevators.

I managed to get through the checkout process, into a cab, and through airport security without much thought. Once we were seated at the gate, I popped my earbuds into my ears and closed my eyes, trusting that Brianne would let me know when it was time to board.

Evie had arranged for first-class tickets. I'd never flown first class before. I hoped that it meant I would be able to stretch out and recline my seat, especially because the flight wasn't scheduled to arrive until what would be tomorrow morning in England.

When we stepped onto the plane, Brianne hesitated. She stared at everything: her eyes flicked from the passengers around us, to the view out the cabin windows, to the controls in the cockpit, to the attendants, to me, and around again before pausing over the seat-belt mechanism.

"Are you good?" I whispered to her when we reached our seats.

"This is how humans transport themselves?" She kept her voice low as she scowled down at the fabric looped through the metal buckle on the seat belt.

I couldn't tell if she was horrified or impressed. "Some people think this is quite luxurious."

She raised her eyes to meet mine and frowned. "How long must we sit in these chairs?"

I checked my ticket. "About nine and a half hours."

Her eyes lifted to the little lights above our heads and the fan blowing recirculated air down on her head. "What do we do?"

I shrugged as I pulled the sleeping mask out of the sealed plastic pouch that had been waiting for me on my seat. "Sleep. Eat. Watch movies. Read."

"You should have let me take you back."

As much as I was enjoying the first-class accommodations, Brianne's way would have been faster. Still, I had to keep up appearances if I didn't want people asking questions. At least, this way, I'd be able to get some rest before I had to face Evie and the Fae Court.

I woke up when we started our descent. By the time the wheels of the plane touched the ground, I was as ready as Brianne to be back at Lydbury. When I could finally allow my phone to connect to the local cellular service, I turned it on and waited for an update from Evie.

"Didn't you say that Evie was going to pick us up?" I asked Brianne. "Are we early?"

I checked the time, then typed a quick message to let her know we'd arrived.

Brianne dug her fingertips into the plastic covering the

arm of her chair. "I'm sure she'll be here. If not, we have other ways of getting back to Lydbury."

Once I noticed Brianne's fidgeting, I couldn't ignore it. She shifted in her seat as the plane taxied to the gate. When the door finally opened, Brianne nearly jumped out of her seat.

I gripped her arm and held her back. "We have to wait until the passengers ahead of us go."

She perched on the edge of her cushion, waiting. Then stood when the couple sitting in front of us stood to depart. I grabbed my tote bag and followed her off the plane.

I waited until we were in the terminal before pulling her aside, out of the way of the other passengers. "Are you okay?"

"I will be. Something about that plane... I didn't realize I wouldn't be able to do any—" She stopped herself before saying something that might draw the attention of the other passengers flowing around us.

"You tried?"

She nodded. "When no one was looking."

"Come on. Let's go find Evie. We can talk more in the car." I glanced at my phone, but Evie hadn't responded. "Let's collect my suitcase. Then I'll give her a call."

I guided Brianne back into the stream of passengers and led the way to the baggage claim. I was so absorbed in my thoughts—worrying about Evie, wondering why Brianne's magic didn't work on the plane, hoping that Hannah was all right, considering what we might do to get the boxes back from the demons and the wizards—that I didn't realize who was standing near the escalator, waiting for me, when we emerged from the customs and security checkpoint.

Max stepped forward when he realized that I'd seen him. "Hi."

I motioned for him to follow me over to an area where

there weren't that many people. "What are you doing here?"

Brianne kept her head down and moved toward a nearby rack of tourist brochures. She kept close enough to protect me, if needed, but far enough away to give me some privacy. Since Max didn't even spare her a glance, I guessed that he didn't recognize her in her human clothes and glamour.

"I wanted to talk to you."

ANGIE STARED AT ME like I might have come to drag her off to some demon lair where my sister was waiting to torture her. I couldn't say I blamed her. She didn't know what side I was on. I wasn't really sure that I knew what side I was on. I just hoped that she'd at least allow me the chance to convince her that, whatever we were facing, I wanted to face it together.

"How did you know my flight information?" Angie's eyes narrowed.

"When I called your phone, it went straight to voice mail. So, I tried your hotel, but they said you had already checked out. I was worried." I left out the part about how, when I couldn't find Angie, I thought maybe my sister or her demon friends had tracked her down, and then I had felt like an idiot for not realizing that was a possibility earlier. "I didn't know what happened to you. So, I got a hold of Evie."

Angie's eyes widened. "You called Evie? How?"

I grimaced. I hated sounding like a stalker, and people never believed you when you explained how easy it was to find their personal information online. "You said Evie was in England. I told Jayden what I knew, and he used it to find her uncle's phone number."

Angie glanced away for a moment. She sighed. "And Evie gave you my flight info."

"I told Evie I'd pick you up and drive you out to that manor. She gave me your arrival time, but she insisted on coming to the airport, just in case you didn't want to go with me." I watched Angie's face for a clue as to how she was feeling. "I want to talk and apologize properly. Please?"

Angie frowned. "Where is she?"

My heart sank. "In the parking garage."

"You should have called, Max." Angie folded her arms across her chest.

"I know. There was just...a lot going on when I got back. I had to deal with all that. Then, once I was done, I realized how late it was and didn't want to wake you."

"You could have at least texted." She waved to someone.

I turned to look as a woman with a shaved head started walking toward us. She looked familiar, but I couldn't quite remember where I'd seen her before.

"You're right. I'm sorry."

"Do you really want to talk to me? Or are you just here because you've finally decided that you need help and want an introduction to my friends?"

I winced. "Both? I really am sorry. If we can just go someplace and talk—"

Angie held up a hand. "Save it."

"Problem?" The woman with the shaved head had approached so quietly that I didn't even notice she was already standing next to me until she spoke. Her eyes were focused on Angie, but I got the sense that she was still watching me.

Angie waved her hand between the woman and me. "Brianne, this is Max. He wants to talk, but I don't have anything to say to him. I think it's best if you take him directly to Fiona."

Brianne's hand clamped around my elbow. "Now?"

"Wait." I tried to pull away, but her grip was like iron. "Who's Fiona? Angie, please? Can we talk about this? I'm sorry. I should have trusted you."

"You should have. But you didn't, and now I'm tired from staying up all night and then traveling all day and sleeping on a plane." She paused to yawn, emphasizing her point. "Talk to Fiona. If you still want to talk with me after that, you know how to find me."

Brianne tugged me backward into an alcove between the restrooms. I kept my eyes on Angie, and tried to squirm away, but it was hopeless. I blinked, and when I opened my eyes again, I was standing in a forest facing a cottage on a knoll overlooking a babbling stream. One of the Fae stood at attention outside the door to the cottage. His head was shaved, like Brianne's, but unlike the Fae female with the vise grip on my elbow, the guard outside the cottage door was dressed like he'd just stepped out of a production of Robin Hood.

"Where are we?" I asked, even though I suspected I already knew.

Brianne called out to the guard as she tugged me toward the door. "Tell the queen that Angela of the Sworn has sent Maxwell Hunter to speak with her."

The guard dipped his head in acknowledgment, then hurried into the cottage. After he left, I realized Brianne had dropped her human glamour. With the return of her pointed ears and belted tunic, I recognized her as one of the Fae who had been with Angie in Italy. Before I could confirm my guess that Fiona was the Queen of the Fae, the guard returned.

He held the door open so we could enter the cottage. "Your request for an audience has been granted."

Brianne shoved me ahead of her, and I used the opportunity to wrench my arm out of her grip. If I was going to face the

Queen of the Fae, I planned to walk in like the head wizard's heir that I was and not be dragged in like a criminal. I didn't realize until I was inside that I was going into this meeting defenseless. My magic was strong, for a wizard, but would be no match against the Queen of the Fae.

I'd wanted this meeting. Angie hadn't been entirely wrong when she suggested that I might be using her to get help from the Fae. I'd just expected that I'd have more time to prepare, and that I would arrive with Angie and at least one or two of my friends at my side. Instead, I was alone, without even Angie to vouch for me.

If I turned back, I would have to face Brianne and the guard who had been standing outside. They weren't likely to allow me to walk out without a fight, and I had no idea how strong their magic was compared to mine. Then, if I did somehow manage to defeat them, I'd have to trust that my transporter had enough power left to get me somewhere safe. I wasn't even sure it would work in the Lands of the Fae.

With no choice but to proceed, I made my way down the hallway with Brianne following close behind me. At the end of the hall, I stepped into a cozy study lit by candles and glowing orbs. Four armchairs faced each other with a low table between them. On the center of the table, a porcelain teapot sat beside two cups and saucers on a silver tray.

Staring out the large windows at the far side of the room stood a tall woman with dark-brown skin, pointed ears, and a long, graceful neck. A twisted iron crown, made to look like a halo of thorny vines, lay nestled in her short dark-brown curls.

She turned to face me when I entered. "Thank you, Brianne. Please close the door and see that we are not disturbed."

Brianne bowed low before stepping out into the hallway.

"You must be Maxwell Hunter. I am Fiona of Isleen, Queen of the Fae." She paused and motioned to one of the armchairs across the table from where she stood. "Please, have a seat."

"It is lovely to meet you, Your Highness." I hesitated next to the chair she indicated, waiting for her to sit down before I took my seat.

"Please, call me Fiona." She smiled as she reached for the teapot. "Would you like some tea?"

"Sure, and you can call me Max."

"I've heard so much about you, it's nice to finally meet you in person." She handed me one of the teacups and sat back in her chair. "Now, it is my understanding that you have two wizard-created boxes in your possession. They are a threat to the Fae. I would appreciate it if you would agree to give them to me."

I paused with the teacup halfway to my lips. So much for small talk and refreshments. "Those boxes are as much of a threat to the wizards as they are to the Fae. I'm afraid I cannot just hand them over without some assurances as to our safety. Especially since I believe the demons already have one box, and they are also interested in acquiring the two that we have."

Fiona folded her hands and placed them in her lap. "Two. The demons have at least two boxes now."

"How do you know?"

"We have our ways." She leaned forward. "Are you able to protect the boxes that you have?"

I wasn't sure if she was calling into question the power of the wizards or offering assistance. "My mother would like me to destroy them."

"Your mother is a smart woman." She paused, and her eyes drifted to the objects on the shelves lining the wall opposite the door. "Unfortunately, we have yet to determine a way to destroy the boxes in our possession. If you have managed to discover how this might be done, perhaps you would be willing to share that information with us?"

"Why do you want to destroy them? I would think you would want to use them."

"For what? I have no use for a device that would drain my people of their powers and lock that magic away, endangering the delicate balance of forces that allow life to continue to thrive on this planet." She shivered. "Those boxes are a threat to humankind as well, which is why it is in your best interest to help me destroy them all."

"If you can't find a way to destroy them, what makes you think that I will be able to?"

"They were made by one of you. A human with magic." She set her teacup down on the table. "I can't say I'm surprised, really. Humans have always been keen to find ways to capture and control the Fae. We've only recently been able to free ourselves of one human threat. Then we discovered that the demons have joined the humans in their effort to rid the world of the Fae. I had hoped that you would be different, but perhaps my aunt was right to insist we retreat into the deep forest and eliminate all contact with humans."

I shifted as the extent of her disappointment settled over me. I found that I didn't want to disappoint her, and I worried it was because she'd somehow charmed me. I set my cup on the table and stared down into it, wishing for a bit of Jayden's earth magic.

"I don't plan to harm you." Fiona spoke as though she'd been reading my thoughts, even though I knew that was impossible.

My eyes lifted to meet hers. "How can I be sure?"

"Simple. Fae can't lie. I've told you, and so it is true."

Angie had said something similar. It didn't make sense based on what I'd been told about the Fae. "Prove it."

"Prove that I can't lie?" Fiona's head tilted to one side.

I nodded. "If you prove I can trust you, then perhaps we can find a way to deal with this problem together."

Fiona stared at me for a moment as she considered my suggestion. "When we say something untrue, it physically hurts us. It is as though someone reached into our guts and squeezed." She leaned across the table and, faster than I could react, grabbed the front of my shirt, twisting it with her hand. Her eyes shone with an intense fierceness that frightened me.

I slammed my body back in my chair, increasing the distance between us, but it didn't matter. As quickly as she'd grabbed me, she released me and sat back. My heart pounded against my ribs.

She wrapped her fingers around the handle of her teacup and lifted it off the saucer. "If you would like me to demonstrate, I will. I only wanted you to know what you are asking, first."

Her explanation sounded similar to what it felt like to lie while under the spell of a truth rune. I'd never had reason to try, but I'd seen wizards questioned by the Council attempt to lie and find themselves punished for it in that way.

Angie trusted Fiona, and I trusted Angie. "That won't be necessary, but if I give you the boxes, will you agree to resume contact with humans? At least the wizards, if not all humans?"

20

EVIE and I didn't talk much on the drive back to Lydbury from the airport. She didn't ask why I hadn't agreed to go with Max, and I didn't tell her I sent him with Brianne to see Fiona. A part of me felt bad about refusing to talk it out with him, but the other part of me didn't want anything to do with him as long as he insisted that the Fae were the enemies. If he couldn't see that we were on the same side, then there was no hope of a future for us. It didn't matter how sorry he was about not trusting me.

When we arrived at Lydbury, Liam was waiting for us outside the carriage house. He opened the doors so Evie could pull her uncle's car inside and park.

Evie opened her door as soon as she took the key out of the ignition. "What's wrong? I wasn't expecting you back until tomorrow."

"Fiona's called a meeting of her Court." Liam's eyes broke away from Evie's long enough to glance at me.

"Go ahead. Don't worry about me. I'll unpack and hang

out with Salty until you get back." I pulled my suitcase out of the back seat and shut the car door. I was Sworn, but I'd never been given an official position on the Faerie Queen's Court. Evie and Liam would need to attend, but I could put off facing Fiona a little longer.

Liam and Evie exchanged a look. I could tell Evie was worried about me, but she didn't need to be. I really was looking forward to seeing my guard dog, and I hadn't had any time to finish reading Jayden's sister's book. I planned to make a fire in the guest room fireplace, take a long bath, and then curl up with Salty and the adventures of Emma Fierce, international woman of mystery. By the time Evie returned, I'd probably be ready to talk.

Whatever silent eyeball communication was occurring between my best friend and her Fae mate, it ended with a shrug from Liam. He turned toward me. "The injured wizard has been transferred to the Queen's Guard barracks to rest while she recovers. Gwawr has been looking after her, but as our guardian, she'll be attending the Court meeting. Your friend will be alone. I can take you to see her, if you'd like."

I realized that Hannah had been whisked away by complete strangers, and Fae strangers who she might think meant to harm her. She would probably be relieved to see a friendly face, and I would feel better knowing that she was okay. My plans could wait.

I set my suitcase down next to the car. "Okay. Let's go."

Liam left me outside a long one-story building, but only after I'd reassured Evie that I would be fine and that I wouldn't wander off.

Once they disappeared, I walked toward the single door positioned at the center of one end of the wooden structure. The whole thing looked like a saggy old barn that might fall down at any moment. The walls were dotted with windows, but the inside appeared dark and empty.

The guard nodded at me and stepped aside to let me in when I told her who I was and that I'd come to visit Hannah.

"Only two patients at the moment. Both are near the far end. Won't be hard to tell who's who." She lifted her eyebrows like that was supposed to mean something to me.

I thanked her and hurried inside to avoid further discussion. Cots lined both walls in a configuration that I'd only ever seen in movies with old-time hospitals or orphanages. The building was wide enough to allow for a spacious aisle down the center, between the ends of the beds. As the guard said, all of them were empty except two at the far end of the room.

The only light inside came from the windows. I was nearly to the middle of the building when I realized that one of the two patients was sitting up, leaning against the wall at the head of their bed, watching me approach. Based on their silhouette, it wasn't Hannah. Whoever it was had broad shoulders, short hair, and pointed ears. They were in the last bed on the right, next to the windows on the far side of the building. On the left side, a few beds closer to me, Hannah lay curled on her side. I recognized her long dark-brown hair, which was the envy of her followers.

"Here to see the wizard?" The face belonging to the low voice in the far corner was still shadowed, and I couldn't make it out.

I swallowed. "I am."

"Don't get many humans visiting." The speaker's accent was vaguely European rather than English, like most of the Fae. I couldn't quite place it. "Don't get many human patients, either...or any patients, really."

"How long have you been here?" I stopped at the end of Hannah's bed.

The figure at the far end of the room turned to look out the window. "Too long."

"Well, at least you have a bit of company, now." I motioned toward Hannah.

"If you mean your friend, it will be a while before she wakes up and starts talking. But, you're here." The figure shifted forward into the light, and I realized I was speaking with one of the most beautiful male Fae I'd ever seen. He had wavy light-brown hair, a chiseled jaw, and a bare broad chest thick with muscles and lined with scars, some old and some still healing. He caught me noticing his body and grinned.

I turned away and edged closer to where Hannah's head rested on a thin pillow. "Has she woken up at all since they brought her here?"

"No." His voice was closer.

I turned to meet his gaze, wanting to show I wasn't scared of him. Then I worried that might somehow give him the idea I was challenging him. I hadn't met many Fae outside of the Queen's Court and wasn't sure how to behave.

"I didn't think these Fae associated with humans," he said as he sat on the end of the bed across the aisle from Hannah's. His chest heaved as he sucked in air, more winded than I would have guessed from such a small amount of exertion.

Before I could respond, a large bird fluttered outside the window for a moment, then disappeared. The Fae's head turned at the sight. He flicked a wrist at the window, and it slid open. The bird reappeared and flew inside.

It wasn't until it landed on the end of the Fae's bed that I realized it wasn't a bird at all. It was a dragon. A blue-and-purple dragon about the size of a hawk. It curved its long neck in my direction and cocked its head to one side as it studied me.

"That's a dragon." I whispered the words as I backed myself against the wall at the head of Hannah's bed.

The Fae limped back over to his bed and sat down next to the creature. "A faerie dragon."

The dragon climbed up the Fae's arm and curled itself across his broad shoulders. It continued to stare at me from its perch.

"Angie?" Someone called to me from the door.

I dared to look away from the faerie dragon for a moment and caught a glimpse of Max and Brianne walking toward me. Their appearance made me forget for a moment about the potential danger posed by the small dragon and the large Fae male.

"What are you doing here?" I asked.

Behind me, the Fae shifted and sighed. "Another human. This queen is rather unusual, isn't she?"

I resisted the urge to turn around and kept my focus on Max. Brianne nodded to me before continuing down the aisle to speak with the male Fae and his faerie dragon.

Max stopped next to Hannah's bed. "Brianne brought me here to check on Hannah."

"She's asleep."

"I see that."

"How did it go with Fiona?" I asked.

"I appear to still be in one piece." Max grinned.

"Is she going to help you?"

"We came to an agreement. She can have the boxes I—we—collected. In exchange, the Fae are going to help the wizards learn to use, and hide, their magic so that we can help them defeat the demons." Max paused and glanced over my shoulder at the figures on the bed against the far wall. "Can we go somewhere and talk?"

"Now?"

"Now."

"I promised Evie that I wouldn't go anywhere until she returns."

"Brianne can tell her you're with me. Please?"

The bed against the far wall creaked. "Aw. Give the bloke a chance, love."

I grimaced at the reminder that we weren't alone. If we were going to talk about our relationship, I definitely didn't want to do it in front of an audience. I looked over and met Brianne's eyes. She nodded.

I turned back to face Max. "Sure."

He smiled as he reached across Hannah's bed and took my hand. "Close your eyes."

I obeyed, and for a moment, the world was silent. Then bright sunlight warmed my skin and a sea breeze whipped my hair against my cheek.

Max tucked the strands behind my ear. "You can open your eyes now."

I blinked against the glare of the sun. It took me a moment to realize we were standing on a familiar balcony overlooking a town square. We'd been here before. In this exact location, with this exact view, or close enough that I couldn't tell the difference.

"Italy? You brought us back to Italy?" I turned around and found the balcony doors open wide. Inside was the room I remembered with the comfortable armchairs and stacks of books. "How did you know that there wouldn't be anyone here?"

"Because I bought it." He walked inside and stood next to

the bookshelves that lined the wall that separated the sitting room from the bedroom.

I stepped through the French doors and ran my hand over the plush velvet back of the burgundy armchair. "You bought the apartment we stayed in on our vacation? When did you do that?"

Max shifted a stack of books so he could reach behind the ones standing upright on the shelf. When his hand emerged, it was holding a small black velvet box. "It was supposed to be a surprise. I was going to tell you after I gave you this."

My heart lurched, then started hammering at a speed that made me think it would be best if I sat down. My fingers dug into the velvet. "Max..."

Max crossed the room in two steps, closing the distance between us. "Before you say anything, will you let me explain?"

———

THE LOOK OF PANIC that had crossed Angie's face added a layer of urgency to my words. I'd realized a few things in the days we'd spent together being honest with each other. I needed her to know what had really happened, and to explain why I was never going to let that happen to us again.

I guided her into the chair, then knelt at her feet before opening the box so she could see what was inside. "I bought this ring five years ago, before we left for our vacation. I had everything planned. I let you think that I rented this place when I'd actually bought it, knowing what I planned to do, and I wanted us to always be able to return to this place. I didn't anticipate how much we would love it here, and I didn't anticipate the visit I received from my mother before we left for our trip."

I paused as memories of that conversation flooded my mind in vivid detail. "I don't know how she found out what I was about to do—some sort of mother's intuition, I guess. I'll save you the details of the conversation, but she made it clear where she stood on the subject of my intentions. She didn't forbid me. She didn't threaten to disown me. She made her case, told me it was my decision, and left."

Angie shifted in the chair. "Why are you telling me this?"

"Because I want you to know everything. I don't want there to be any secrets between us."

"But you're telling me that it was your decision. You decided not to go through with your plans. You chose your family over me."

"Yes. I did. And I have regretted that decision every day since you left me. I convinced myself it was the right thing to do. That it was the best thing for my family and for the Wizard Society that I would someday have to lead. I ignored how much it hurt me to push you away. I was an idiot. I let myself be weak when I should have been the leader I was born to be. I'm sorry. I'm so sorry for every minute that we spent apart when we could have been together. I'm sorry I never told you the truth. I've seen how you guard other's secrets, how you stand by them and stand up for them, even when you barely know them. What you did when you trusted me and handed me that box, even though you knew you were breaking your promise to the queen you serve... I don't deserve you, but I want to. I want to do whatever it takes to be worthy of being your partner."

Tears spilled over her lower lashes and rolled down her perfect cheeks. I couldn't wipe them away without letting go of the box or releasing her hands. I started to set the box on the floor, but Angie slid her right hand out of my grip and reached for it.

"Oh, no. You didn't think you could just show me that and take it away, did you?" She held the box closer and stared down at the emerald-cut ruby bracketed by a pair of shimmering diamonds. "You had this for five years and just left it hidden behind some old books in an apartment you never visit?"

"Who says I never visit?"

Her narrowed eyes flicked up to meet mine. "I was almost ready to forgive you."

My chest warmed at her words. "Okay. You're right. I haven't been back since we left. There's no way I could have come here without you."

"Better."

I plucked the ring out of its cushion and held it up between us. "What do you think? Is there a chance for us?"

Angie's eyes softened, and the corners of her lips pulled up in a smile. "I think you're worthy enough."

"Worthy enough that you'll marry me?"

"Yes." She leaned forward, and her lips crashed into mine.

I slid the ring onto her finger, then released her hand so I could wrap my arms around her waist. She slid forward and down until we were both kneeling on the floor. Her fingers curled into my hair and teased the skin on the back of my neck as I pulled her tight against me.

For a moment, everything was perfect. Then Angie shifted back to meet my eyes. "Now would be a great time to tell me that you didn't go through all this trouble just because Fiona has decided to kill me for giving you that box."

I laughed. "Wow. You're dark. Your queen has no intention of killing you. But I'm not sure I can say the same about my sister. Fiona suggested that someone named Nigel might be able to talk some sense into her."

"Did she explain that Nigel is Emilio and Lilium's son?"

"I believe you mentioned that." I had been listening to what she was saying just before I'd kicked her out of the Silicon Moon office. Though the reminder of my unsympathetic reaction made me cringe.

"Well, if anyone can get through to Morgan, it will be him. He served Lilium until he realized that she'd been lying to him about his father. He's one of the Sworn now."

I nodded. "Your queen can be very convincing, even without the assistance of her Fae charm."

"Oh, I don't think it was Fiona who did the convincing there." Angie smirked.

There was definitely more to that story, and I looked forward to hearing the rest of it.

Angie tugged on the waistband of my jeans. "Do you have enough charge left on that transport device of yours to get us back to Lydbury? Or are we staying here tonight?"

"Oh. That's the other thing I worked out with Fiona." I released her so I could push up my sleeve and show her my forearm.

She grazed the markings on my still-tender skin with her fingertips. "Evie has a tattoo like this. Did Fiona give it to you?"

I pressed my finger against the tip of the compass rose Fiona had marked me with. "I doubt that Evie has one exactly like this. This is the first of its kind. Fiona modified the Silicon Moon transport device technology with her magic. She basically embedded the device in me. It still only works for humans with Fae blood, but it uses that energy to charge, and it's much more efficient than our original design."

Angie dragged her fingernail up along the center of the

design until her finger brushed against mine. "I'm surprised you didn't convince Fiona to take a seat on Silicon Moon's board as part of the deal you made with her."

"Don't think it didn't cross my mind. I still might try, once this war is over." I interlaced our fingers and brought her knuckles to my lips to kiss just as my watch buzzed with an alarm. I turned my forearm over and bent my wrist to glance at the notification.

I'd set the alert so long ago that I'd almost forgotten. On any other Tuesday, I would have been in the Silicon Moon office. On this particular Tuesday, I was supposed to be with our engineering team. That was before everything had gone sideways, and I'd ended up having tea with the Queen of the Fae.

"Come on." I stood and helped Angie to her feet, then pulled her over to the balcony. I positioned her so that she was facing south, then I stood behind her and wrapped my arms around her waist.

She lifted her hand to admire her ring in the sunlight. "It's beautiful, Max."

I leaned over her shoulder to kiss her cheek. "You're beautiful. Now, watch the sky, or you're going to miss it."

Angie leaned her head back on my shoulder. "Miss what?"

A white line cut into the blue sky at the horizon and lifted up, higher into the sky. The rumble of the rocket took longer to reach us. "Our future."

Angie twisted in my arms. "Is that a Silicon Moon rocket?"

"Our tech is on that rocket. I'll tell you all about it later, but it's the start of something that I think is going to be huge."

"Did you use magic for that?"

"Shh..." I kissed her temple, then nibbled at the top of her ear. "We can go back to Lydbury now, if you want."

"Now?" She pressed her back against me so that her butt ground against my hips.

"If you want." My fingers found the button on her jeans and popped it open.

Her head tilted to one side, exposing the skin of her neck to my lips. "I don't know... We could stay a bit longer. I'm in the mood for gelato. What do you think?"

"Gelato sounds good." I kissed the tender spot just below her earlobe as I slid her zipper down and slipped my hand inside her underwear.

She sucked in a breath as my fingers found their mark. "Hmm... Maybe gelato can wait."

If you enjoyed this book, don't miss the other books in the
Modern Fae series:

Vivian's Promise
Eve of the Fae
Eve the Immortal
Dawn of the Fae
Will of the Fae
Rogue Assassins

To be the first to know about new books, discounts, give-
aways, and behind the scenes book info, sign up for my
newsletter at
http://bit.ly/MagicForMortals.

ACKNOWLEDGEMENTS

THIS has been quite the year. Without the community of awesome people I have in my life, you probably wouldn't be holding this book in your hands right now, dear readers. I am forever grateful for their and your support.

Starting with my Tuesday night virtual writing group, who kept me laughing while I tried to figure out where Emilio hid those pesky boxes. Shannon, Alex, Adrienne, Anne, Kilby, Kara, Dafina, and Jackie are all rock stars. Thank you to Shannon for organizing and hosting, and to the whole group for being so inspiring and encouraging.

To my first readers, Kaitlin and Carolyn, thank you for your enthusiasm, your critiques, and your sharp eye for details. Without you two looking forward to seeing the next set of chapters, I would probably still be writing this book.

Thank you to my copy editor, Michelle Hope, and the Artful Editor team for helping me take my final draft to the next level.

Thank you to my cover designer, Elizabeth Mackey, for creating the perfect magical Seattle vibe for the cover.

To my friends and extended family, especially my mom, who remains my first and biggest fan, I have missed seeing your lovely faces in person this year, but I thank you for cheering me on and cheering me up over video calls. And a special shout out to our friend Mandy, who, while I was writing and editing this book, found us a new home to settle in, complete with the perfect writing room.

To my husband who encouraged me and kept our pantry stocked with all the best treats, thank you for everything. This year has proved that I couldn't have asked for a better partner.

And to you, my lovely readers, and especially my Magic For Mortals crew, thank you for continuing to join me on this journey.

ABOUT THE AUTHOR

Elizabeth Menozzi is an award-winning writer of science fiction and fantasy with romance. A former Midwestern girl, she currently resides on Orcas Island with her husband. In her spare time she is a competitive swimmer, reluctant runner, and devourer of books.

You can follow her on Twitter (@emenozzi) and Instagram (emmenozzi), or contact her via her website at http://www.elizabethmenozzi.com/.

Made in the USA
Middletown, DE
18 May 2021